PRAISE FOR NATHAN PONSOR

* * *

"...beyond great ... this guy had me interested the whole time."

—gabe1108, *reddit.com*

"Nathan's fantasies might not be too impossible."

—Royboy, *earwolf.com forums*

"This guy was good."

—TvsPhil, *reddit.com*

ABOUT THE AUTHOR

Nathan Ponsor is originally from Marina del Rey, California. He currently lives somewhere between Washington Heights and Inwood in Manhattan. This is his first novel.

HUMAN SATELLITE

NATHAN PONSOR

TOYNS BOOKS

TOYNS Books | New York, NY

FIRST TOYNS EDITION, November 2019

To purchase copies of this book in bulk, please contact us by email at the address below.

toynspublishing.tumblr.com | toynsbooks@gmail.com

If you enjoyed this book, please consider rating it online wherever you can and telling your friends about it. We love word of mouth and social media.

Book design by Tony Golde.

ISBN: 978-0-9970678-1-1

10 9 8 7 6 5 4 3 2

Thank you for picking up this book and looking at this page.

HUMAN SATELLITE

EXPLANATORY NOTE

The manuscript you hold in your hands was discovered in the closet of a recently-vacated apartment in New York City and taken down to the communal laundry room by the building's superintendent, who put it amongst the books, small pieces of furniture, and other cast away items that were up for grabs by tenants. I first came across it in 2015, although it had been in the common room since 2010, when its author disappeared from the building suddenly, leaving no forwarding address or other means of contacting him.

Curious while doing laundry one morning, I opened up the packet of papers and began reading the extraordinary tale. Although my only previous experience in the publishing industry was as author of a gossip column for a student newspaper in high school, I decided to take up the task of translating and editing the manuscript. I was able to find little information about Ilya Zamyatin online, but many of the historical details he mentions are true, which lends some credence to his story. He grew up in the U.S.S.R. with limited access to Western culture. In the course of translating this book, I discovered many cultural references which were factually questionable. I have not changed them, in order to preserve the integrity of his book and to capture his portrait of a life in 20th Century Russia. His outmoded views about women and the world also remain, for the sake of accuracy: Zamyatin is a product of the toxic masculinity that was prevalent throughout the world well into the 21st century.

I have generally left the work unedited, although I have used the English term "blowhard" as opposed to the more linguistically sound "armpit f*cker" in passages where Mr. Zamyatin refers to Soviet leaders. Additionally, for the sake of readers, names, nicknames, and patronymics have been made uniform to Western naming conventions. Some historical notes and corrections are included at the end of the narrative. If anyone has knowledge of Ilya Zamyatin's whereabouts since 2010, please contact me via the publisher so that we may share with him the royalties from this work and celebrate his survival.

— N. P.

HUMAN SATELLITE
by
ILYA ZAMYATIN

"Going to Russia was like going into outer space."
—*SEBASTIAN BACH* [1]

"People have raised the question: are we going
to stay there forever?"
—*MIKHAIL GORBACHEV* [2]

"In space, no one can hear you dream."
—*GEORGE LUCAS (Star Wars)* [3]

00 / PROLOGUE

My country disappeared twice. The first time was when I left Earth's atmosphere and entered outer space, where the borders that mark territory on a classroom globe are no longer visible. From up there, you can see only land and sea and cloud, and none of mankind's self-imposed boundaries. The second time my country disappeared was two months later, when the Soviet Union literally ceased to exist, as its government crumbled and the mighty nation I had known as a boy became a collection of independent states. It was a sad and scary time for all my countrymen. I was still in space, living in a capsule orbiting the Earth, a capsule where I stayed for 14 months. Would I ever get back home? Did my *home* even exist anymore? And would the government blowhards stop arguing long enough to consider the plight of one lonely man trapped in space? I had been a soldier and a pilot and, finally, a Cosmonaut. Would there be another chapter written in the story of my life?

If you're holding this book, then you know the answer is *Yes*.

I nearly died as an exile in space, but returned to Earth as a hero, and became a famous novelist. I founded the Space Discovery Theme Park in the former training center of the Soviet space program. I beat John Glenn in an arm-wrestling contest. Finally, I insulted Vladimir Putin at a dinner party and went into hiding, where I composed this book. I am still in hiding today. I no longer drink tea for fear that I will be killed by radioactive poison my enemies placed inside it. Whenever there is a knock at the door, I wonder if it is the Fresh Direct groceries I ordered or a Kremlin hitman come to take my life. And then I look through the spy hole in my door and see that it is the Fresh Direct delivery person. *But what if it is a K.G.B. assassin dressed as a Fresh Direct person?* I ask him to leave the box outside my door, and later have a neighbor open it for me, in case it is a bomb. In any event, I live in fear. This book harkens back to an earlier time in my life when I was also afraid: the months I spent stranded in a satellite above the Earth. It also describes my childhood and training to become a Cosmonaut, and my adventures after returning to the ground.

I have not been back to Russia since that ill-fated dinner party with Putin.

I suppose my country has disappeared a third time.

01 / I AM BORNE

I ran through my equipment at least twenty times. I couldn't sleep. It was my last night on Earth before I became a true Cosmonaut. I had technically been in the space program for three years already, and a Cosmonaut for the last 18 months. But you are not *really* a Cosmonaut until you go to space, just like you are not a *real* man until you break a woman's heart or *really* a strongman until you kill your first dissident. I must confess, going to space gave me an erection. I was supposed to stay calm and focused on the mission, but I was too excited. I checked my equipment again. Food pellets? Check. Water purification system? Check. Data recorders? Check. And I made sure I had my black market equipment as well. Tape player and Beatles cassettes? Check. American blue jeans to re-sell as "space jeans" when I returned to Earth? Check. Vodka? Check. I even had a copy of *Moby Dick* packed in there in case I got bored. I was as ready as I would ever be.

So I left the airfield and went to a bar. As a Cosmonaut, I usually drank for free, and women tore of their skirts when they saw me in my uniform. Often I even had intercourse while wearing my uniform. It was against protocol, but who cares about protocol when a lovely Ukrainian lady wants your manhood? Plus, Russian winters are cold, so it helps to wear a warm jumpsuit rather than make love in the nude.

I took a jeep to Uncle Sasha's. It was barely a shed with a coal stove, but it served its purpose as a tavern. It had vodka and hookers. A word about prostitutes—after my famous interview with *Moscow Gentleman Monthly* where I said I never slept with whores, many women wrote to the magazine to say that they had made love to me and that they were indeed whores. First of all, who can trust a woman who proudly tells a magazine she takes money for sex? Second of all, I never paid for sex with these ladies, so I did not consider them prostitutes. They might have charged other men for sex, but they did not charge me. It is not hard to understand. Even today, I look at myself naked in the mirror and think, *I would have sex with myself for free.*

At Uncle Sasha's, the wind was bitter cold and the peasants were grumpy. *The new leaders were a bunch of blowhards*, one said. *We should not have gone to Afghanistan*, another said. *My wife's family died at Chernobyl*, added a third man. I guess old men always have to complain about one thing or another. Why couldn't they be happy? I was happy. I was about to go into outer space! I did not follow politics back then. I joined the party when I became a Cosmonaut, but only because it was required. I thought a voting booth was a good place for sex, but not much else.

The bartender at Uncle Sasha's was a one-legged veteran who had fought back the Germans at Stalingrad. He told people he lost his leg in the war, but really he got drunk and fell asleep on the train tracks. A locomotive amputated it for him. His name was Gorky. He was always excited to see me. "Ilya!"

he cried, "Come get warm with a drink. When you come back from space, tell everyone to visit Uncle Sasha's so they can be a Cosmonaut like you." I took a drink and sat down next to a blonde beauty who was eating a sausage.

"Are you Ilya Zamyatin?" she asked.

I said I was.

"I am Zlata. I work at the butcher's. You should not go to space on an empty stomach. Would you like sausage?"

I nodded and she gave me the rest of her dinner.

"Tell me," she said. "Are you scared to go to space?"

"No," I said. "I am scared of nothing."

"I am scared of wolves and cancer," she said.

Later that night we made love in my space capsule, on the airfield. She left her underwear inside and told me to think of her when I was in space. I did indeed think of her often. I also wore her panties many months later, not because I desired to, but because my own underwear had grown dirty when I was stuck in space for over a year.

She snuck out and walked back to town just as the sun was coming up. The sky was like a foyer filled with cigarette smoke. I still had a few hours before launch. I checked my equipment again.

Five. Four. Three. Two. One.

That is how they count down to launch someone into space. I knew the countdown by heart. Ever since I was a boy and Sputnik[1] was launched, I wanted to go to space. So I memorized all the numbers in the countdown, from five-thousand-four-hundred all the way down to one. I knew them forward and backward. I still remember some of those numbers today. Beautiful numbers such as *six-hundred-thirty-seven* and *three-thousand-thirty-thre*e and *eight.*

But before the countdown started, I had to say goodbye to Old Viktoravich, the white beard in the space tower. He was so old, some say he was friends with the dinosaurs. Personally, I don't believe that mankind was ever alive at the same time as the dinosaurs. And furthermore, even if they did walk the earth together, I don't believe that reptiles can really be friends with anyone, even if we're talking about a friendly, friendly man like Old Viktoravich. So he might have been old, but it strains the imagination to think he was friends with a stegosaurus. How could a dinosaur even express friendship? *Be serious.* A human friendship bracelet would never fit around a giant dinosaur claw. I won't argue, however, that Old Viktoravich was old. He was at least as old as the space program, where he handled ballistic trajectories, and he had wished luck to every Cosmonaut who had left the Earth and then welcomed him back home safely after the trip, if he survived.

His office was at the base of the space tower. It was filled with math books, computing machines, and sardines. It smelled like old fish.

"Greetings, Old Man," I said as I walked in. "I'm going to space today. Wish me luck."

"You don't need luck," he said. "With Mother Russia's best scientists planning your mission, you need only trust in Moscow and the Academy."

"I will trust you, but you must do your calculations carefully."

He pounded his wrinkled hand on top of a pile of ledgers.

"We've planned for every possibility, child. Have no fear. But if you are suspicious, I will wish you luck." He found a bottle of sardine-flavored vodka and poured a bit into his coffee cup, and a another bit into a tumbler for me. He raised his cup to me. "Good luck, Ilya Zamyatin, in your journey to the stars!"

"And you will be here to welcome me back?" I asked, wiping the fishy vodka from my lips.

"This I cannot promise. I am an old man. The doctors, fuck their mothers, tell me I have only two months to live."

"I am sure they are lying cowards. And I will be back on Earth in five weeks, so even if they are right, you will be here to greet me. We will drink your vodka and celebrate my return."

"It will be so," he said. And then he began coughing, and pulled a handkerchief from his pocket. Soon he was coughing blood into his white handkerchief. "Those fucking doctors," he said weakly.

"It is a good omen," I said. "That bloodstain on your kerchief is shaped like the port wine stain on Chairman Gorbachev's forehead." He laughed, and then coughed some more. As I walked out the door, he was coughing. I'll never forget the last thing he said to me: *Cough, cough, cough, hack, cough,* and then the sound of spitting.

Next I had to check in at mission control so they could start my official countdown. If you find men in vests attractive, then mission control will give you an erection. Twenty men in red vests sat behind computers monitoring my ship and my rocket. My life was in their hands. Commander Vulkov was wheeled out to greet me. He had lost his arms and legs in Afghanistan, and he wore a rubber prosthetic hand on a chain around his neck. I grabbed the hand and shook it, as was customary.

"Captain Zamyatin," he said. "If you are ready for your mission, I will begin the countdown."

"I am ready,' I said. "I will not disappoint the Soviet Republic."

"Begin ninety-minute countdown, on my mark."

All the men turned to their computing screens as he spoke.

"And ... mark."

A machine beeped and the countdown started. On every computer screen in the room, numbers flashed in green letters. I was less than two hours from space! The countdown had started.

I walked to my capsule and strapped myself into place. Then the crane lifted me into position at the top of the rocket. This was to be my home for the next five weeks. Or so I thought. In fact, I would be there for over a year. If you had opened the capsule door at that moment and told me, "Ilya Zamyatin, your trip will actually be 14 months because of the collapse of your government," I would have said to you: "I don't believe you, and for God's sake close the capsule door! What are you doing outside my space capsule on top of the rocket? Don't you know how dangerous it is? Fuck off!"

Commander Vulkov's voice came across the radio.

"All systems go," he said. "We are at fail-safe launch point. Begin final preparations for launch. One-hundred. Ninety-nine. Ninety-eight..."

I was sweating in my space suit. I put my helmet it on and secured it to the bolts around my neck. I turned on my oxygen. And then I waited.

The rockets began with forty-five seconds left. It felt like an earthquake or a disastrously large fart. My whole body was rocked and the capsule shook. At thirty seconds, the boosters kicked in and the noise became so loud I could not hear the rest of the countdown. I can only assume that Commander Vulkov counted down the numbers in the order I knew them.

Then I was moving.

Fast.

The clouds rushed towards me.

Imagine being hit in the back with a sledge hammer. It would most likely kill you. But if it didn't, and instead you found yourself in outer space, then you'd know how I felt. The sky went from blue to white to black. I was in space, just like Ziggy Stardust in that David Bowie song.[2] Ground control was calling me.

"Zamyatin, confirm rocket separation."

I checked my monitors.

"Rocket separation confirmed."

"Apply thruster boost to reach orbit."

"Affirmative."

I ignited the thrust engine until the coordinates in my altimeter were correct. I was in space! I was doing space things! This was what I had dreamed of since I was a small child. It was like my life was a story book. I wondered what the next chapter would be about.

02 / MOSCOW HAS A PROBLEM

While I was dreaming of space, trouble was brewing on Earth. The Soviet Empire collapsed. I should have seen it coming. After all, I fought in Afghanistan. I knew how rickety the Russian military was. I knew how poor the space program was. Our country was out of money. We could not keep up with the West, who made millions off of Disneyland, Wheel of Fortune, Mr. Pibb and Knight Rider.[1] My people finally got tired of not having bread or prune soda or awesome television, and they forced the leaders to change things.

But I did not get newspapers in my orbit, so I knew little of this. My mission was a secret, so I had very little contact with Earth, other than the voice of mission control speaking over my headset. At the start of each morning, Commander Vulkov would read the headlines on the front page to me. Then he would read the beginning of each story. Then he would stop, because he lacked the ability to turn the pages. I guess the rumblings of revolution among the population were buried on the inside pages, if they were mentioned at all, because I never heard about them.

Then one day, Commander Vulkov said "Ilya, we are having a bit of a problem on Earth. The hard-liners are fighting against the change, and the regime is in chaos. What do I care? I hate the blowhards as much as anyone. But if you lose contact with us for a day or two, then it means someone is fighting for control of this building."

"Commander Vulkov," I said, "tell me what is going on. Is it another revolution? How will I get back to Earth?"

"I cannot predict the future," he said. "Just sit tight."

It was a long night up there, wondering what was going on. When I say night, I mean the night as measured in the Soviet Union. My own hours were less important than the hours of my home country. When they were awake, I was awake. While they slept, I slept. Only I did not sleep that night. You know those nights when you can't sleep and you lie awake in bed staring at the ceiling, fearing that you'll be tired the next day, too tired to face the obstacles in your way? It was like that, except instead of a bed, I was in a space capsule, and instead of the ceiling, I was staring at the other side of the space capsule. Another difference is that when you pee yourself in bed at night, you have to wake up and change your clothes. But I had a vacuum tube attached to my penis, so I could pee all I wanted and not have to change clothes. That's one thing I miss about being in space!

The next morning, Commander Vulkov's voice woke me up again.

"Ilya, there is no newspaper today. It might have been printed, but it was not delivered to the base. Something is happening in the country."

"You must read something to me, Commander," I said. "If I

don't hear another voice, I may go mad."

"Relax, relax," he said. Then he read me the front page of the newspaper from the day before.

The next day, he did the same.

He read me that same front page for two weeks straight. While old men in the Kremlin battled for supremacy, our airfield was cut off from the world. At first, the old guard kept us cut off, with their tanks and Kalashnikovs. The younger generation did not even know I was up there. The K.G.B. had kept my mission a secret from all the untrustworthy elements of the government. Only after the government fell and the people stormed into secret rooms and vaults did they discover the existence of the airfield and the small town around it. It was a mirror space program, a hidden duplicate of the public Cosmonauts league.[2]

Many people complained that this second space program was a horrible waste of money, the kind of costly, useless secret that bankrupted the U.S.S.R. into oblivion. I still believe our program was fine and heroic. It was that other space program that was not needed. Ours was more cost effective, since we spent no money on publicity. Yuri Gagarin had his ugly face plastered on posters and lunch boxes and children's vodka canteens. What a waste of money! Every April 12, the huge Cosmonautics Day parades wasted valuable ticker tape celebrating that guy's short trip to space. No wonder we fell behind the West – we had no more ticker tape to monitor stock prices after we threw it all into the street for parades.

So then the world found out about secret mirror space program. But getting me back to Earth was not so easy. Even staying in touch with me became impossible. Certain high ranking blowhards quit the space program when they realized the old

Communist regime had lost. Among those men was a radio tower technician who I'll call Goatlover because he seemed like the kind of guy who loved goats. Maybe he liked it when goats loved him. Goatlover broke the radio tower on his last day, and took with him a bunch of circuits and vacuum tubes as souvenirs. Some of those parts hadn't been made in over a decade, which made them pretty much irreplaceable. Without them, the radio tower could not communicate with me, and I could not communicate back.

Some of my readers may be scientists saying to themselves, that does not seem plausible. Couldn't any radio be rigged to send and receive signals from this man's capsule? These scientists should scrub my toilet. I will tell them what is plausible. I spent 14 months in space without human contact! The K.G.B. was worried about American infiltration of Soviet Union. Especially they were worried about American space program doing something tricky in outer space, which they could not watch all the time. They had spies in the United States, but what if a N.A.S.A. soldier broke into a space capsule and replaced a Cosmonaut with American secret agent who had plastic surgery and voice modulator implanted in throat to perfectly mimic the Cosmonaut? To prevent this treachery, they made capsules impregnable to outside. Once I was locked in, no one could get me out unless I released the hatch mechanism. Otherwise I would be blown up and killed. So far, so good. But what if a crafty American tricks me into opening hatch? Maybe they broadcast radio message telling me they were flying by in their space shuttle and saw my capsule was on fire. "Don't worry," they say, "we can rescue you if you just open the door." Then when I open the door expecting a rescue mission, I am killed and replaced by a man who used to look like Nicolas Cage.[3] This was a big concern for K.G.B. (It is also why I am wary of the Fresh Direct delivery man who looks like Nicolas Cage.) To foil this sort of operation, my radio was scrambled by a mechanism so secret that only Goatloaver knew how it worked. So when he left and broke the radio tower, I lost contact with Earth.

I barely survived. I had enough protein pellets and water, but my mind almost crumbled under the strain. I have seen many documentaries about the famous American criminal Steve McQueen, who escaped from two different prisons.[4] Often, he is put into solitary confinement where his will is nearly broken. This was how I felt, trapped in my space capsule. I wondered if I would ever return to Earth to become a famous art thief or a renegade cop named Bullitt.

The first two days without radio contact, I was still hopeful. I knew from Commander Vulkov that there was turmoil in Moscow, but I thought it would be resolved and I would hear from mission control again. On the third day, I lost hope. For two days after that, I had the shakes and sweats and punched the walls of my capsules until my hands bled. Some of my comrades say a space capsule is like a woman because it doesn't fight back when you punch it, but I say that a woman's face is not made of steel and aluminum, so they are not the same.[5] Also, I tell them, you should not stay inside your woman for weeks at a time like you do your space capsule.

After five days of radio silence, I calmed down. I knew I had enough food for a long wait. The endless horizon of day-night churned towards me and I was only alone.

So I decided to read *Moby Dick*. It seemed like a good novel for someone floating through the darkness of space. If you wanted to say that the U.S. Space Shuttle was my white whale, then you could, although a whale could not survive in outer space. Imagine if it could! That book would be much more exciting than Herbert Melville's story.[6] Imagine: *A space whale comes to Earth and only one man can stop it, a grizzled sea captain who lost his leg to the space whale. But his daughter is in love with one of the sailors on his ship and he doesn't want to close his eyes, because he would miss her and he wouldn't want to miss a thing.*[7]

That is another story, though.

The book I had in my hands was *Moby Dick*.

I opened it, and decided that, despite the uncertainty and fear, there was something wonderful about floating among the stars reading this great book. It began: *It was a bright cold day in April, and the clocks were striking thirteen.*

What a powerful beginning! I knew I was in another universe, one filled with lies, because there is no number 13 on a clock. And April is not a cold month. I was fascinated and riveted by the story. After a couple hundred pages following Winston Smith, I wondered when the whale would show up. And when would he meet the man who insisted on being called Ishmael?

He never did. There was no whale. In the end, he fell in love with Big Brother. As it turned out, I was not reading *Moby Dick*. I was reading *1984*, by George Orwell. In the height of the Soviet empire, that book was strictly forbidden, along with many other works that were critical of the U.S.S.R. Yet those books circulated in Russia as samizdat, underground copies passed from reader to reader much like a Grateful Dead concert bootleg, except actually important in this case. Some of these samizdat works were disguised, so that curious cultural censors would not notice them on the shelves of secret dissidents. Which was how I ended up with a big bound book that looked like *Moby Dick* on the outside, but was actually *1984*, *Howl*, and *Shaft* on the inside. It was my first glimpse of Western literature, which seemed to be very gay and black, unlike Soviet literature, which was dominated by old white men.[8] This was a taste of the freedom that decades of Communist rule wanted to keep hidden. And it was delicious.

03 / NIGHTS IN THE MACHINERY

"I hear America singing."

–Walt Whitman[1]

Y ou could say I became an American in space. Not just because I became an exile, when my country disappeared, or because I was like the poor huddled masses* America welcomes to its shore. No, I mean that I earned my cultural citizenship in space. I read those American books, and I listened to my American rock and roll music. I discovered the fierce heart that beats in the American chest. I began to dance! Not ballet dancing like Russia is famous for, but sock hopping and jitterbugging, right there in my capsule. It was like being a teenager again. Nobody could tell me what to do. Even Com-

---

*In Russia, as a form of brainwashing, we were taught America was so pitiful it was populated by beggars, and that the Statue of Liberty even *requested* them, with a poem branded on her base declaring:
> Give me your tired, your poor,
> Your huddled masses yearning to breathe free,
> The wretched refuse of your teeming shore.

Nowadays, I laugh at the nonsense our Soviet government tried to tell us about the United States, as if a powerful nation would actually request for the human detritus of the world. Ha![2]

mander Vulkov was gone. I had the capsule to myself. Forget about my scientific missions and my spying assignments. The K.G.B. was falling apart. It was freedom. I could do anything I wanted.

I spent hours, staring out the tiny window at the brilliant black night, the endless well of darkness. I thought of the women I had known, and imagined the women I might know in the future. I listened to the timeless music of The Beatles over and over again: "Last Train to Clarksville," "I'm a Believer," and "Zilch." If God had a favorite band, it must have been The Beatles.[3]

I was lonely, too. Sometimes I counted stars. Other times I wrote letters. I wrote letters to my parents that I had never known. Both disappeared in purges when I was an infant. I am told my father was reported by a neighbor for complaining that his bath water was too cold one day. His voice boomed out through the window of our little home, "Ach, my globes are frigid in this water!" Gregorin next door heard him and realized that a complaint about bath water was an insult to Josef Stalin, who was obviously doing everything in his efforts to make sure the people had warm bath water.[4] Father disappeared in the night. Mother scratched his face out of all our family pictures. She became the man of the house—she had no choice. She plowed the fields and chased off wolves and thieves in the night. When the front gate broke, she got tools and repaired it herself! A great woman, the townspeople later told me. Repairing the gate, sadly, she hammered her thumb by accident. "Stupid hammer!" she yelled out in pain. Gregorin heard this and reported her to the secret police for insulting the people's hammer, a fine tool, one that appeared on our flag. They dragged her away the next morning. I became a ward of the state.

It was some small comfort, to know that I had no grieving

parents on Earth suffering at the same time as me, wondering about their poor son's fate. If a passing space shuttle were to attempt a rescue, they would only find another orphan.

As it turns out, I was not rescued. But I was contacted.

Six months had passed.

I was wearing Zlata's underwear and reading aloud from *Shaft* when I noticed something twinkling in the night sky. A new star perhaps? But it was not twinkling so much as blinking. And regularly. The light would go on. Then go off. On. Off. On. On. Off. On. Off. On. On. It was Morse code! Another craft in the night was sending signals to me. I tore a page out of *Shaft* and wrote down the dots and dashes. Then I consulted the encryption key I wore on a ring around my finger and translated the message.

ILYADONOTFEARYOUARENOTFORGOTTEN...
ILYA DONOTFEAR YOUARENOTFORGOTTEN
ILYA DO NOT FEAR YOU ARE NOT FORGOTTEN

Just eight words. But a hopeful message! It repeated over and over until the light disappeared. A ship orbiting was broadcasting that message to the whole atmosphere, to me, and to the space junk surrounding me. It was a beacon. I slept peacefully that night. And the night after.

I was not forgotten!

On the third day, I looked at the message again to encourage myself. I stared at it all day. After a while, I began to doubt.

Where did the message begin and end?

Ilya, do not fear: You are not forgotten.

If that was correct, it was a message of hope and encouragement. But maybe it was:

Forgotten Ilya. Do not fear: You are not.

Oh no! That would be a message of despair and existential doubt. And that wasn't even considering all the other possibilities...

Yo! Ua: renot forgot. Tenil, Yad, Ono, TF. Ear.

Now what did that mean?

I'll tell you what it meant: I was starting to suffer from space madness.

Even the strongest man can fall victim to the disorienting fear. I remembered training for it, back when I first joined the Cosmonaut team: In the middle of the night, sleeping in my bunk, I would be startled awake as someone threw a burlap sack over my head. Then I was carried through the darkness. I tried to count the steps, figure out where I was using my knowledge of the facility. But it was no use. I was twisted and turned and spun until I lost my bearings. And then, just as the dizziness began to fade, I was dropped. I fell in a panic, reaching out my hands and legs into space and finding nothing but air around me. It was only a fraction of a second, I'm sure, but I lived the fear of a void for what felt like hours in that instant. Next I was underwater, having been dropped into a pool. I swam towards what I thought was the surface and felt my hands clawing at plastic under water. There was a tarp above the pool! I became entangled in it and sank towards the bottom. When I finally gave up hope, I was pulled from the water by strong hands and rolled out on the edge of the pool, where I gasped for breath like a dying fish. Traumatic as it was, this provided excellent training for the mental and emotional rigors of space travel. Although, it's possible this was not actual training, and that it was just elaborate hazing on the part of the older Cosmonauts. At the end of the night, I was given a key to the secret Cosmonaut brotherhood building and the whole thing was never mentioned again. So, it was probably fraternity initiation.

In any case, a few hours of terror in in one night were not enough to prepare me for the terror and torture of my ordeal in space. First I doubted the hopeful message I had seen in the night. Then I began to see visions. A woman appeared to me, just like in the famous Monkees' song, "Let It Be." I thought it might be my mother, though I was not sure what she looked like. She whispered that I was a star child, and that I might marry the moon Titan. If I wasn't going crazy, then this hallucination certainly was. How could a man marry a moon?

Next I saw a bear. The stars of Ursa Major coalesced into a pure being of white light that ate brilliant pink space salmon. Circus music accompanied this vision. *Come with me*, the bear said. *We have much to see.*

I followed it into some space woods. After we walked a while, I looked back and saw only one pair of footprints in the snow. I said to the bear, "Why did you leave me alone there?" The bear answered, *Ilya, that is where I carried you.* But I think the bear was lying because I don't remember being carried, and besides, they were footprints, not paw prints. Lying bear!

I knew I was going insane, but I also believed each vision I had. Commander Vulkov opened the door of my capsule and talked to me from space. He had both his arms and legs. *Russia loves you*, he said. "Where did you find your arms and legs?" I asked. *They were built by a robot maker*, he answered. *I am a robot now.* Then he closed the hatch again.

Then I saw the face of an Afghan soldier I had killed in the war. He was covered in dirt, but he cried out to me. *Soon you will join me*, he said. *Please bring some clean towels, because I am covered in dirt.* His eyes began blinking rapidly. I was transfixed by his face. His eyes continued blinking. Open. Closed. Open. Open. Closed. Open. Closed. Open. Open. I knew that from somewhere. I fell asleep. When I woke up, his eyes were still in front of me, blinking. His face was black now. He only had one eye. He kept blinking that same pattern. His face was made of glass. He looked like outer space. His eye looked like the light of a space ship. His nose did not exist. Oh, now I got it. This wasn't his face. This was the light I had seen before. I was still looking out the window of my capsule. The message was repeating. *Ilya, do not fear. You are not forgotten.* I cried. Not in a girly way, but in a redemption sort of way. A manly cry. If tears could have a huge hairy dick and balls, that's what my tears would look like.

I was alive and knew where I was, but I could still see the face of the dead soldier. I thought back to my time in Afghanistan, which was a completely different chapter of my life.

04 / THE NEVERENDING WAR

"I will fight now! More! Forever!"
    –Chief Joseph of the Nez Perce[1]

I joined the army when I was young. It wasn't patriotic: I did it to impress a girl. Natasha Babel was the beauty of St. Martyrsburg, and everyone knew it. I joined the army because of her. I should have just learned to play guitar.

St. Martyrsburg was the small town where I ended up after my parents were taken away. Built in the 1950s, it was supposed to be an agricultural outpost, a hub for farmers growing potatoes and wheat to feed the nation. Never mind the bitter cold and lack of fertile soil! Stalin's science minister had said he could change the weather and make the icy crust arable land. He failed. So the town existed with no purpose once the farming efforts failed. Rather than admit its mistake, the Soviets stood their ground and insisted the city remain–*it must survive! It should prosper and be an example to other cities. If this town, with no natural resources, can be productive, just think what could be expected from towns more favored by the Earth!*

My orphanage was built inside of three large empty silos

that had been built to store food that could not grow. If it could not produce grains, St. Martyrsburg could at least produce children. Our bunks were in the silo. In the mornings we got out of bed and slid down the central pole before heading to school in the empty hangar-sized barn next door. Nights were the worst. After spending a day beneath books, studying literature and science and judo, we had to climb ladders to our beds, hundreds of feet in the air. You can tell the orphans of St. Martyrsburg by their muscular forearms.

Natasha Babel was not an orphan. Her father taught chemistry at the school and she lived just outside of town. How many teen boys drooled and fantasized about her normal sized forearms! Natasha! Such a sweet young thing, saying hi to all the boys. We were all in love with her. There were girls at the orphanage, but none were the objects of our affection. We wanted Natasha. She inspired great feats of daring. Marathons were sprinted for her love. Juggling learned for her pleasure. Poetry memorized for her satisfaction. As we approached adulthood, it became more urgent that we win her affection before she fall for another boy and marry him. On her 17th birthday, someone saw her kissing Peter Sukharin by the frozen lake. This would not do! Sukharin was ugly, and looked like cactus might one day sprout from the desert of his face. He had, we assumed, impressed her by his decision to join the young brigade of the K.G.B. So we all tried to one-up him. I rode my one-wheeled bicycle to the Army base and signed up. "Come back tomorrow," they said. "You'll leave the orphanage forever. The army is your new family."

I rode home excited and scared. I stopped at the Babels' house and told Natasha I had joined the army for her.

"Ilya Zamyatin, why do such a thing?"

"Because I love you, Natasha."

"But you will never see me. Men join the army and disappear to far off places. I think you wanted to get as far away from me as possible!"

"No, no, just the opposite. I want to be near you, always. I only joined... I joined because ... how else could I show I was more of a man than Peter Sukharin? He is going to be in the K.G.B., but I am going to be in the army!"

"Why would you want to be like Peter Sukharin?"

"Because you kissed him. Everyone wants to be like Peter Sukharin now."

"I kissed him because he had photographs of my father picking the people's flowers from a municipal field. He said he would have father arrested if I did not kiss him. I hated every tongue-filled minute of it! He is a weasel! I kissed a weasel, but only to protect my father."

I did not know what to say. I felt like I had been punched in the stomach by Natasha. Except it was worse, because it hurt like I had been punched in the stomach by someone with strong forearms, which she did not have.

"Please, Natasha Babel, tell me you will wait for me. I will join the army and become a hero. When I return to St. Martyrsburg, we can be together."

"I will wait for you. Be a brave soldier for me."

She was lying. I knew she was lying. She knew I knew she was lying. But it was for my own good. A white lie so I could leave happy and hopeful. God bless her for that lie.

That night I packed up my thing and put it next to bed. As an orphan, I did not own more than one thing, which was half the bicycle I shared with Dimitri Orlov. Rather than take turns riding it, we had sawed it in half and made two smaller bicycles. We each had one tire with a short half-chain and one pedal. Some called it a unicycle. But I was not a clown. It was a half-bicycle to me. I slept poorly, dreaming of Natasha Babel growing old. In the morning, I put the wheel on my back and slid down the orphanage pole for the last time. Goodbye, orphans. I had new parents now: My mother would be a tank, and my father a rifle. My brothers and sisters would be the soldiers of the Russian army. My children would be bullets, and I would shoot my children into the enemies of my country.

Rich people did not join the army. They hired others to take their places, so the recruits I trained with were all poor like me. We were astounded at the free food we were given in the giant cafeteria where we trained. Soup twice a day. Bread with every meal. Clean water, sometimes milk! This, I thought, must be what it's like to live the millionaire's life.

It was not easy, however. They tried to break us down, from the very first day. A truck picked us up and drove deep into the cold. We shivered in the back, protected from the howling wolf winds by only a green canvas tarp. Everyone was cold but the sergeant in his parka, the fur collar keeping even his face warm. We huddled into small fetal shapes, trying to keep every ounce of warmth with in our bodies But each bump in the poorly paved road threw us into the air, letting the cold air beneath us, freezing the hard bench before we landed again. It was as if we were being spanked repeatedly by a snow man. One comrade passed around cigarettes, which gave us a breath of warmth for a moment. Hours passed. We stopped for gas. We climbed great hills, then rolled down the other side. Every half hour or so, we rotated so nobody had to sit near the back for too long. It was warmest close to the cab up front. Someone tried to sing, but we were too cold to join him.

Just as we were nodding off, drained and tired from the effort to keep warm, we heard gunfire. Panic and madness took over. We grabbed our things and jumped out of the truck. Nobody had much. A few small bags, a personal item or two, and me with my bicycle wheel. As we crouched down low to avoid being shot, we heard the laughter of a superior. A hard-faced man was doubled over giggling. He held a Kalishnikov and pointed at us. "Look at you sad dogs, peeing yourselves like war has broken out! A few gun shots and you lose all control of yourselves. I am sorry to say I don't think you'll amount to much as soldiers."

He fired a few more shots into the air, sending us all into panic again. This was how the *stariki* treated new recruits.

"I am Lieutenant Vulkov! I will turn you babies into men, or I will kill you trying!" He threw his rifle to an underling and dropped down to the ground with us.

"Let's do some push-ups! If any of you infants can do more push-ups than me, I will let you eat dinner and go to sleep without running the obstacle course. You don't see an obstacle course nearby, do you? That's because it's a five-mile run from here. Now, push ups! You'll see my arms are quite strong!"

He began doing push-ups and we tried to keep up. Some of the farm boys actually kept pace for a while, until we got into the 70s, when most of us had to quit. Others had thrown up but kept going, lowering their faces toward their vomit over and over again. By 120, only two recruits were left. Then Vulkov began doing one-armed push-ups. "You see, girls, showing you how weak you are is my job, and I could do it with one arm tied behind my back," Vulkov laughed. How could a man laugh after 120 push ups, I wondered. How could he even talk?

The two recruits collapsed soon after and Vulkov hopped to his feet. "Well, it's time for a run, except for these two, who have proven themselves. They can go to the mess hall now." The rest of us groaned. I think the two men would have smiled if they'd had the strength. Vulkov bolted off into the night. "Follow me, children, if you want to be men!"

We began jogging haggardly after him.

The sergeant laughed from the back of the truck. "Better follow even if you don't want to be men," he said, and we ran faster, hoping not to lose Vulkov's trail in the darkness.

It had all happened so fast we forgot our cold until a mile into the run. But then he led us through a stream and our feet got wet. He was wearing boots, but we had the shoes we brought from home. Some of us had sturdy work boots, but many had threadbare dress shoes or hand-me-down sneakers. The first man into the stream cried out but did not stop. We all looked at each other and then plunged in after, every one of us crying out just the same as the freezing needles hit our feet. On the other side of the stream, we all ran faster: *Let us get away from this cold wet feeling.*

We nearly caught up with Vulkov as he turned from the beaten path and into an untamed field. "Look out for wolves," he said. "They like the taste of young recruits."

It is hard to panic and search the horizon for predators while running on cold swollen feet, but we found a way. Our group suddenly looked like an army of rag dolls, stumbling through the tall grass, looking this way and that, fighting to stay in the center of the pack where it seemed safest. The full moon over head did nothing to calm our fears. Then one of us fell completely, smacking into the cold hard dirt and rolling to a stop. All of us slowed and looked at him on our way by. "Grab him! Carry him!" yelled Vulkov. We did. If he had not injured himself falling down, he was certainly beaten and bruised by the way we hoisted his limp body onto our shoulders and plowed on into the night. We still did not know each other's names.

We continued forward. Would we end up in some other

country? How far could we run? Then a murmur passed through the bunch and a few arms lifted weakly to point towards the horizon. In the moonlight we could see the silhouette of an obstacle course. Giant pillars, raised platforms and, as we got closer, thick webs of rope connecting the entire thing. We didn't know it yet, but this monster would feel like our home after a few months.

"Listen, peasants. As soon as everyone runs through this course tonight, we can go home and eat," Vulkov said.

"What about this guy?" asked a man with the slumped soldier on his shoulders.

"Him too!"

We groaned. We ran the course. We threw up. We jogged back to base. That was the easiest night we had.

We didn't train for Afghanistan. Perhaps we would have, if we'd known we would go there. I don't know whether to blame poor training or poor planning for that situation. It could have been either.

Most of our training involved invasions of mock cities made to look like American towns. I got to be very good at bursting through the window of a malt shop and shooting mannequins sitting on bar stools. I practiced infiltration, too. The fake cities were populated by our soldiers with the best English skills. We would try to hold conversations and not reveal our origins. It was difficult. Our accents were heavy, and we knew very little of American culture. Good thing we never invaded. I think many of our troops would have stopped at K-Mart and gone shopping instead of fighting. When I think of this American city I live in now (I don't want to say which one) and compare it to the simulation cities of Russia where I trained, I laugh. Whoever built those fake towns had no idea.

At night, we smoked and played cards. I often thought of Natasha Babel and wondered where she was. In the barracks, I was renowned for the strength of my orphanage forearms. While I was no good at pushups, I could give Vulkov a run for his money in the pull-up department. The first time he respected me was at the gym, when he saw me doing pull ups. He jumped up on the bar beside me and began doing pull ups himself. "I love to use my arms," he said, barely breaking a sweat. "I don't know what I'd do with out them." When he had done about 50 pull ups, he asked me how many I had done before he started.

"I don't know," I said. "Maybe a hundred? I don't count."

He laughed heartily. "Was your father a ladder maker?"

"I don't know what a ladder maker is," I said.

"A man who makes ladders, idiot."

"Oh, that makes sense," I said. "I didn't know there were people who just made ladders. In my town, a carpenter made ladders, but also fences and tables and night stands."

"Did he make end tables?"

"Sure. I mean, he made all kinds of tables."

This conversation seems boring on paper, but imagine it as a contest of wills between two people who don't want to show any weakness or signs of being tired as they continue to do pull-ups in an exercise facility surrounded by army recruits.

"I have two tables myself," Vulkov said. "I like to put things on my tables."

"What sort of things?"

"Books. Breakfast. You know. Table stuff."

"I never had a table, as I was raised in an orphanage."

"What? Couldn't orphans have tables? Where did you eat?"

"On long planks of wood propped up by legs made of wood connected to the planks with corner joints."

"Those were tables!"

"Ahh! I never knew what they were called," I said.

"Say, how many pull-ups do you think we've done?"

"Not enough!" I said. "I'm hardly breaking a sweat. I'd like to know what other things you put on your table."

"Oh, you know... the usual. Heavy weights. Sore-muscle reliever. Painful shoulder ointment."

The crafty dog! He was naming items that would make me aware of how tired my arms were getting. I doubted he put any of those things on his table. Eventually I grew tired. I was not tired enough to quit, but I also did not want to risk beating him at this contest of muscles. So I gave in.

"I think I have done as many pull-ups as I can," I said, and dropped to the floor.

Vulkov did five more, then dropped down next to me.

"I like a strong man!" he said. Then he put his arm around my shoulder. "I like a smart man even more. You could have done more pull-ups, Ilya. But you choose to save your strength and possibly my face. This I appreciate." He grabbed my hand. "I enjoy shaking your hand to acknowledge your strength, and to make use of my perfectly functioning hand, which God saw fit to give me, and I shall keep until I die."

Now some of you readers are probably doubting that he actually said that. I know what you are thinking: *How unlikely!* And yet, I tell you, it is true. He did, in fact, mention God in front of me and the other recruits. Officially, there was no religion in the U.S.S.R. But Vulkov cared little for rules unless they made sense to him.

So the months passed for us recruits. When we scraped together some money and had a weekend of leave, we went into town for the ladies. They gave us a soldiers' discount. In a brothel, you could find vodka and a woman for every type of desire. Someone who looked old, someone who looked young, someone who pretended to be your sister or dentist. No fantasy went unserved by the professional women. A particularly popular request was for American women. The madame of the establishment we frequented had a connection with the army base and obtained access to the fake American towns where we trained. On certain nights, when no exercises were being conducted, soldiers would lead prostitutes to the artificial villages and make love to a woman at the public library, or in the movie theater, or at the McDonald's. The more American the location, the more exciting the sex! To paraphrase Neil Simon's song "The Boxer," I must declare there were periods when, due to my lonesome state, I sought comfort in such places.[2] The most erotic and patriotic night of my basic training was when I bedded Anya Magazanin at the facsimile of the Daughters of the American Revolution meeting house, while I wore my soldier's uniform and she cried out "Oh, Ilya, you are so much better than my American husband Mr. Abraham Lincoln!" I had asked her to role play that she was a married American woman, and that was the only American name she knew. At first it was distracting, but after I got used to it, it was empowering.

Sex and fighting and running and shooting. We became experts at all these things. Yet we were still unprepared for Afghanistan.

The war had started a long time ago and was almost over. I was still a boy when the Soviet Union invaded the desert wasteland. I remember because we did so well at the Olympics that year when the Americans boycotted. At the orphanage, we got good TV reception because the antenna was at the very top of the tallest dormitory silo. We savored every minute of that

Olympics. It was the only good thing that came out of Afghanistan, unless you count kabobs. They call the country the Graveyard of Empires because all empires go there to die. It is a poetic phrase but not quite accurate because the empires are not actually buried there, while dead bodies are buried in a graveyard. It is more like a Hospice for Empires. When imperialist powers are on their last legs they go there and die. Although a hospice is a place to die peacefully, so it's not quite a hospice either. I would say it's a Killing Field of Empires. But more sand than grass, so Afghanistan should really be called the Deadly Sandbox of Empires.

The arc of Soviet history was feeling gravity's pull by 1986, when I climbed aboard a military transport bound for Kabul. Those of us in the army were never very optimistic, and this assignment did not help. It was clear we were losing the war to the *mujahideen* who were backed by America. Morale was low. Commander Vulkov did his best to keep our spirits up. He was promoted just before we left. This was a big achievement! I had discovered by now that he had been an orphan like me. With no family members to pull favors or kill off his competitors, Vulkov had to earn every stripe on his sleeve. During the revolution and later in the purges, many families of power were destroyed. But the rich and powerful are impossible to entirely destroy, like cockroaches, they find a way to survive. By the end of the Twentieth Century, our country's royalty was the elite Party Leaders and K.G.B. secret collectors. But Vulkov was not one of these men. He was a hard worker with a good head on his shoulders that his superiors appreciated. That head on his shoulders is one feature he never lost.

Bumping its way along the broken roads of the U.S.S.R., the convoy took us through the heartland south along the Caspian sea. No townspeople waved at us or welcomed us with their daughters. We might just as well have been ghosts in the wind. When we stopped to rest nobody made eye contact with us. It's easier to ignore a war you don't see. We were not attractive by any means, with our stench of exhaust and thundering engines. But this part of the country was no beauty queen either. They should have thanked us for buying candy bars and vodka in their towns! Instead we rolled on deeper into the continent. Plains gave way to mountain passes and Europe gave way to Asia. Squared buildings became rounded domes, church steeples became minarets, white skinned men became browned skin men. One wrong turn would take us to China with its tigers and wontons, another would lead us to Persia with its magic carpets and saffron. Maybe a wrong turn would be a welcome gift – following directions would lead only to Afghanistan with its warlords and opiates.[3]

We sang songs as we rolled. Starting off, it was Russian anthems. After a while, we hesitantly broke into some Western tunes. As we picked up steam, we got more into the songs. A soldier would stand up and play vicious air guitar solos in place of the real ones. We drummed the rhythms on our legs and on the benches around us. We used steel canteens to replicate high hats. We were right in the middle of a killer version of "Born to Run" when Vulkov stood up and screamed at us. "You fucking idiots!" He pounded on the back of the cab and made the driver stop. He seemed close to firing his weapon, he was in such a fury. Veins bulged from his head and neck. "Listen to you idiots! I've never heard such nonsense in my life!" He jumped out of the truck and onto the road behind us.

"What the fuck did you men just say?"

Nobody answered.

"You were singing. Don't pretend you weren't."

More silence.

He stared at us. It was clear the convoy wouldn't move again until we answered.

"We were singing 'Born to Run', sir," I answered. "By Bruce Springsteen."

"Were you?"

"Yes. I know it's inappropriate."

"Would somebody care to tell me the lyrics you just sang?"

Rachnoyvitch cleared his breath. "It goes 'Maybe this clown rips the bums from your pack, it's a deaf track, it's a suicide rack.'"

"I can't believe you pitiful men. You might as well die in Afghanistan, you have nothing to live for." He fired his rifle into the dirt in front of him. The echo inside the truck kicked our ear drums. "Listen closely," he said. "I'll only tell you this once." Then he told us the actual lyrics to "Born to Run", which seemed equally silly. "Is that clear to all of you?"

We nodded.

"If you're going to sing The Boss, at least do him the honor of getting the words right." He climbed back into the truck. "Now let's take it from the top." We rolled on, and we sang every song our unit knew, even "Born in the U.S.A." which was a criminal act. But we were headed towards war. We had nothing left to lose.

Kabul. If you think Russia is bad, then you have never been to Kabul. Kabul is so shitty, it doesn't sit around the house, it *shits* around the house. How many Kabul residents does it take to screw in a lightbulb? None, they like it better dark so they don't have to see how crappy their homes are. How did the Kabul hockey team die? They killed themselves because they lived in Kabul.

These were the jokes we traded in the bunker. Like all jokes, they have a bit of truth to them. Perhaps if you visit Afghanistan when it's not at war, you might enjoy it. If you can find a time when it's not at war.

I say these things, not to insult Afghanistan, but to make clear what a bunch of blowhards our leaders were in those days. Who invades and occupies such a place? The Kremlin found the only place more desolate than Russia, and tried to take it over. And you know the Afghans were prepared to defend it with their lives! For only someone who truly loves his country would stay in such a place. People who live in Afghanistan are like victims of domestic violence. They should leave, but love keeps them where they are, despite the bruises and suffering.

When we got to our base in Afghanistan, we found the soldiers who had been there for years and were about to go home. They showed us the ropes and we told them what had changed at home, which was not much. We ate goat and soup. We played soccer in the sand. Our ankles were twisted and sprained. The generals knew a few days of rest and adjustment would be helpful when we went into the hills. We fell asleep easily.

We woke up hard. Giant gunships swooped in and rattled us with wind and steel. Mi-24s looked like wasps had mated with warthogs and given birth to giant metal helicopters. The sound startled us that first morning. Within a year it would not even register, the deadly birds were so omnipresent.

That first full day in the desert is a kind of blur. We suited up and headed into town. All day long we heard "Glory of Love" by Peter Cetera playing on small radios. It was popular at the time. But listening to it for so long, I can understand why the Taliban outlawed music after taking power.

The markets smelled of sweet fruit and burning oil. Our rifles knocked fruit off carts and to the ground as we walked past. The people looked at us askance. What were we doing in their country? Why did we think we'd have any more luck conquering this hellhole than any civilization before? Did we hate this song as much as they did? Why was it playing so often? Was it on Afghan radio, or did somebody own a tape?

Of course, American readers, that last paragraph applies to your country now, except you should replace *tape* with *CD* and "Glory of Love" with "All the Single Ladies."[4]

Then it was time to patrol. Vulkov volunteered us for one of the most dangerous valleys in the country. He liked to quote Confucius: "If you're going to die, better not to die as a woman."[5] And so our parade of force marched and then drove out of town to the mountains. The enemy was hiding in caves waiting for us: Imagine a surprise party when it is not your birthday and every present you receive is thrown at you faster than the speed of sound, and the gifts are bullets, and you receive thousands of gifts. That is what it was like.

We charged over humps in the ground and tumbled into ditches. We dug in. We tore out. We shot and ran and shot again. War is exhilarating, yes, but so is sex and there is far less chance of death. I would not go to war again unless I had no choice. By nightfall we had driven around the same cave three times, drawing out rebels and shelling them back into their holes.

"We'll keep them pinned down for the night," Vulkov said.

"What if they have exit tunnels?" I asked.

"Tomorrow we'll chase them down those tunnels to hell."

Men were assigned to launch flares periodically towards the mouth of the cave. That way the men inside couldn't sneak out or really even see where we were. The blinding light kept them pinned inside.

"Get a good night's sleep, men," Vulkov told us as he went

from foxhole to foxhole in the blue light. "Just before dawn, we'll take the cave."

Fear kept me up all that night. But it also gave me time to think back on my life. I was 19 years old and this was my first time traveling out of the country. I bet other children of the world traveled in their childhood to Paris and London and summer camps all over Europe and America. They owned berets and wrote poetry and made love to thin severe ladies. I had only known the round severe ladies of the Steppes. And yet, all things considered, I had not done too poorly for myself. I had escaped my hometown. I sat back on the hard dirt that was my mattress and stared up into the night. I could not see stars for all the light from the flares landing near the cave. In future weeks, I would stare into the vast unpolluted cosmos above Afghanistan and wonder about the stars and the worlds beyond this one. The winking stars would call to me. *Leave this place*, they would say. *Come to us.* I did not know what they meant at the time. I thought maybe my parents were up there in the heavens. Perhaps they wanted me to visit and communicated with me through light, a direct connection to my mind and soul from the ether of space. Does this sound fanciful? I was, remember, still a teenager naive to the ways of the world. And I had lost my parents when I was young; certainly it was not unusual to search for a connection with them in the heavens above? Also, I was smoking a lot of opium those weeks. I guess that more than anything else explains the voices I heard.

Still, for all the death and blood and mayhem that followed, what I remember most about Afghanistan was the feeling I could not shake, the one that said, *Your parents miss you and wish they could be with you... they are in the stars above.*

Earlier this year, I broke down crying in a grocery store the first time I heard the song "Somewhere Out There." It was in New York. I dropped my orzo back onto the shelf and fled the market with tears in my eyes. I stumbled into a bookstore and managed to find the song's origin – in the form of a DVD of *An American Tale*. I took it home to my apartment and watched it. I had been crying before, but when the film was done, I was pounding my sofa with fists, sobbing and slobbering like a dog. I missed my parents so much. The cartoon made me see the truth: I was alone in the world. I had not wanted to admit it before. I had believed that my parents were up among the stars, but that was a joke, a fiction, as unbelievable as a talking mouse. And yet I had talked to them so many times when I was trapped in space, when I was a floating orphan.

05 / WHEN WE WERE ORPHANS OF THE FLOATING WORLD

When I recovered from my fit of madness in space, I still faced an abyss of despair. My hallucinations were gone, but I was still far from home. I could not communicate with my country men. All I had to guide me was the occasional message in morse code from a passing star ship. I learned later that it was not just the American space shuttle. Television and radio satellites were rewired to send me messages of comfort. The transmissions were short: usually the date and a brief message about plans to bring me home to earth. How I longed to be on the Soyuz! Russia's public space program would not have suffered such trouble. The entire planet would have rallied to its aid. But nobody knew about my suffering save the intelligence agents and space officials of the world. Together, they decided it would be too terrifying to reveal the truth to the world. Russia was worried about the anger its citizens would feel that one of their countrymen was stranded in space. As for America, the government feared panic if U.S. citizens discovered that the evil Soviet Empire had not just one, but two space programs, and that one of them had been operating in secret all these years. So my existence was hushed up. The only civilian to find out about me was a vice president at Hughes Aerospace, who hand coded the messages of comfort that his company's satellites passed on to me.

And how did I pass the nights? I must confess that I jerked off a lot. I can count it among my accomplishments that I am one of the few men alive who have masturbated in space. I doubt any American astronauts did such a thing. Some of them may have ejaculated during wet dreams, ruining their spacesuits with semen. But the close quarters and prude attitudes of your N.A.S.A. pretty much guarantee there is no self-pleasure on your space craft. But with a capsule all to myself and nothing to occupy my time, I tell you I touched myself in all kinds of ways. If you have never reached orgasm in zero gravity, then you have not led a full life. After all, that is what separates us from the animals – our ability to build rockets, launch ourselves into outer space, and then use our opposable thumbs to rub our erections to completion.

I've heard of Americans in the space shuttle watching DVDs to pass the time. I wish I'd had that luxury. Instead it was *1984*, and *Howl*, and *Shaft* for me. All those books, however, left me with a sense of metaphor. Despite all the amazing experiences I've had in life, you'll notice that I compare events to other events. I cannot sum up my experiences without analogy. When I came back to earth, I was reborn, from the period I had spent floating like a fetus, now going forth into a planet of comparisons. For being in space is like being in a womb. And just as all babies being born find themselves confused to be on the planet earth, I too, was alarmed and began crying when I found myself on solid ground again.

But I'm getting ahead of myself. I must first relay how I returned from space. This is a story of orphaned countries. The fractured satellite nations of the U.S.S.R. were in turmoil. Without the central iron fist of Moscow pounding down on them, they yearned to be free. The nations with natural resources kicked the hardest at the their Mother Russia, waking her in the night. But like any mother, she did not want to let them go. They were her children after all. When a child leaves home, there is shouting and the slamming of doors. In this case there were troops and invasions and threats. But the breakaway republics managed to declare independence on paper. Those were the children Mother loved and she refused to let them go, no matter how much they shouted that they were grown-ups and ready to live their own lives. The runt children, the countries with nothing to offer, found themselves on the way to the orphanage. They clung to their mother's legs crying out not to be sent away. They grabbed at their brothers' arms. If those other countries did not leave, maybe the family could stay together. The whole world was watching the domestic struggle because this family was armed with an arsenal of thermonuclear weapons.

It was even rumored, later, that I had been orbiting with a hydrogen bomb at the time. The story went like this: Russia, having won the space race, began hurling nuclear bombs into orbit, keeping them circling the globe in case they should ever be needed. If a U.S. first strike destroyed all of Russia's vast atomic stockpile, we could still rain down annihilation from above, destroying key cities as retaliation. This topic was broached in your American film *Space Cowboys*, which is one of my least favorite cowboy movies. It is not a classic of the justice and the western plains like *High Noon*, *The Searchers*, or *The Cowboy Way*.[1]

I do not think I my capsule was a nuclear weapon. I say *think* because I cannot be sure. It is just like the secretive Soviet government to send a man to space on a bomb without telling him that vital information. But if that had been the case, could not the trigger mechanism have been used to bring me down to earth sooner?

My presence in space was still a guarded secret. I owe my life to an anonymous source that notified *Pravda* and *The Washington Post* about my existence. Suddenly I was on the front page of newspapers around the world. Russian people clamored for my return. America showed its humility about winning the Cold War by offering to help bring me back to Earth. Boris Yeltsin was coming to power in those days, and he pushed to launch a capsule full of vodka so that I might drink away my sorrows until they could figure out how to get me back to earth. I did not know about any of this. But the best scientists in two countries were now working to get me home. Recently, while being interviewed by *The New Yorker* for a story about that blowhard Vladimir Putin, I talked to the former *Washington Post* reporter about the anonymous source who had contacted him and shared my story with the world. I don't want to reveal the reporter's name, but he is currently the editor of *The New Yorker*.

"This anonymous source," I asked, "did he sound like a man with no arms or legs?"

The reporter stared at me. "I don't know what that kind of man would sound like," he said. I understood perfectly. He could not reveal his source, just as I could not tell you this former *Washington Post* reporter's identity, or point you towards his books on Muhammed Ali, Russia, or The Devil Problem. There is a certain code of honor among reporters and their sources. I believe, though I could not confirm it, that Commander Vulkov was the source who saved my life. I would have asked the reporter from *Pravda* who their source was, but they were shot to death two days after running a story critical of blowhard Vladimir Putin. Putin is such an elbow-fucking blowhard that his dick smells like Old Spice.

Why, you ask, would Vulkov have risked his neck, his last remaining appendage, for me? Because he is a great man, for one thing. And because I saved his life during a thrilling battle in Afghanistan, a gunfight so exciting that it would make you want to read the next chapter of this book even if you were starting to lose interest in my tale.

06 / THE MOUTH OF HELL

"Counterrevolution and imperialism have turned
Afghanistan into a bleeding wound."

—Mikhail Gorbachev

Once I was being interviewed by David Remnick of *The New Yorker* when he asked me "What the scariest moment of your life before you were trapped in space?"

The answer was easy – a certain battle in the Afghan hills, where life is cheaper than poppy seeds and death comes so rapidly you would think there was a two-for-one special. At the time he asked, I didn't tell this story as an answer. I thought it would sound more masculine to joke about my fear.

"When I saw horror film *The Exorcist*," I answered. "That was the scariest thing. It was scarier, even, than being trapped in space." A short blurb about me appeared in the magazine's opening pages next to a line drawing of my face and a cartoon about homeless cats.[1] I was in Washington, D.C., at the time, and I told Mr. Remnick how I had recently visited the stairs featured in the film's climax. "They were so dizzyingly high," I said. "Like Odessa but steeper and sharper. We are students of filmed stairways in our country."

That made for a nice literary anecdote, but it was not the truth. I saved the truth for you, the reader of my life story.

All wars are scary. Soldiers who are unafraid are the ones who have gone insane. But this battle I shall tell you about was more terrifying than anything I have ever seen involving men and guns.

We had followed the Afghans through the tunnels, starting the morning after the long night of the flare and the cave. Waking from weary, dreamless sleep, we pounded the mouth of the cave with mortars, then charged in with our guns blazing. They escaped. Over the course of the next few months, we became the Soviet army's specialists at clearing out mountain caves and other guerilla hiding places. We chased a particular band of rebels from one cave to the next, beyond the Khyber Pass and up into the white mountains of Tora Bora.

The outlaws rode hard, breaking and killing horses as they fled from our tanks and gunships, the devastating firepower tearing up green fields and laying down stitches of bullet holes in the countryside. As night fell on the sixth straight day of chase, we pushed them into a well fortified cave and halted outside of it.

Commander Vulkov pulled me aside.

"We can't go into that dry cave at night," he said. "It's like a woman. She must be lubricated first. We must begin the foreplay."

Shouting orders, he quickly dispatched groups of men to the other openings of the cave we knew from stolen maps. The men laid down gasoline trails, soaking the rocks and walls. Then we lit the fuse.

We smelled death before we saw it. Smoldering flesh and

smoke poured out of the cave and traced the mountain breeze into our faces. Then we heard the wheeze of the mountains as the air swirled in a deathly tornado. Fire was pouring out of caves on the other side of the hills, but the main entrance in front of us was still dark. We tensed on the perimeter, fingers on triggers. As soon as the warriors came running we would mow them down.

But it was not men that we saw. It was something else entirely. It was apocalypse. Thundering hooves of burning horses brought fiery orange flames into the night, rampaging towards our position. Riderless beasts set ablaze, the horses let out an unearthly cry and we began firing before we knew what they were. It was as merciful an act as it was confused. Only as the creatures fell to the earth, cartwheeling in flames, did we recognize them. The rebels had set their animals on fire and chased them out towards us, armed with explosives. Now they lay smoldering in the dirt. A few eager men ran towards the cave, charging despite the cries of Commander Vulkov. Then the beasts exploded, sending man and horse meat alike into the sky. I was still in shock. The true nature of what had happened only became clear as I reloaded my rifle and heard the sounds of bone and skin falling to earth around me, deathly precipitation. Charred pink bits landed all around us. Smoking tatters of camouflage whispered down into the night, swaying with the wind. Then it was quiet. The blasts had put out the fires where the horses had been, sucking away the oxygen. All we could hear was the cleaning and loading of guns.

"It's time to go, men." Vulkov was speaking in a normal voice now. "These cowards sent their animals to do their dirty work. A man who will harm an innocent creature does not deserve to live. It's time to take the cave."

He fired his rifle once into the air, then aimed a burst at the cave and began running. We trailed behind him, screaming with fury, blind in the dark and smoke. It was madness.

Inside the cave we tore off down different tunnels shooting at anything that moved. I was with Vulkov. Six of us charged through the black smoke and into a clearing. It was a portion of the cave that had been ventilated somehow. Artificial lights illuminated the rocky chasm. A lone Afghan warrior was laughing: *Soon you will join me.* He held no weapon, only a detonator connected to a pile of explosives on the ground behind him. I remember stopping short. It was a standoff, I thought. But Vulkov did not stop. He kept running, dropped his rifle, and threw himself at the rebel. He wrapped his arms around the man, chest to chest, and dove towards the explosives as the man pushed the detonator. Light filled the room. Only silence followed as our eardrums were rendered numb by the concussion. I saw the bodies of the two men suddenly change direction, thrown backwards now, somersaulting away from the blast and past us as we turned our faces away from the blast. I fell face first into the ground and felt my back scorched by a wave of heat. As soon as it passed, I stood and ran towards the opening we had come through. This was where I found Vulkov's remains. I knew he was dead. Until his eyes opened.

"Kill me," he said.

I gasped and threw up.

"Quickly," he said. And then he passed out.

The spine of the rebel was lying on his chest. Vulkov's arms were gone, and his legs were mostly shorn away by the blast. His limbs had been unprotected, but the Afghan's torso and skull had protected Vulkov's trunk. He was bleeding from his legs and shoulders. I had no time to think. It was pure instinct and training that made me grab a burning ember from the wreckage and cauterize his wounds. Vulkov always said it was my quick thinking that saved him, but actually he had saved himself by training me so well. Endless nights of Russian drills had prepared me for this moment of darkness. I stumbled away from Vulkov and saw the head of the rebel in on the ground in front of me. His hair was smoldering. I shoved the ember into his face. Then I kicked his head and collapsed to the floor of the cave. My hand was screaming with pain. I still couldn't hear. The night went black.

Fever dreams carried me through the night.

In sleep, I found myself locked in dungeons, where skulls screamed at me and said I would pay for making a wreck of this country. Horses charged toward me, or in other versions of the nightmare, I would be riding a horse when it reared up and threw me to the ground as punishment for having been burned alive. "It wasn't us," I'd scream. The horse would stare down at me and say, *If you hadn't surrounded the cave, I would still be alive.* I hope I am conveying how terrifying this dream is. I should make clear that in the dream, the horse has a rough angry voice, like a throat torn in half. It does not have the pleasant warble of Mr. Ed or many other talking horses you may be familiar with. If he did, I would enjoy such a dream, which would probably be funny. Even if a horse says something terrifying and demands vengeance, you can't take it seriously if it sounds like Mr. Ed.

In order to make Mr. Ed talk, they rubbed peanut butter on his teeth. He wasn't really talking, of course. But the movement of his lips matched up with words added in later. In the darkest years of whispering in the Soviet Union, a similar trick was used to get confessions out of dissidents. We would see them on the television, in flickering black and white light: a former minister admitting that he had lied and stolen and dishonored the country. It was all a puppet show. If you had got on their bad side, the politburo could find a way to make your lips move and they would put any words into them that they wanted.

These bleary eyed confessions were such a part of the world I knew that I saw them in my sleep, too. After the fight at the cave, my night terrors included visions where I saw myself on a television revealing my crimes. It was a green tinted tube at the end of a rock tunnel. As my talking head droned on, describing every bad thing I had ever done, I tried to turn off the television by turning its knob into the off position. For my younger readers, I should point out that the lack of a remote control was not a harrowing part of the nightmare – those devices simply didn't exist in the Russia of the time. Anyways, in the dream, the knob doesn't work, so I try to unplug it. I grab the cord out of the back of the box and pull ... it comes toward me but never ends, a dangling cord of rope that is warm and slippery in my hands ... it is covered in blood, I realize, and I drop the cord. My voice still echoes in the cave, ticking off items on the list of my crimes. I look at the screen and my face looks up at me suddenly. The words continue, but my mouth stops moving and I am just staring at a green avatar of myself. Then my voice begins describing sins I had not yet committed but that I would in the future. I look for a weapon to shoot the television, trying desperately to make it stop. Then suddenly my face disappears and I see Laika, the dog that had first ventured into space. He barks at me but I can understand him because it is a dream. *Some missions end in death*, he says. *But do not be sad about it. Is it not better to die out among the stars, or in a distant exotic land than to grow old and die in your hometown?* Then he begins licking himself. *I did not survive more than three years on this Earth*, he barks. *But I am not sad. I am a celebrated hero! I am most famous dog in Russia! And I can suck my own balls when I want to. You can fear death, but do not be sad about it.* I begin crying in my dream. "Where are you, now, Laika?" I ask. "Still in space?" *No,* he barks back. *I am in heaven. And if you die, you can join me here where everyone is happy, everyone has two loving parents, there are no orphans, and all souls can sexually pleasure themselves orally if they want.*

When I finally awoke, I was in a desolate field hospital, tattered canvas hanging from wooden posts. Gun shots and artillery could be heard in the night. The doctors and nurses were tense, shouting at each other in hushed tones. The other patients who could move their heads looked at each other nervously. But I was at peace. The dog had told me everything was going to be fine.

At first, I thought the bed next to me was empty. Only when a nurse came and changed the intravenous drip did I see the small lump of flesh starting with a head at the pillow and fading away below the blankets less than halfway down the mattress. Vulkov. What remained of him was snoring only a few feet away from me. Should I be happy that he had survived? Or miserable? What kind of life would he lead? In my head, I pictured him outfitted with two stump legs and hooks for arms, yelling at recruits, but unable to move on his own. Maybe, I thought, he could swing around on ropes held between his teeth. This image made me laugh, and a nurse quickly shushed me and gave me a shot of something. I fell back into sleep.

Later, I discovered that we had barely finished surveying the cave and setting up camp when a counter attack pounded at us. Weakened and without a leader, it was almost the end of our division. The caves, which had almost killed us the night before, now provided salvation. We fell back into them and radioed for help. As we were bombarded by the cousins and brothers of the men we had killed in the cave, we waited for the gunships to arrive. I say "cousins" and "brothers" but not friends, because there are no true friends in Afghanistan. There are only temporary allies and enemies. You could choose to call *friends* those who were not your enemies. But would they come help in your time of trouble? When your goats are dead and you have no meat to feed your family? When your goats are dead and you have no milk for your baby? When your goats are dead and you have nothing to put your dick in? In Afghanistan, only your family will truly help. Alliances are temporary, family is not.

The field hospital had been set up inside the cave. We were safe from gunfire, but the echoes of war reverberated loudly around us, making it hard to sleep without drugs. Whenever a man was given morphine, I thought how funny it was that we were using the opiate of this country to help us in our efforts to subdue it. As loud as it was in the hollow mountain chamber, we could still hear the beautiful sound of the Mi-24s rumbling through the night on vector to our position. They lit up the night with fire and phosphor. Soldiers near the mouth of the cave could see the silhouettes of dying warriors, the shadows of falling men illuminated by deathly flames. We were like Plato's philosophers who suddenly knew that the deaths we had seen in the cave were just a representation of the many different ways a man could be killed in the world outside.

I think Plato is the guy who killed himself when soldiers entered the city in which he lived. Or maybe it was Socrates? Whoever it was, those old philosophers really committed to their ideas, unlike the ideologues in Russia. As soon as a communist came to power, he started collecting goods for himself. I guess I can't blame them – power corrupts, and if I was in their place, I would build a palace for myself, a grand dacha in the woods. Maybe the ancient Greeks and Romans remained truer to their ideals because they didn't have to sacrifice much to do so. What would a man of great power get in those days? Designer robes? Taller columns? If they had television and sports cars, I bet the ancient Greeks would have been more decadent. Assuming, of course, that they also had electricity to power the TVs and petroleum-processing plants to make gasoline for their cars. And enough broadcast networks to create decent programming. Otherwise, you could plug your TV in and it would still be useless. For the sports cars, too, they'd also need roads and driveways. Half the fun of owning a Porsche is watching your neighbors drool about it. Imagine if Augustus Ceasar owned a plasma-screen TV but didn't have electricity and there was no such thing as television programming. That would be a pretty useless item! Maybe he could hang his robes on it. Also, the Porsche would be of little value to him. Maybe it would be fun to open the door. He could have sex with young Greek boys in its backseat. That is one use for a car that is timeless. I bet even Adam and Eve had sex a few times in the back of Adam's car in the Garden of Eden. And, yes, he definitely had a cool car in Eden before the fall. But my point was that Soviet leaders gorged themselves on the people's sweat. When I stumbled out of the cave and saw the remains of the rebels, I realized that our firepower was vastly superior to theirs. If only the Kremlin had built more of those helicopters and not wasted money on nuclear weapons trying to make up for their small, boy-sized penises. With enough helicopters, we might have won the war in Afghanistan, and then the country would not have begun crumbling.

Three years later, I went back to Russia. My first memories of returning from the war are peaceniks at the airport spitting on

soldiers, calling them baby killers, and giving dirty looks to anyone in a uniform. That's because the country had changed while
I was gone. Gorbachev's Perestroika had opened up the doors
of the country to the West, and travelers had smuggled back
bootleg tapes of movies and music. My first night back, we
watched *Born on the Fourth of July*, which is where I saw the
behavior I just described. Man, those hippies were really mean
to the soldiers coming back from Vietnam! Luckily the citizens
were too terrified to mistreat army veterans in Russia, so everyone was polite to me. That movie struck a chord, though, as I
watched it on a Betamax cassette in my friend Piotr's apartment. I had recovered from all my wounds, but my friend
Commander Vulkov had been crippled like Tom Cruise.
Vulkov was even worse off, for his arms and legs were gone.

In a similar situation, most men would lose the will to live.
Vulkov was no ordinary man, however. He became even harder
than he had been before. After being released from the hospital,
he used all his military contacts to get a job in Star City. For a
man who specialized in motivating young soldiers but had only
a torso at his disposal, this was actually a perfect assignment.
Calling to cosmonauts over a radio, he could talk his men
through tough space missions. Because of his disfigurement, the
leaders assigned him to the secret mirror space program, where
he could be hidden from view and still do his job. Despite
Vulkov's stellar record as a military leader and the sacrifices he
had made, the Engineering Minister still resisted giving him
the post. "I refuse to hire a man who can't even shake my
hand!" he reportedly told another minister. Vulkov had some
K.G.B. contacts convince the minister to reconsider, by taking
pictures of him doing things he should not be doing. Confronted with the pictures, he magnanimously changed his mind
and decided to hire Vulkov. When Vulkov showed up in his

office to receive the appointment, he was wearing the rubber hand around his neck. "Thank you for the post," Vulkov said. "I have made arrangements for you to shake my hand." The minister did, and it became a tradition to shake Vulkov's rubber hand as a sign of respect afterward. I have heard some young cosmonaut recruits whisper that Vulkov's actual hand is encased inside the rubber, preserved as a grisly reminder. I don't correct them, because the story amuses me, but I know it to be untrue. I saw his hand disintegrate in a bomb blast in Afghanistan. His current hand is merely a rubber ornament, and a reminder of his political skill. The kind of skill required to leak news about my presence in space to the media and then cover his tracks.

If you're reading this book and keeping track of how often people saved each others' lives, you might think to yourself: *Sure, you saved Vulkov's life in that cave, but he had saved yours moments before. So you were even, right? He had no debt to repay any more.* To which I would say: When you read books, you should look for symbolism and poetic language and not be so busy keeping score on who is living and why. Did you read *Anna Karenina* and say to yourself *That railroad won by killing the most people in the book, including Anna herself?* If so, you are a horrible reader and did not appreciate the novel at all. If you haven't read that book yet, then you are an illiterate scoundrel, and also I apologize for revealing how it ends. Regarding Vulkov: Maybe we were even when it came to saving each other's lives, but he also felt responsible for my being in space in the first place, since he recruited me to the cosmonaut program.

07 / WIND OF CHANGE (LOVE PUNCHES ME IN THE JUNK)

I was home and finally free of the army. I'd completed my service and now had to figure out how to live my life. The old orphan home was no place for me anymore, so I stayed in Moscow. At first I drifted around the streets restlessly. Getting used to the lack of gunfire was difficult; not that I missed it, but it took some time to finally feel at ease on the streets.

Freedom was the spirit of the times. Before I had left, rock music was all underground, along with subversive literature and Hollywood films. Now you could hear it playing on boom boxes down every street. Bookstores put works by Solzhenitsyn right in their front window. We could even watch *Tron!*

But the biggest event of the year was the Moscow Music and Peace festival, featuring Bon Jovi, Skid Row, Motley Crue, Ozzy Osbourne, and the Scorpions! All these Western hard rock bands coming to Russia to perform for the workers, to break down the Iron Curtain with their guitars, smash the Berlin Wall with their bass guitars, and build a path to the Finland Station with their drums. I don't know what they did with their keyboards, but I'm sure the keyboards helped too.

Clearly this was a hot ticket, but I was able to secure one as a veteran for the big concert in August. Thousands of youth filled the Luzhniki Stadium around me. In traditional Russian fashion, we were drunk and wild and reckless like wolves. I had survived a war, but I was not ready for what happened when Skid Row took to the stage. Sweat-covered bodies surged forward in a mass, charging against the barricades. In some ways, it was like a rehearsal for the storming of the gates in 1993 when the Old Guard gasped their last dying coup filled breath. But that was later.

Now was the concert, the ringing chords, the throbbing rhythm, and I found myself flung across the concrete from one body into the next.

It was a mosh pit, developed by American dance scientists during the 1980s. We had nothing like it in the U.S.S.R. I cartwheeled and bruised myself against the throngs, then saw the most beautiful woman's face in the world. Even more beautiful than the Skid Row singer Sebastian Bach, who is a very lovely lady.[1] The face I saw was even more stunning. Suddenly it was gone, and I was in another section of the mosh pit. How could I get back? I had to find that face. It was Natasha, I was sure. I had glimpsed her face. My sweet angel of the orphanage was here in the throng, another one of the youth gone wild with frenzy and rock. I fought against the surge and made my way back to where I had seen her. She wasn't there; she was moving too! I forgot about dancing. I was on a mission. I had to find her. I saw her hair twenty feet from me and darted towards her. She was thrown to the right. Had she seen me? I elbowed my way towards her. I toppled smaller kids. It was rough, but love doesn't care how well you dance, it only cares who you dance with. I had to find her before the song ended and the dancing stopped. Moving through the crowd would be impossible then. The guitar solo started – I had no time to lose. I began lifting long haired rockers and tossing them out of my way. They knew more about music than me, but I knew more about fighting. Then she was in my sights, on the periphery of the mosh pit, just dancing by herself. I pushed past the shaking hordes and drew up beside her just as the final chords of the song rang out. There we were in the shadow of a giant Peter Max banner as the crowd screamed and cheered.

"Natasha," I said.

"Ilya?" I could have died: *she remembered my name.*

"I can't believe I found you."

We were practically reading lips in the thunderous noise.

"I missed you after you left the orphans' home," she said.

"I thought about you all the time I was gone, Natasha. I saw a lot of horrible things but the thought of you got me through it."

Then our voices were interrupted by Sebastian Bach, the pretty singer for Skid Row.

"The song we're going to do now is about a boy who got in trouble with the law," she said, as she readjusted her torn black shirt to reveal more of her chest for the screaming Russian fans. "He fell on the wrong side of the tracks, if you will." I remember every moment of the concert and the words that Bach spoke just then. The words could have been just for me. The band started playing. It was a ballad. I put my arms around Natasha and just swayed. I didn't know the song; I didn't know any of this music. It didn't matter. I had found my girl. We were together.

All through that head-banging night, we held each other. Through Mötley Crüe and the Scorpions. Through Cinderella and Bon Jovi. In the dark, the stadium swelled with feeling, as if the world was ours and were the children of tomorrow. Maybe Marx and Engels had it wrong; it wasn't communism that would drive us forward. It was power chords, long hair, and spandex. No one would join our cause if we remained austere, square jawed and dressed in gray. What people want is the flash and pomp of an electrifying stage show! It is just as dangerous as war – ask Michael Jackson or the singer from Metallica, both set ablaze by the artillery of stadium rock. Still, given the choice between dying in a desert at the barrel of a gun and dying in a pit of youth while a semi-literate drummer swirls upside down playing a drum solo and his band mates shout single-entendres into microphones surrounded by big breasted dancers, I would always take the second death. The magical part was that I was not alone. I was in love, but every young heart in the stadium felt something just as powerful. One hundred thousand people finally felt alive for the first time in their lives.

The spirit of change was in the music and it had lived in our bones before Perestroika. The first time I heard heavy metal music, it was not on cassette or even a record: It was on an X-ray of a terminal elderly man. Once he was diagnosed with lung cancer, his doctor gave the X-ray to a friend who secretly ran it through a machine and embedded circular grooves in it. Cassettes were still a novelty and required too much illegal technology to enjoy. But record technology was easy to create. All you needed was a needle (thanks again, *Doctor*) and something to amplify it with. Plastic discs were hard to come by, but square sheets of X-ray plastic were readily available in the sick wards of hospitals. So bootleggers copied records onto X-rays and distributed them widely.[2] The man with lung cancer gave his X-rays to *Metal Health* by Quiet Riot. I stared at a spinning broken leg the first time I heard Black Sabbath. I owned a copy of Queen's *Sheer Heart Attack* on a dislocated elbow X-ray. Now this forbidden music was being performed live. We couldn't go back to listening to the bones. We would demand our heavy metal records; if that meant capitalism, then we would be capitalists.

I'm not the first person to claim that rock and roll helped bring down the Soviet Empire. Vaclav Havel was a fan of underground music and a crackdown on it led him to become a revolutionary. I met him once at a dinner party. He kept going on and on about his good friend Frank Zappa. That did not impress me! If he had known Dweezil Zappa, I would have been more excited. Dweezil was in *The Running Man* with Mick Fleetwood. How I would have liked to have been a bug on the wall secretly recording conversations between those two!

Back at the Moscow Music and Peace Festival, after the bands performed, everyone came out on stage for a wonderful rock and roll jam. The people in the stadium held hands and sang and chanted and wished the night would never end. But it did, and rather than push our luck, we filed back into the streets. Natasha said I could ride with her in the back of a friend's car. I had hitchhiked to the show. We climbed into the tiny East German car and enjoyed being cramped together by need and a lack of raw materials on the assembly line somewhere else in the Soviet Empire. Her hair was in my face. It smelled wonderful. My mouth was pressed up against her ear. I told her I loved her and wanted to spend the rest of my life with her. I told her secrets, too, things that will always be shared only by the two of us. When you truly love someone, you can create a secret life together and have no secrets except those you keep to yourself and hide from the world. A true love is a hiding place for the vulnerable part of you.

Now that she has left me, I must care for all our secrets by myself. I keep her flame alive inside of me, hoping to share it with her again some day. It is a fire that was kindled in the back of that car that perfect night after the concert. I think that is where most love begins. On a road home.

08 / SCARCITY IN STAR CITY

I woke up on the cold wood floor of a small apartment Natasha shared with her friends. They were artists. Dancers, painters, writers. Beautiful antiques decorated the space. I was curled up next to my love underneath a heavy wool blanket. I knew that I wanted to stay there forever. It was time to decide what to do with my life. I didn't care what it was as long as it included Natasha.

Sometime in the night, she had left a glass of water beside me, knowing I would be thirsty when I awoke. She had known exactly what I needed and I wished to wake up beside her for the rest of my days.

I gently pulled the blanket off our bodies and stood. Early morning light hinted at the day to come, spilling softly through the frosted windows. Years in the military had made me an early riser. If you like to look through people's things, I recommend waking up early in their house to do so. Most likely, they'll sleep through the investigation. If by chance they do wake up, you can claim you were also tired and were looking for something (bathroom, coffee mugs, a pen) depending on where you're caught snooping (behind a closed door, in a cabinet, in a drawer). Which is not to say that I snooped through Natasha's things. I only mention it in relation to waking up early. I looked around, certainly. But I did not snoop. I looked at pictures on the refrigerator. Natasha with her friends. Pictures of people I didn't recognize. And then a snapshot of Mr. Babel the chemistry teacher, older than I remembered him, standing in front of a blackboard covered with equations I had never properly learned or understood. Soon enough, I would get my fill of science and classrooms.

I walked down the hall and opened the front door. Only old women were up at this hour, shuffling through the building and making their way, like turtles, down the steep stairway to the front door. Buildings erected by Communists were made as cheaply as possible. It saved space and time to build a single steep staircase rather than two more gently rising sets of stairs. They cut every corner possible, metaphorically – in reality, the buildings are filled with corners because they were easier to prefabricate than curves and arches. A rounded edge takes grace; you can join a corner through blunt force, which was one natural resource we had in abundance.

In the street, gypsies were rousing themselves to face the day. Old babushkas dotted the city scape. For everyone else this was home, but I had spent my life in a grain silo and the desert. This place was unfamiliar to me. I felt as if all the people could tell. They stared at me, or they averted their eyes. I didn't fit in here. They even pointed. Moscow, I thought, you are so cruel to a young Russian boy. Then an old woman yelled at me, "Put on some pants, you whore's peacock." I realized I was naked. Moscow wasn't ungracious, it was just modest. In the army, you didn't have to put on pants until the day really started. Why pull on trousers just to walk 30 feet and take a dump? Realizing my first mistake (no pants), I was lucky to understand my second (looking for an alley where I could take a shit). Truly, I forgot about indoor plumbing that morning. I was not thinking straight. I had a hangover; not the painful kind that makes you regret drinking, but the pleasant kind where you are still a little drunk and feeling your skin buzz around you and another drink would be welcome. Also, it was love, not alcohol, that I had indulged in the night before.

Back inside the apartment, I found Natasha on the floor, her eyes dreamily looking towards me. "I knew you'd be back," she yawned.

"I left you once. Never again," I said. Then I went into the bathroom.

"Liar!" she laughed. "You just left me again!"

I came back out and picked her up, throwing her over my shoulder like a sack of beautiful potatoes.

"I will keep my promise. Even in the bathroom, you'll be with me." She laughed and protested merrily.

I carried her inside and put her in the bathtub, then pissed into the toilet. I can still close my eyes and see her in that tub.

It was the first time she had seen me naked. The night before, we had made love in the dark. I was not ashamed. When you're in love, you don't mind standing naked before your partner. Also, I have a huge cock. Sure, all Russians boast of their length and girth, but I tell you truly – the book you hold in your hands is not half the size of my member. And I'm talking about the hardcover version of this book. If you're reading a small mass-market paperback, then my manhood is at least twice as big as this book. Try this: Hold the book out in front of you. Pretend it's a penis. That's how big my manhood is. (No, it is not book shaped, that would be ridiculous.)

I was there in the bathroom with Natasha, both of us laughing.

"What are we going to do with ourselves?" she asked.

"We are going to stay together forever," I said. "And then after that, we'll still be together. I will find a job. We will be married. I have seen the future. Do not worry about a thing."

I flushed the toilet.

"I must get ready for work," she said.

She showered, and put on her make-up. She wore perfume smuggled in from America. "I want to smell like freedom," she smiled. And she did. Every time I breathed in her scent, I knew I had found freedom. I had been imprisoned by loneliness and finally escaped with Natasha.

Finding someone in Russia was nearly impossible, unless you were in love, or had the K.G.B. working for you. So many thousands miles of land. Empty spaces and cold vast tundra, it was so easy to disappear. Millions did, during the Twentieth Century. Lost to time, slipping through the cracks of history, crushed in the fist of Stalin. But before they were lost, they were found by ministers of state, dark men in shadow jackets, knocking on a door in the middle of the night.

Since childhood, I had been taught to fear that late-night knocking on the door. After three weeks with Natasha, I was working as a bodyguard for important tourists. My military skills came in handy on the fledgling job market. We were new to capitalism and new to employment. I'd follow rich foreigners around the sights of Moscow during the day, keeping them safe, sometimes partying with them the following evenings, then return home to Natasha every night. Dead tired, I'd collapse beside her and sleep the contented sleep of working men. In America you have better dreams than the rest of the world.

That is because you work harder during the day and are more tired at night.

When I heard the knocking, I thought it was in my dream. It was a soft wrapping, not the demanding rap of the secret police. The knock was a question. Nevertheless, I got up and answered it. Better that I should face the night visitors than Natasha or her friends. Looking through the peephole I saw nothing. Not a good sign. Was it a ghost? Or a spook? Kremlin agents would know to hide off to the side so I could not see them. I opened the door.

It took me a second to see Vulkov there, sitting in his wheelchair. He had been too low for me to spy him through the hole in the door. One of the men to his side must have knocked on the door with the rubber hand hanging around Vulkov's neck.

"Ilya," he said. "I have come to take you away."

I pulled the robe tightly around myself. Could I fight my way past his two escorts? Did I want to?

"Have I done something wrong, Commander Vulkov?"

"Nothing, my son. I have come to offer you a job."

"I have work as a bodyguard."

"Psssh. That is not a job. That is a waste. You were meant for better things."

"I am an orphan."

"Even motherless children can make something of themselves. Think of Oliver Twist. Or Arnold Drummond, the young black boy on 'Diff'rent Strokes.'"

I eyed his escorts.

"I don't know this book or this television show," I said warily.

"Relax. We are not the culture police. If you don't know these works, you are a poorer man than I, bankrupt of culture."

"What are you talking about, Willis?" I asked.

We both laughed. I had seen "Diff'rent Strokes" a few times, and was familiar with Charles Dickinson's famous story of the singing orphan Oliver Twist.[1]

"I want to take you on a trip."

"Where to?"

"The stars," he said. If his hand functioned, I'm sure he would have pointed skyward dramatically. "I am working in Star City. I need men I can trust for a special mission."

And then Natasha woke up and called from the other room.

"Ilya, come back to bed. Your woman needs you! She is so cold alone."

I smiled at Vulkov. "I would like to live in Moscow for a while."

"You can bring your woman. You can marry her and live in splendor. You will live like a czar with his wife in Star City. You will be like royalty, all the best for you and her."

It was a magnificent offer, although I should have remembered what happened to the last Czar.[2]

"Think about it," he said. "I'll contact you again."

His minders rolled him backwards into the hallway, and the darkness. I went back to Natasha's side.

"Who was that, Sweet One?" she asked.

"An old friend," I said.

"What did he want?"

"He wanted me to marry you and treat you like a queen. I think I will have to do what he said. If we left Moscow, would you be sad?"

"Not if I am with you," she said. Then she closed her eyes and slept, content.

So our honeymoon began. Her friends threw us a party and we

were wed. There were flowers and borrowed clothes. I wore my military uniform because it fit well and looked better than any of my other clothes. We took a train to St. Martyrsburg and visited her father at the school near my orphanage. It was hard to walk through the streets without yelling, *I have gotten her! I have gotten Natasha! You fools, how could you let her get away? She is the only thing in the world!*

The city had not changed much, only gotten emptier in the years we'd been away. It was sad and forgotten. If I never returned, I'd be happy.

Vulkov had gotten us a house in Star City, a big one, where we spent our first full week as newlyweds. We made love in every room. We went for long walks, holding hands. My training wouldn't begin for 14 days. After the war, and the crazy love of our reunion, it was nice to take a break from the whirlwind and spend time together. Neither of us had to work during the day. Our only job was to enjoy each other, and that was hardly work. We set up our house and prepared for this new life in this new town. I would become a cosmonaut, Natasha a cosmonaut's wife.

At night, we sat on the roof of the building, a blanket beneath us, staring up at the stars.

"Would you like me to bring one of those back for you?"

"No, I wouldn't have anywhere to put it," she said.

"I'll bring you just a small star."

"Aren't the small ones the hottest stars? I'm afraid it would set our nice new home on fire."

"True. Perhaps I will just bring you back a comet or meteor."

"As long as you bring yourself back, you don't need to bring me anything from space."

I share this sappy talk with you as a way of proving how

utterly in love we were. If I didn't love her, I would have pushed her off the roof of the building for speaking such ridiculous drivel. Then I would have jumped off myself for also being such a hopeless romantic. But what could I do? We were in love, and we talked this way, saying meaningless things with our faces pressed close to one another as if we were the only two people on the world.

My first day, I showed up early at the main administrative building in Star City.

At the check-in desk, I presented myself to a burly woman behind a typewriter.

"Ilya Zamyatin. I am here for cosmonaut training."

She looked at me, unimpressed.

"I fought in the war." Here I made a muscle with my bicep. I'm not sure why – it's not like I lifted heavy barbells to defeat the enemy. I guess it seemed more manly than making a fake gun with my hand and shooting. I needed some physical gesture to accentuate my statement.

She dug up a binder and flipped through its white pages protected by clear plastic sheets. Finally she found my name.

"Zamyatin, Ilya?"

"Yes. That is me."

"It says here you are assigned to janitorial duties. Report to Building 12, lower level."

"There must be some mistake. I'm supposed to train to be a cosmonaut, to go into space. Commander Vulkov told me so in person."

"Commander Vulkov? Do you mean Old Stump Vulkov? He's in charge of janitors and maintenance."

"I thought he was part of the cosmonaut program."

"You thought an old man in a wheelchair with no arms or legs was in the space program? Tell me something, soldier.

When you were in the war..." here she made a muscle with her bicep, which was at least as big as mine, " ... did you get shot or otherwise injured in the head? Because your story sounds mentally impaired."

"I should talk to someone in the space program. I am a fit veteran who was assigned to the cosmonaut training program."

"According to this, you're in the janitor staff. Of course, if you're sure there's a mistake, I can call the K.G.B. and have them pull your personal file to see where you belong."

"What?! Call the K.G.B. my asshole! Don't think of it. I will take this up with the janitors and Commander Vulkov. It's obviously some sort of mistake."

"The binder doesn't make mistakes," she said. Then she pointed out the window to the north. "Building 12 is three miles that way."

I walked out with my shoulders slumped. How could I have gotten my hopes so high? It didn't make sense for a cripple to run the cosmonaut program. And yet, he had told me so himself. Had the war and the wounds made Vulkov crazy? Even if he was insane, those two men with him seemed like officials. Would they let a crazy janitor run loose telling lies in the hallways of apartment buildings?

Walking across the campus this way was a sad affair. In a good mood, you could really enjoy the beauty of Star City. It was like a modern, efficient American college. Vast dormitories and research buildings mixed with grassy quads, statues of great men, and shade from trees. You could take off your book bag, curl up on a lawn and get lost in a book. Except if you were hurt and disappointed. Then you failed to see the possibilities. You saw only failure.

I found myself at the door of Building 12. I couldn't find an entrance to the lower level so I walked in the front door. This time the desk was guarded by a bulky man who sat in front of a computer watching a bank of TV monitors. His arms barely fit in his shirt, he was so muscular. I certainly wouldn't pump my biceps for him – he would be unimpressed. *Shit*, I thought, *they must throw all the meat heads into this building.*

"I'm Ilya Zamyatin," I said. "Through some mistake, I've been assigned here."

He typed something into the computer.

"No mistake, comrade. You've been assigned to janitorial staff. Take the second elevator on your left to the lower level."

He motioned towards a wall of metal doors.

"But I don't–"

"Go. Second door on the left."

A small chime sounded and the doors opened. As I walked towards it, I noticed there were no call buttons on the wall. How did one request an elevator? I stepped in. There was no button for the lower level. The doors closed. I felt the car drop suddenly and continue falling for about five stories. Then the doors opened into a vast warehouse space. It was filled with custodial carts. There were rows and rows of mop handles sticking out of plastic buckets on wheels. Along the distant walls were small doors labeled "Supply Closet" and marked with a string of numbers. One of them opened and a voice called out to me. "Zamyatin! This way."

There seemed nothing to do but follow the instructions. A man in a jumpsuit stood inside the doorway. In the small cramped space, there was only a sink and some containers of soap. He looked at me closely, then pulled a picture from his pocket and compared my face to it. Satisfied, he put the picture away and reached for the faucet.

"Are you filling a bucket for me to mop with? It's all a mistake!" I protested.

As he turned the knobs, however, no water came out. Instead, the shelf of soap swung away from us with the wall and revealed a large polished steel hatchway like the door of a bank vault.

"What kind of janitors are you?" I asked in astonishment.

"The kind that provide a clean cover story," he said.

The giant hatch opened and behind it was Vulkov in his wheelchair, flanked by the same two men who had visited us in Natasha's apartment.

"I apologize for the deception. It is, I regret, a necessary arrangement for now. If anyone asks, you were mistakenly assigned to the janitorial staff, and are now stuck on it. No one must know you are a cosmonaut."

"But I told Natasha and her family and our friends!"

"Yes. You had to. It would have been unbelievable for you to move to Star City to be a janitor. This is a common cover story we use. We must account for intelligent, talented men coming to join us. Let me explain."

We entered the cavernous underground fortress and he told me this story:

The secret space program was launched soon after Sputnik, he said. At first, our leaders thought we must publicize our space triumphs in order to strike fear into the hearts of Americans. Otherwise, what use was our space program? And yet, it did have other uses. The men in charge soon realized that they wouldn't want to announce every satellite they launched, every weapon that might provide a tactical advantage. If they only announced missions with no secret agenda, the Americans would become suspicious of the rocket launches in between. Better, they thought, to start an entirely separate program.

This second program could draw on the trajectory and ballistic knowledge of the public program so it would be less expensive. But instead of scientific payloads, it would launch only military and intelligence projects.

Here the vast undeveloped wasteland of the Russian interior became useful. In America, where railroads and highways make the landscape accessible to all, keeping such a huge secret would be impossible. We knew about the Manhattan Project, after all. Not every detail, but we knew it existed. Too many people were involved. In Russia, you can bury an entire town and few people will notice. Even the disappearance of citizens has a plausible cover in the frequent purges of the people.

This, then, is a secret shadow space program. We share equipment and facilities with the public program, but launch our rockets from deeper in the wilderness, away from prying eyes.

Alas, the spirit of Glasnost has forced us to find new cover stories for our supply of workers. In the past, our recruits simply disappeared from their normal lives and joined us here in the shadows of Dark Star City. Nobody asked any questions about where they went: they were too afraid of the answers. In a train full of prisoners bound for Siberia, nobody would notice the dozen men who slipped out at a station. The other passengers were too busy being afraid. And the men we took were so happy to find out they were not bound for the Gulag that they had no qualms about abandoning their former lives.

Now, in this new era, the people will ask questions and want answers. Fear is no longer a useful tool, but bureaucratic incompetence is. We tell recruits that they are desired by the space program. They tell their friends and families and everyone understands when they move to Star City. Upon arrival, they are told there has been a mistake and they are assigned to menial duties on the support staff. It's a disappointment for everyone, but their loved ones understand. These kinds of clerical errors are unavoidable. Nobody asks too many questions. Now the world thinks these men are living in Star City but not participating in the Space Program. This is what we want the world to think. Meanwhile, they are training and preparing for missions in the dead of night while everyone else sleeps. It works better that way, since it is always night time in space.

In the end, there is good news and bad news. You get to be among the privileged few who leave the earth's surface and soar among the stars. The bad news is you must lie to your family and keep your work a secret. Only history will know of your accomplishments. That is not such a bad bargain, I think. One hundred years from now, after all, only history will remain of anyone.

There he stopped.

"What if I refuse to lie to my wife?" I asked.

"It is too dangerous for her to know about this program. If you tell her, you risk her life. It is dangerous for you to know, too. If you don't wish to join us now, you will have no future. Boris!"

Here, one of his bodyguards drew a finger across his throat, symbolizing that I would be killed. Although I doubt they would have slit my neck in that way, as it a messy fashion to kill a man. More likely they would have shot me and thrown me into a river. But it is difficult to mime shooting a person in a threatening way. Usually it comes across more like "Hey good job, pal. You hit the bull's eye." On top of that, trying to use charades to imply that you would throw a corpse into a river is nearly impossible. Any thug or henchman hoping to make such threats accurately would have to be accompanied by a trained mime, whose presence would obviously detract from the threats. So Boris made the throat-slitting gesture. I got the drift.

There was no spite or venom in it. Vulkov (Boris too) was just being matter of fact. He'd let me in on a deadly secret, putting my life in danger, because he felt sure of my answer. Who wouldn't want a chance to go to space? And he knew I was an orphan, so I had little family to disappoint with my fictional janitorial job.

What he didn't know about was Natasha. He knew she existed, since he found me at her apartment. But he didn't know how much she meant to me. Could I just lie to her about all this? I had to consider it carefully. I didn't want any secrets between us. But telling her the truth would be putting her life in jeopardy. Mine would be in jeopardy as well. It would be like Double Jeopardy. I had to make my wager carefully because I wanted to survive to the next round.[3]

Vulkov could tell I was on the fence about my options.

"Think of it this way," he said. "In a few years, Gorbachev will probably give away all of Russia's secrets anyway, and this program can come out of hiding. Why even today, the children can enjoy the hard rocking sounds of Bon Jovi and Mötley Crüe. The world is changing faster than we blink our eyes. Bob Dylan will soon have to sing about this, the times a changing once again."[4]

"Alright, you crazy bastard," I said.

And here I shook his rubber hand for the first time.

I would enter the basement, moving downward so that I might soar up to the sky.

Natasha was not happy to hear about my new job. She cried and yelled and cried some more. I did my best to soothe her. I described how there had been confusion. I talked about how I was still part of the Space Program. I said the cosmonauts couldn't travel to space if it weren't for the people keeping their precious instruments and equipment clean.

She was not convinced. She had left her small town and

moved to Moscow to be among the artists. Now here she was in Star City, married to a janitor. And on top of the disappointment was my guilt at lying to her. We were no longer as happy as we had been in the bone-crushing mosh pit when Skid Row played their hard charging rock music.

With this heavy heart, I began my training to become a cosmonaut.

Here is what I recall:

Running. Swimming. Physics lessons. Astronomy. Codes. Propaganda.

Running. We did so much running. Why? I do not know. Perhaps because all training of any kind requires running. It's not like you can run in space. You can hardly even walk in space, unless you are attached to oxygen and heavy equipment or you are Michael Jackson.[5] But I ran miles and miles on the indoor track. Every morning, as soon as I arrived at work, I'd run five miles. At night before I went home, I ran another five miles. Before long I had run enough distance to cross Russia on foot. I hate running.

Swimming. This makes a little more sense than running. Buoyancy in space can be disorienting, so time in the pool is a good preparation. Doing laps in different strokes is another story. The only conceivable time you'd need to swim in space is if you're separated from your craft and trying to find your way back like in a science fiction movie. This would never happen. Based on my experiences in space, the best preparatory training would be to sit on a floating chair in a pool, eating candy bars, drinking nutrients, and pissing and shitting right into your swimsuit. Little children would have no problem adapting to life in space.

Physics lessons. Now we get to the important material. Figuring out orbits and escape velocity and leaving enough of a window for return is no easy task. You can leave it to the nerds in the math department but if you find yourself in space without communication, you'll be glad you paid attention and can calculate your own way back to earth.

Astronomy. Stars are to space navigation what stars were to sea navigation in the time before compasses and chronometers. Knowing the difference between a comet and a meteor is important because if you see one coming towards you, you'll know whether to be scared (comet) or scared shitless (meteor).

Codes. We lived in a land of secrets. It was impossible to write the plain truth. You had to hide it in enigmas and ciphers. Reading coded plans for a space mission is like trying to unravel the mysteries on a child's menu at Denny's, but much more difficult.

Propaganda. There was no end to the political lies we were shoveled like so much horse shit on a farm. Surprisingly, our teacher was an African immigrant. Maybe you had to be from the Third World to truly believe the Soviet Union was a great place. He had been raised in a country led by Milton Obote and backed by the U.S.S.R. We used to say that the teacher of this course offered propaganda on demanda from Uganda.

So many hours in and out of the basement training facility, my classmates and I became automatons who could complete space missions in our sleep if that was required. Then when the sun rose, we'd come out of our underground lairs and return to our disappointed families, pretending to be janitors. Really we were like reverse vampires: coming out in daylight to intermingle with the living while we spent the night underground in a giant tomb.

And like any vampire will tell you, it is hard to find love among the women of the earth. Sure, it is easy for pale young teenagers with brooding eyebrows and fragile non-threatening bodies to win the affections of a woman. But for big burly vampires it is much harder. And staying in love is the real trick. A woman wants a man who can take her out into the sunlight. If the man cannot do this, trouble ensues. Silences become meaningful. Resentment builds. I was so busy studying physics that I failed to notice the problems I was having with chemistry.

Natasha grew sad. She withdrew. I can't blame her. I came home too tired to even talk to her.

"Quit your job," she would say. "Being a janitor should not take so much life out of you. You already gave yourself to the army for years. Wasn't that enough?"

If only I could have explained to her that I was not a janitor cleaning floors! But that truth was swept under the rug. Instead, she understood me less and less with each passing day. I had left the orphanage with such big dreams, and now I appeared to be dying slowly in a dead-end job in a nowhere town just as the Soviet Union was opening up and our generation had all the opportunities our families had never known. The world was in our hands and the light of Perestroika was shining through, but I was sleeping the day away, hitting the snooze button on revolution. That was how it looked to her, anyway.

We celebrated our first anniversary by driving to a small lakeside village. I used the space program's connections to get a cabin there. Someone must have thought I was a high-ranking janitor. Natasha packed a bag of cheeses and wine, fruits and bread. I brought candles and some books for us to read. Maybe we could fall in love again, I hoped, if it was just the two of us. Instead the weekend cemented the cracks between us.

"I don't know you anymore," she said. "Or maybe I never knew you. Maybe I imagined you to be the man I wanted to meet." She stood up.

This was on the porch Sunday morning as the coal-mine fog rolled across the lake towards our cabin. It was quiet and calm and horrible. I ate the last of our bread. She ate strawberries from a bowl. I considered fighting, arguing. But I knew the truth was the only thing I could tell her that would make her stay. And the truth was too dangerous. Even as Gorbachev moved us towards freedom, the K.G.B. was marshaling its forces and guarding its secrets. It was (and still is) a deadly, vindictive army. So I could no more tell her about the secret space program than I could choke the life out of her with my bare hands. I wanted her to live, above all else. I wished it would be with me, but if she had to leave me to stay alive, I would understand. She told me what was wrong and I offered no answer. She would leave me. The fog hit the shore and drifted into the porch, covering us. Natasha was just three feet away from me, and I could no longer see her. I heard the door open and close. When the fog cleared, she was no longer there.

Back inside the cabin, I found Natasha packing her belongings into a small bag. We had brought one shared suitcase, but somehow she had squirreled away an extra duffel to make her getaway. She had come knowing she would leave alone.

"Isn't there a way we can make this work?" I asked.

"Only if you quit your job. Do you really love cleaning more than you love me?"

I had no good answer, none that I could tell her anyway.

"I love you," I said. "But I made a commitment to this job. And to Commander Vulkov. He saved my life. I just wish you weren't so unhappy."

"I'm going back to Moscow," she answered. "I hope you and the commander of the janitors are happy. Don't try to find me."

She walked out the door and I was alone again.

Russia is a country of orphans. The West acknowledged this when they dubbed Stalin our "Uncle Joe." We had lost our parents and were left in the disastrous care of a harmful relative. Life is hard, loss comes easy, and the peasants end up with nothing.

I stood in the cabin. I was heartbroken. The only consolation was that I could now leave the toilet seat up after I peed. That is not a good trade: true love for bathroom ease.

I almost ran out into the street to tell her the truth. I wanted to shout it out at that moment and bring her back to me. It was in my power. But I couldn't risk her life. And she said I should not try to find her. So I sat on the floor and wept.[6]

In America, I understand, broken hearted lovers compile mix tapes of depressing songs so they can sit and mope in their sadness. What wonders of technology! I had no such collection of music at my disposal. On the wall of the cabin, however, there was an old balalaika, the traditional Russian instrument. Triangle shaped, it had three strings, half the amount of a Western guitar. Three strings is enough. Only the excess of the West demands six strings, or even 12 on some guitars.

Pulling the instrument down from the wall, I accidentally knocked over a decorative vase full of flowers. It shattered on the floor and seemed a fitting symbol of how I felt. I played a spare melody. I had no musical training. For all the knowledge crammed into my head in school and in the underworld of the shadow space program at Star City, there was not a bit of musical theory or practice. Yet, as you say in America, the blues is not nothing but a feeling. So a miserable Russian cosmonaut trainee could play the blues and wail a sad song towards the lake, which is what I did. Here are the words of the song I wrote that day:

Natasha's Song (for Natasha)[7]
by Ilya Zamyatin

I should have told you the whole truth
No more secrets, pretty girl
In my rocket craft I'll think of you:
I'm a spaceman, soon I'll leave this world

Natasha, I'm really going to space
Oh, Natasha, unpack your packed suitcase
Natasha … shit, I broke a vase

I was just an orphan when at first we met
You were the apple of a teacher's eye
Now I'm a secret cosmonaut
But you have just said goodbye

Natasha, I'll think of you in space
Oh, Natasha, unpack your packed suitcase
Natasha, I should pick up this vase

I'm glad you didn't take the car
Because it means I'm not stranded here
Natasha when you walked away
I cried looking at your rear

Sweet Natasha, I'll soon be in space
Oh, Natasha, time to pack my own suitcase
Fear not, Natasha, I will leave some rubles on the kitchen
    table with a note explaining that I accidentally broke
    the vase.

You probably know this song if you have my first album, "Russian Back From Space (As Quickly As I Can)." That was recorded many years later, and the song became famous on television. Right after Natasha left, I was too raw to share this song with anyone else. So it was my secret.

In a way, there was an upside to the end of our love affair. When the weekend was done, I went back to Star City alone. She had gotten home before me and taken all of her things. The house was empty – I had been an orphan and a soldier until I met her, so I had not accumulated many possessions. In the empty house, it was easier to forget her. I plunged headlong into my training for space. This sudden energy, this redirected sadness, put me at the top of my class. I spent extra hours in the water tank, running on the track, mastering codes, studying astronomy. I redoubled my efforts at everything but the propaganda. In doing so, I moved from the middle of the pack to the head of my unit.

So far this story has focused on me. What can I say, it is an *autobiography* after all. And yet I realize I might have given the impression that I was the only trainee in the shadow space program. Nothing could be farther from the truth. Dozens of men like me were competing for a few shots at space. Some were soldiers: men from Afghanistan or other outposts of the Soviet empire. They had the same advantages and disadvantages as me. We were in good shape overall, but lacking in any special skills relevant to a cosmonaut's jobs. Better equipped were the navy men, veterans who had served on nuclear submarines. Having spent years cooped up in metal cans, they excelled at the psychological screening tests. You could lock them in a space capsule for days at a time and their heartbeat maintained a cool steady pulse. Finally, there were the scientists. Nerds, as they are known in America. Scrawny pencil necked geniuses, they struggled to swim even a lap or two in the pool. Yet they aced every written test we were given. They groaned every time we were told to run a lap; the rest of us groaned when a pop quiz was produced. Let me describe a few of my comrades specifically. These were the men in my assigned group.

Fedor Korovich was a fellow infantry man. We hadn't known each other in the army, but we shared a common language. He had a bullet-shaped head and could smash a bottle in his bare hand without batting an eye. Often he would drink a beer in one gulp, then crush the glass container and throw it in the air. Depending on the bar we were in, the lights would sometimes hit the shards of glass in a pleasing way, creating an array of lights above our head. *I've made you children some stars*, he would say. Then he'd wipe his hand on his pant leg and slap someone on the back, laughing as they recoiled from the bits of glass being pressed against their spine. Fedor was tougher than me for sure. Once, when we tried to play soccer in a field, he uprooted a small tree and threw it off to the side of the grass because it was in the way. If we ever made contacts with fist-fighting Martians, Fedor would be the best possible cosmonaut to represent us in space.

Lev Gorsky was a sailor, specifically a radar man. He understood equations better than any of the non-scientists. Lev was most at home hunched over a desk; he looked uncomfortable when he stood up straight. This was from years of hunching over in the low-ceilinged tubes of a submarine. Lev was six-foot-five. Whenever he sat in a space capsule, his knees jutted up towards his face. Mostly he was known for his love of animals. At least once a week he would bring a wounded creature into our locker room and nurse it back to health. Everyone would get into the act, secreting away extra servings of dinner to feed the kitten or squirrel or puppy. He named each animal after a star in the sky.

Evgeny Pulkin was an astrophysicist. At first I mocked him. Any number of young children could learn all the stars' names and identify the constellations. I thought Evgeny did the same thing. Only after a few months did it become clear that he had a much greater knowledge. When we began courses on radio interferometry or dark matter, everyone clustered around Evgeny's desk for help. Evgeny wrote poems that he tried to hide from the rest of us. He was right to hide them – as a man of science, he did not have a terribly lyric mind. Still, it was nice that he had this poetic side to him, because it helps to distinguish him from the other characters in our unit.

Ilya Zamyatin was an army veteran and well-hung orphan.

That was our group, Section October. We competed against eleven other groups in team exercises. As you can guess, of course, the teams were assigned names based on famous Soviet events. You didn't think we were all named after months, did you? What kind of bullshit would that be? Imagine being sent into space with Section April! You'd be mistaken for a bunch of girls in their Easter bonnets. No, we were sections Odessa, Potemkin, October, Dialectic, Lenin, Brotherhood, Laika, Kossack, Eisenstein, Rublev, Caviar, and Amber Room. Each week, Vulkov or one his comrades would post a list of which unit had achieved the best scores on its assignments.

You competed with your Section comrades at times, and then against other sections at other times. In the view of the K.G.B., you could never have enough enemies. Our leaders thought enemies made you stronger. Which was true, unless your enemy was too strong, in which case you just wore yourself out fighting the enemy. (That is the history of the Cold War.)

So we were friendly in Section October, but also watching out for the knife plunged towards our back.

After Natasha left, I became the clear leader of our group, with the best scores on physical and mental tests. I didn't have the education that Lev and Evgeny had, but I had time and no distractions. I studied all through the day. I didn't sleep. When I stopped working, I became sad, so I never stopped working. Soon enough Section October was the unchallenged leader of the dozen sections in the shadow space program. I could tell this pleased Vulkov, who wanted someone he could trust to rise through the ranks. When you have no arms and legs, it's important that your right-hand man be a true friend.

When the next year ended, the other groups washed away and the men of Section October were elevated to the next level. Here we all had a chance to go to space. We were no longer fighting against each other. The decisions about who would be launched depended now on other factors: Sometimes a tall man was required for a mission, sometimes a short one. Sometimes they needed an astrophysicist, other times a poet. (Looking back now, Lev Gorsky would have been better suited for my mission. If the authorities had known how long I would be in space, they would have sent the man who'd spent years under water hiding from the American navy.)

We graduated and left the underground lair. Now we would train in the daylight, still hiding from the American spies we assumed were in our mist, but a small enough contingent that we could get lost among the more public figures of the space program. As for the other 11 teams, I am not sure what happened to them. Perhaps they actually became janitors? Maybe they went back to Moscow and forgot about their times in Star City. I never saw any of them again. Part of me wonders if they weren't permanently disappeared, sacrificed to the need to keep the program secret. It was not something I considered at the time. I doubt my mind would have let me consider it, as the implications were too grim.

Like rats burrowing up from the ground, we were startled by the light of day. We felt safer in our underground facility.

Among the living, we didn't know how to behave. We were clumsy on the airfields, and shy in front of the other cosmonauts. It was a time of mumbles and apprehension.

Not until our first mission was announced did we gain confidence.

Our moment in the spotlight came sooner than expected. The team that had preceded us died in a tragic space accident, whose details have only recently come to light as the Kremlin archives are finally opened and examined. At the time, we were told that the crew had died in a car accident. They had only accomplished three missions to space. Of course, their careers were still a secret, so their families believed the men had died as janitors in a car accident. Section October attended their funeral dressed in dark suits, civilian clothes rather than the official cosmonaut uniforms we all kept secretly in our closets. Were it not for my ordeal and the end of the Cold War, we might never have worn those uniforms. I think about the generations of secret officers, cosmonauts, soldiers and police who had unworn uniforms in their closets. Why even bother with the uniform? Such were the unanswered questions of the Soviet Union, the wasted labor and goods that told the story of poorly programed economy.

Recently, I read a story about the actual deaths of the cosmonauts before me. All four of them were launched in a capsule to circle the planet, but their control rockets failed and the ship accidentally launched itself out gravity's pull, beyond the reach of earth. They continued on deeper into the galaxy. One can only assume they died out in the distance, having run out of food or oxygen. At one point their ship was designated as a comet by some British astronomers who saw it twinkling in the night sky, but soon it vanished into darkness.[8]

I read this tale last summer while sitting at a coffee shop and began twitching. Discovering their fate reminded me of my own brush with oblivion. I would have died like they did. Unable to return home, to communicate with your fellow man, like drifting off to sea as an old eskimo on an ice floe. Did they compose messages to their families, messages that will never be delivered? Love letters that will be found and read by some alien race light years away? Or maybe they embraced each other and died as brothers on the sea. Did they live out their time? Or perhaps they found some way to end their own lives, by creating an air leak, or cutting their air supply. What a horrible death! I couldn't finish my coffee. I became pale and gaunt. A man standing nearby asked if I was alright. I said I was. Then he asked if I was going to be long, or if he could have my table. I didn't seem to be drinking my coffee anymore, he said, so it wasn't really fair to still be sitting there. I wanted to shout at him, "Who cares about coffee and tables, when there is so much living to do? We are not adrift in space, we are surrounded by mankind! Isn't it wonderful?" Instead, I slipped my coffee slowly, grimaced at him, and made him wait another ten minutes before I got up to leave. That guy was an asshole.

When mission control realized the capsule had reached escape velocity and was never coming back, they did two things. The first was to orchestrate a car crash in Star City, one so bad that no bodies could be recovered. That way, empty coffins could be buried without raising suspicion. So an explosion sounded later that day (staged by the K.G.B. most likely) and the press reported that a car full of drunken janitors, having recently left a petrol station with a tank full of gas, accidentally drove into a fuel depot and crashed into a larger tank of gas, causing an enormous fire. They were labeled as drunk, not to explain the accident, but because the high alcohol content in their bloodstream offered even more reason why their bodies burned away beyond the chance for recovery. The second thing mission control did, after arranging the fake accident, was to call Commander Vulkov and ask him if his new recruits were ready to go to space.

"But they're just trainees!" he said.

"Haven't you trained them well?" asked a general. Vulkov had to admit that we were very well trained.

"And besides," the general said, "sending students into action worked well for America's pilots in *Top Gun* and their astronauts in *SpaceCamp*. Both of those documentaries tell stories of great triumph."[9]

"You're suggesting a trial by fire?" Vulkov asked, as the fuel tank burned uncontrollably outside his window.

"Yes. We have no choice."

So we were promoted early. It was like Christmas in July for October that year.

Instead of training for missions, we began preparing for them. What is the difference? In training, you practice things over and over until they become second nature. In preparation, you are told once what you must do, and if you fail to do it correctly, you will most likely die.

At a secret ceremony, Commander Vulkov awarded us our cosmonaut badges. He had somebody load them into the rubber hand around his neck, and then he rolled towards us. We took our badges from him one at a time. They were squeezed into the spaces between his fingers so they wouldn't fall out before we got them. We pinned them into the uniforms hanging in our secret lockers. Now we were officially cosmonauts.

09 / HEART OF DARKNESS

All my bags were packed, and I was ready to go. I was standing there, just outside my door. Now that we were no longer trainees, it was time to ship off to the hidden launch site near Siberia. We couldn't share the facilities of the actual space program any longer. My comrades packed small bags of clothes but left their lives behind. For me, there was nothing in Star City to come home to. The house reminded me of Natasha, but all of her things were gone. I had decided to make a new start wherever we ended up. Why not? There, presumably, I could be myself and not need to maintain the charade of working as a janitor. I could live my life openly as a cosmonaut. As the saying goes, *Better to be a big fish in a small pile of fish than a small fish in a bigger pile of fish, but best of all to be a fish in the ocean.* I hoped the launch site could be my ocean.

A dirty sky-blue truck rumbled up to my front door. Fedor, Lev, and Evgeny were already in back. Commander Vulkov was sitting up front in the passenger seat, with one of his bodyguards driving.

"Come on!" he yelled to me. "We haven't got all day."

The men helped me load all my things in the empty space of truck's cargo bed.

"I've got a little something for the road," Vulkov said.

We all braced ourselves for a shot of vodka from up front, but instead we heard music.

The opening drumbeat of Bruce Springsteen's "Born to Run" blared out of the tinny speakers in the dashboard. The sound quality was horrible but still it sounded miraculous to us. I had only heard the song as performed by Russians in underground clubs, and by the soldiers on the way to basic training. Now here was *The Boss*, telling me how much he hated his hometown just as I was leaving my home looking for a new one. In America, by the age of 17, everyone has driven through the streets with the top down listening to the E Street Band, but in Russia it was a new kind of ecstasy. We shouted along with the chorus, our voices strained in the billow of dust surrounding us. Our truck was headed deep into the soul of Russia, where the darkest wilderness lies.

It had been early morning when we left, but we drove straight into night. It was a familiar feeling for me. My life had become a series of journeys by truck. The K.G.B. kept tabs on the whole country but its claws did not grip as tightly in the sparse uninhabitable patches of dead earth marking the road to Siberia. Anyone who has seen the American comedy *Deliverance* will know the sorts of crazy residents who make their home in the unsettled land of a large country and are left to live the desperate life they desire. Our path twisted through tall forests, past ramshackle flats, into unsettling villages. Ugly faces stared at us from the tops of hulking oversized bodies. Freaks were the norm there. The Central Soviet cared so little about these beings that there were no billboards or propaganda messages here. Aside from the odd diesel engine in the yard, it might have been the 1800s. We laughed and smiled at the maniacs. The sheer terror of these folks is what kept the prying eyes of spies away from the secret launch pad. Even the most courageous American spy would never dare to venture into this part of the country.

I managed to fall asleep in the back of the truck. Years of war had trained my body to ignore rumbling and bumps in the night. That evening I dreamed I was on a great naval vessel, a wooden ship sailing across the Atlantic ocean armed with cannons. The other sailors tried to console me because I had been in love with a mermaid but she left me for the sea. I tried to climb the mast and throw myself down to my death, but they caught me in a fishing net. Then they told me to sleep on the deck of the ship where I could see the stars. I did, and rested peacefully until I felt the ship suddenly veer off course. In a panic, I woke up, and bolted upright in the back of the truck.

Our vehicle had turned off the main road and into a secluded grove in the woods.

"Someone open the gate," the driver yelled back to us.

Fedor jumped out and rolled back a heavy barbwire covered barrier. The truck drove slowly forward into a small pen where a gun tower climbed forty feet into the air. Fedor closed the gate and we were enclosed in concrete and barbed wire.

"You'll have to take turns on watch," the driver said. "I'll sleep. If you see anything move, shoot at it. The locals won't be scared off by anything other than .50 caliber bullets."

He tossed a set of keys to me, and pointed to the gun tower.

"The tower is locked so the bullets and gun should be safe inside. There's four of you. Everyone take a two-hour shift, then wake me up, and we'll get out of here."

I climbed up the steel ladder and reached an armored door

that was padlocked shut. A number of scratches and dents decorated the space around the bolt, suggesting that intruders had
tried to break in at some point. I was comforted that the lock
had not given way. Hopefully the fences and gun were as trustworthy. When I opened the trapdoor, I found a battery powered lamp and turned it on. Fedor and I took charge, as men of
the infantry. He unloaded ammo from cases and I ran the belts
into the gun. Lev and Evgeny climbed up the ladder and back
down, trying to decide whether to sleep in the cramped gun
tower or on the ground below.

"It's no safer up here than on the ground," I told them. "The
gun can't swivel too far down. If they break the perimeter, we're
all done."

"Couldn't we lock ourselves in?"

Fedor laughed. "I'd rather be torn apart by wolves and men
than starve to death in this can. It's not like a space capsule
where you have air and water supplies and can see the stars.
This would be solitary confinement. It would drive a single man
mad. Six of us would be insane within an hour."

From below, we could hear Vulkov and the driver snoring.
Like any good soldiers, they knew how to fall asleep quickly.
Once the heavy machine gun was loaded, Fedor unlatched the
iron shields and opened the windows on all four sides. The
blinds pulled inward, with a hinge at the top, and could be
latched into place on the gun tower's ceiling. If you were being
overrun, gravity would help you keep the iron shields down
until you could latch them. Then you could wait and hope that
the cavalry came before you surrendered to madness and took
your own life. Along one wall was the ammunition stockpile.
Along the opposite wall were four giant batteries and four Klieg
lights in case it got dark.

I called Lev and Evgeny up to the tower.

"One of us will sleep up here on your shifts." I pointed at Fedor and myself. "If you see anything, pull the trigger. The first shot should wake us and we'll take over. If the first shot jams, kick us awake. Although if that happens, we'll probably die anyway. And most important, don't shoot the pillars." I slapped one of the four heavy iron bars on the corner of the tower holding up the roof. "The bullet will ricochet and maybe come back to kill you." Their eyes went wide. "Now try to get some sleep."

Fedor grabbed Lev by the shoulder and then climbed down the ladder. Evgeny remained in the tower with me. On the ground, they refilled the vehicle's gas tank before joining the chorus of snoring men. Evgeny rolled up in a ball on the iron floor. I tucked the gun under my arm and began my slow rotation. The trick was to view all 360 degrees every 30 seconds, but at random intervals so approaching hostiles never knew when to advance. If you caught their movement, you fired and killed them. If they got to the fence wall, you were in serious trouble. If you had enough bullets you could hope to kill them all. But if you were low on ammo, or the enemies were too numerous, they would eventually break through. Inside the perimeter, you couldn't reach them. They would surround the base of the tower and wait you out. You could close the iron blinds to keep out grenades and fire but then you were trapped inside. Better to shoot them all outside the wall.

What would they be after? Perhaps the supplies inside, the batteries, the gun, the ammo. Or maybe they were just territorial, angry that the Soviet Union had invaded their turf. You wouldn't have time to ask them as they tore you to pieces. Maybe they were the creative type. They could start a fire below and try to cook you out.

I scanned the trees. Some enterprising captain had ordered

his men to clear the low branches for fifty yards in any direction. That gave us a leg up. Still, I couldn't keep a watch on all sides. If anyone attacked by stealth, sneaking up one tree trunk at a time, they could make it pretty far before I caught them, if I ever did.

It is just another peculiar fact of Russia that its soldiers are not safe from its own countrymen, and must build defensive posts along the roads to keep from being attacked. American highways are dotted with squat buildings known as rest areas, which are quite the opposite of an armed sentry post. Built by the government, they offer comfort to all and are staffed by locals. They serve coffee and cinnamon rolls and hot dogs. You can buy souvenirs and sunglasses there. You can even get a hand job in the bathroom if you know the right signals. In short, the people welcome travelers. That's the only way to travel. Of course, I didn't know much better back then. My first long trip was to Afghanistan. This was my second. I assumed any journey of great length was fraught with peril.

Genetics probably play a role in that fear. While modern man has learned to travel in airplanes and relocate with ease, for our ancient ancestors, any land beyond eye sight was the great unknown. Even Christopher Columbo, the detective who discovered America, must have been afraid of what he would find.[1] Did the ocean disappear into a void or was there just one more thing somewhere over the horizon, a land he could claim as his own?

So there we were, explorers in the Russian wilderness. I watched the woods wondering if the savages would attack. Reader, you've probably never sat on a ridge, scanning the distance with a rifle in your arm, trying to pick shapes out of the haze. To give you a sense of what it's like, try to remember the first time you saw one of those Magic Eye posters at a shopping center. At first there was nothing. Just a jumble of colors. But you had to keep staring. You thought something might show up. All the indicators suggested there was an image. But you couldn't see it. *Wait, is that it?* You kind of see something, but then it disappears. Now it's just the jumble of colors again. *Shit.* You try staring at the same spot as before, where you thought you saw something. *What's it even supposed to look like?* It would help if you knew. *Wait, what's that?* You think you see something. Don't let your eyes wander. You're pretty sure now. Finally, you can see it, a fire truck or something stupid like that. You're standing there in the mall and you can see the image in the poster. You're really sure this time. Also, you have a rifle with you. Maybe you bought it at a sporting goods store. So now you fire the rifle at the image on the Magic Eye poster. Suddenly the poster is in shreds. You can no longer see the image. But is that because you shot the fire truck, or because there was never a fire truck there in the first place, and it was just your mind playing tricks on you? And while you're thinking about that, you don't notice a real fire truck crash through the doors of the mall heading towards you and it runs you over.

My eyes watered. I got chills in my arms and legs. My breath came out in foggy patches. I kicked the machine gun's iron mount to hurt my foot and keep myself awake. I tried to count the trees in the forest around us. Some zen masters teach their students to look into the woods and see the nothing that is there. In a way, I have achieved great levels of zen proficiency, because I stared into those fucking trees for hours and didn't see a thing. When my time was up, I nudged Evgeny with my foot. He sat up and I motioned for him to stand. He rubbed his eyes and yawned. I was about to entrust our safety to a sleepy astrophysicist. Luckily, as he woke up and remembered where he was, fear took hold of him and opened his eyes wide. He might not have known anything about war, but his nerves would give him a hair-trigger finger and as long as he didn't freeze up, we might survive. If he fired even one shot, I would wake up and take the gun. Or if he cried out, I would jump up to help. The only danger was that his muscles would lock and his lungs would not work to scream –that he'd stand there like a statue while Russian barbarians stormed the gates of our small fortress. I could take that chance. I went to sleep.

Earlier I skimmed over the story of my last three years in Afghanistan. They were mostly spent on days like this, and nights of the same. Terrifying outposts in a strange land. I stood on ridges, or crouched in a ditches, waiting for onslaughts that never came. The battle raged elsewhere in the country. But we lived in fear that it would return to our provinces, death on horseback, delivered by men with rocket launchers that could now take out even the great Russian warships, the predatory helicopters. As the war dragged on, those Afghan rebels became a fierce resistance, armed by America to fight back against our Soviet forces. We wondered if some new weapon would find its way into their hands, a laser cannon or pulsing phaser. How could we fight against that armed only with machine guns?

Generally, we believed that such technology did not exist. But a few high ranking military officers had seen *Star Wars* and some *Star Trek* films. What if, they asked, those science fiction films were created as a cover story to disguise the existence of actual laser blasters? This was how a nation raised on propaganda viewed the world. Any good story was a possible smoke screen, even the stories of television and movies. They imagined a secret weapons lab in the New Mexican desert where children of the Manhattan Project had developed photon weapons.

Realizing that news of the futuristic pistols would soon spread into the world through the loose talk of scientists and researchers, the C.I.A. created a special program to create popular stories about lasers for the public. That way, any whispers or gossip about the actual lasers would be mistaken by Soviet spies for conversation about *Star Wars*. The movie was so popular and cleverly constructed to tap into collective consciousness and human mythology that it could only have been created by the C.I.A. Such conspiracy theories seem silly now, although you can still find a few cranks discussing this nonsense in modern day Russia. They note that the recent fall of the American intelligence community and its spectacular failures to predict terrorist activity coincide with the release of equally disastrous prequels to the *Star Wars* franchise. They ask: Could not both messes be the result of the same poor leadership?[2]

Those ridiculous fears were still with us in the waning days of the Afghan war. By the time I found myself in the Russian woods, though, I knew better than to expect a laser attack.

I wish I had learned more about the Afghan people while I was in their country. Such knowledge would have been profitable later, when I could have gone to work for Blackwater or other American companies engaged in war. Those firms can always use experts to tell them how to more efficiently lose a war in Afghanistan. But I did not speak to the locals. Instead, I got to know a parade of recruits, new soldiers on their first tours, old soldiers returning to the field. Green men and gray men. In talking to them, I learned a bit about Russia and how it was changing when I was gone. The military was becoming less of an escape valve and more of a slaughterhouse. Only the poor wound up there, because they had nowhere else to go. Some of the men considered it luxury to sleep on the floors of sand covered huts outside Kabul. It was warmer than they had ever known. Getting three meals a day and rides on horses was like being at the circus. Backwards people, penniless beggars. That was our new army. The days of a proud warrior class were fading.

I felt someone shaking me. I looked up to see Fedor smiling at me.

"We're halfway through the rest stop," he said. "It's my turn to watch."

Evgeny was already halfway down the ladder to the ground, a nervous wreck. Lev waited until he made it down to climb up. When there were three of us in the tower, it was very crowded, and I realized how difficult it would be for six men to survive in there, even if one of the men had no arms or legs. I hoped it wouldn't come to that as I climbed down to the ground. Evgeny was shivering next to the passenger door of the truck. I unrolled a scratchy wool blanket and bundled myself up at the bottom of the ladder.

With two hours to sleep, I had enough time for real dreams. I imagined myself on a warm beach, somewhere in the tropics. I was under a great metal umbrella and I could see the blue sea in the distance. Beautiful women in black bikinis frolicked in the surf. Tall blond Amazonian models played friendly games of volleyball. I was the only man around for miles. Motherly old island women brought me cold bottles of beer. From the forest behind me came the muffled sound of a steel drum band – normally infernal racket, but transformed through the power of dreams into a sweet lullaby. On the horizon, I could see a great wooden sailing ship bobbing up and down. Powerful women rowed in boats toward the ship from the beach, carrying loads of fruits and other supplies. It was preparing for a long voyage, and I was to be the captain. Nobody had told me this, but I felt it in my bones. That was my ship to sail. Then I saw a great cannon hoisted up from a smaller boat onto the deck of the great clipper. It raised the red flag of the U.S.S.R. Some movement near the shore caught my attention. Was it a fish jumping out of the water? It disappeared before I saw what it was. The motherly women who had brought me beer arrived again, this time bearing maps. I looked at the charts and saw not coastlines, but stars and planets. My ship's destination was the reaches of space. I looked up and saw that the sailing ship was now a rocket being hoisted out of the ocean and stationed on a launch pad jutting from the water like an oil rig. Great tons of water poured from the rocket as it was lifted into place. Another darting black movement caught my eyes near the surf, where the women were playing. Was it a shark? I concentrated my eyes and saw a great dark shape burst forth from the water, overpowering one of the women and pulling her into the ocean. It must be a shark. I watched to see if it would release her, but then it came up again. This time it was clearly a man in heavy black coat. He was holding a giant hatchet and I saw two halves of a woman's corpse floating in the waves behind him, in a part of the sea turned red with blood. Alarm clawed at my brain. Something was wrong, I knew, but what should I do? Could I help the women? Should I attack the man? I found I could not move. I was stuck on my beach towel in the sand. Then I heard a gunshot and the man fell into the water, dead. I was relieved. Then three more men appeared in the surf. I tried to cry out, but my voice was overpowered by the sounds of a gun behind me as the three men recoiled back into the water, bleeding. A longer gun blast rattled me and I was awake, staring into the forest where the ocean used to be.

Great tree trunks were being ripped apart by gun fire as leaves sputtered in the air and then fell to the ground. Fedor was yelling savagely; Lev whimpering beside him. I climbed up and took his place, feeding the ammunition belts into the gun, praying it wouldn't jam.

"Go see if the driver has any grenades," I told Lev as he climbed down. I doubted that was the case, but at least it would keep him occupied.

"They're coming on," Fedor yelled to me. "But not very heavy. I think we'll be alright." I continued feeding bullets into the giant machine gun.

Through the opening in the floor came Lev's hand and a revolver.

"This is all he has," Lev said.

I took the pistol. It would be pretty useless if the machine gun jammed, but could offer some protection if we had to load a new belt of ammunition. And it would let the marauders know we were well supplied, with at least two guns on our side. Or if we became trapped in the gun tower, we could kill ourselves, one bullet for each man.

Fedor was firing in short bursts now, spinning this way and that, taking careful aim before pulling the trigger. This saved ammunition, and also, hopefully, scared the enemies because of our precision. Pausing between clusters of fire also let the woods settle and allowed Fedor to pick out new movements in the trees. If he was firing non-stop, everything would be a blur of wood chips, broken branches, and falling leaves with movements of men imperceptible in the chaos.

"I think they're starting to doubt," he yelled to me. "They're falling back."

This was good news. The first belt was getting near the end. We only had two more strings of ammunition to feed into the hungry weapon. As I unraveled the chain of ballistics, I checked the revolver with my other hand. I turned the safety off and made sure all six barrels were loaded.

"Sixty shots left," I called out as the end of the belt left my hands. "Then I'll switch belts."

"That's when I reach for the revolver," Fedor yelled, still spinning to shoot in all directions of the forest.

Then the belt clicked through empty on the other side of the big gun.

"Now!"

I grabbed the fresh supply of ammunition and loaded it into the chamber. I felt the blazing heat of the overworked cannon in my raw hands. As I did this, Fedor watched the woods, now letting loose single bullets and calling out his accomplishments.

Headshot! Turn, fire. *Chest shot!* Another shot. *Head again.* Two shots. *Stomach. And neck. I was aiming for the head. Last bullet.* He spun around 180 degrees and fired one more time. I heard the sound of a bullet ricocheting off of metal. *Hit him in the machete.*

He handed the revolver back to me and wrapped his arm around the big artillery piece, firing a burst in the same direction he had just fired the pistol.

"Got him in the back. He was going to die anyway, but at least now his friends know we aren't completely out of ammo. Maybe that will keep them away."

The tension eased out of both of us, though he kept his eyes open and alert as he scanned the perimeter, conversing with me in the eerie silence following the gunfight.

"That last pistol shot snapped the machete blade back into the man's chest. He was bleeding bad. It wasn't a trick shot. I aimed for his heart and got the knife instead."

We watched the trees for another fifteen minutes as the

driver, now awake, refueled the vehicle with gasoline canisters from the back. When he had the tank full, I called Lev and Evgeny back into the tower.

"On my signal, we'll each close one of the screens. Fedor will leave first. Then Lev, then Evgeny. I'll come down last and lock the lower hatch behind us. As soon as you get down, get in the truck. We're most vulnerable when the gun is locked up and the gates are open. They could still rush us then and take us down without much fighting. Fedor will open the main gate. Have the driver roll out the length of the truck, and I'll climb on the back, then pull the gate shut. Any questions?"

There were none.

"Are we clear?" I asked Fedor.

"All's quiet."

I tucked the revolver into my belt.

"Now!"

We all grabbed our screens from the ceiling bolts and closed them. I began detaching the ammunition, closing the chamber so dust would not get in before the next soldiers ended up on the outpost. By the time I was done, all three others had dropped through the hatch. I climbed halfway down, sealed the iron door, and jumped down to the ground. I sprinted to the truck, hopped on the rear fender and slammed the main gate shut. Then we sped off onto the road, and into the darkening night.

It was not safe to stop in the woods after dark.

10 / HUMAN SATELLITES

We rumbled into the small village, not listed on any map, where the shadow space program launched its rockets and satellites.

"Welcome to town," Vulkov said. "The first round is on me."

The six of us entered Uncle Sasha's, the wretched excuse for a bar in the shadow of the launch pad. It was a dark shadow, as it was night time. The stars and moon could not cast even their glow onto the ramshackle hut. We downed shots of vodka. Vulkov, in his wheelchair, grew drunk right away. Without arms or legs, his body offered nowhere for the alcohol to hide, so it dove straight into his bloodstream and went to his head. He yelled out a few times, declared that he missed his limbs, then passed out in the chair.

The rest of us took turns drinking in the sweat and steam of the tavern. We'd stand and lead a toast, then down our drink and slam the glass on the table.

The driver started:

Brothers! I call you brothers, for we have made it through this mess alive. The road is no place for a man without a family. When I invite a man into my truck, I am asking him to join my family! So you are now my brothers! (Loud cheers and clapping.) *I will not travel with you into space, but I will look up into the night sky and see you pass in orbit. Then I will say, "That shining light is my brother." We have traveled together across the great wilderness of Russia and fought off the hordes together. I wish you well on your missions, all of you! Listen. When I was a boy, I dreamed that I would be the first man on Mars. I wanted to be a cosmonaut when I grew up. Instead I am a truck driver. We cannot all have our dreams realized. The world is not large enough for our appetites. Many people must be disappointed. Yet I consider myself lucky to be your brother, and I hope that one of you might set foot on Mars some day. And when you do, think of me, your humble truck driver. That is all I have to say. My name is Ivan Lubavich Tarkovsky.*

He swallowed his vodka and pumped a fist in the air, his hands enmeshed in fingerless driving gloves. We all cheered as the driver refilled his glass. Next, Fedor stood up. He said:

Warriors! I call you warriors, for we have made it through battle alive. (Loud cheers and clapping.) *Not every one is lucky enough to fight in this life. Lucky? Yes, lucky! We were born to hunt and struggle against the gods to make our way in this world. Nature loves a warrior. But the modern world coddles us and treats us like babies. Too many people are born to soft mothers and kept from all harm, crying from fear as they pass from school to marriage to the nursing home. That is not living! You must see your life threatened to appreciate it. Only on the edge of the great mountain of death can you appreciate how high you have climbed, how much your ancestors struggled to get you out of the foothills and into the great peaks. To-day we made it to the mountain top. Did you enjoy the view?* (Hearty cries of Yes!) *Remember that view always. You saw be-yond the veil of fear. You had a glimpse of death. You didn't like it!*

(We cried "No!)" *You want to keep it at bay!* ("Yes!") *You must fight, then! You must remain warriors until the day you die! Death cannot come for you while you hold a sword. Some of us were warriors before today. But now we are all warriors. We battled with death and death retreated. We will drink to that!*

He finished his drink, and took a swig from the bottle for good measure. Evgeny stood up next. He pulled a pair of spectacles from his pocket and set them upon his nose. He held his glass of vodka up in front of his face, as if to inspect it. He shook it gently, then raised it higher.

Satellites! Human satellites! I call us satellites for we have circled the planet alive. The earth spins and we are caught in its gravitational pull. Even now, when I seem to stand still, I am spinning. ("Maybe it's just the room, comrade!") *No, Fedor, I am spinning for sure. Every day we make a complete rotation 'round the center of the earth. It often feels effortless, because the crust of the earth is doing all the work. But some days, like today, an obstacle gets in our way. The earth's pull is so strong that we forge ahead, pushing trouble out of our way. We work harder than the moon to keep our selves spinning. We never quit. When Galileo had the good sense to build a telescope and see the world, he found that the earth itself was spinning around the sun. Looking at satellites is a way to find out where you are and where the center of the universe is. So I will always look to you, comrades, to know where I am. For you are my fellow satellites, and I shall proudly watch your orbit and make judgments about the universe. And I drink to that!*

He drank half his drink and threw the glass into the air with its bottom at the center of a revolution... by some force of physics, the remaining liquor stayed in the bottom of the glass while it spun round and round until he caught it gracefully and pulled it to his lips, finishing it without spilling a drop.

Lev stood up next, looking uncomfortable as he stretched

his spine all the way up – he was only comfortable hunched over a radar station.

Blips! We are all just blips on God's radar. Some of us are friendly. Others are enemy contacts. It's hard to tell. I am drunk, friends. A radar is a faulty instrument. It can tell you where something is, but not its intention. I wish I had a radar for intentions. I could have used it on my wife. Every day she was close to me, and I knew her position in relation to me. But I did not know what she felt. Which was sadness. She was depressed. She hated our life. She thought she was married to a janitor. Ahh, how I wish she could see me now, getting ready to launch into space. She cannot see me, though. My radar failed to tell me how depressed she was and she took her own life one day when I was at work. She shot herself with her uncle's war rifle. There is no radar that can sound the depths of the human heart.

Here he broke down crying. He set his glass on the table without drinking from it. I looked at Vulkov and he was still asleep. It was my turn. I took Lev's glass and drank it for courage, then stood up.

Revolutionaries! I call us revolutionaries because, as Evgeny said, we revolve around the sun. Without all of its citizens spinning round on the earth, Russia would cease to be! A country is not made by mountains and rivers and beaches but by people. We are the people! We are the great red wheel spinning round and round, making revolutions. The wheel is man's first great invention. Such a long way we have come from wheels to rockets. The world is always changing. Who knows what changes we will bring to this great blue planet Earth? Let us hope they are good ones. May all our revolutions be good ones!

We all drank again.

Somebody roused Vulkov and he said we should be getting to our bunks. The driver weaved us drunkenly towards the launch field and our concrete bungalows there. We hugged each other and said good night. We cried and laughed and talked meaningless nonsense that seemed important to our drunken minds. I carried Vulkov's body into his small dwelling and found his bed. I tucked him in, making sure his head was close to the series of mouth pulleys he would use in the morning to rouse himself in the morning. I remember thinking it looked a little like a bear trap, and that made sense because he once had the ferocious strength of a bear.

I stumbled towards my hut and was distracted by the sight of the launch pad. It was dark. Unlike the public launching grounds in Star City, our facility was hidden. I tripped over a giant refueling pipeline and cursed as I fell to the cracked concrete ground. Blades of grass struggled up through the cement and brushed my face. I thought about sleeping there in the stone field. I felt a strong desire to be tucked in. Why was I born to a world that would never let me know my own parents? I cried a bit and balled my fists, pounding on the pavement in fury. Finally, bleeding from my hands, I stopped and rolled up into a ball. My parents had disappeared. My wife had vanished. Even Vulkov had fallen asleep. I was drunk and alone, a tiny speck on the great Russian continent. I thought I could very well die there peacefully. It was cold enough that I would catch pneumonia if I stayed out all night. I rolled over and watched the stars flicker in the great black canopy of night. I tried to count them, but there were too many. I fell asleep, ready for whatever the frigid night would bring me.

11 / THE RED DAWN

I woke up covered in blankets. Old Viktoravich had seen me in the night and brought out his family's afghan quilts. He draped them over me and left me to my slumber.

Birds sang across the morning sky. Their music had a brittle feel, as if a chorus had performed vespers in a freezer. It was gentle, though, like a stream running peacefully between my ears. As the day warmed with the sun, I lifted my head from the ground and saw again the sky above. My life seemed doomed to a series of unpleasant trips to horrifying destinations. I had no lover, but I was not exactly alone. There were my cosmonaut mates to start with. And then the man I did not yet know who had brought me comfort in the night. He appeared in a few minutes with a stainless steel cup of hot coffee.

"Comrade, you slept out in the field. It can be dangerously cold at night. Luckily for you, Old Viktoravich has trouble sleeping. His back is a relic of another era. So he paces at night and happened to see you out his window." I took a sip and sat up to face him. He pointed towards his space tower home.

"I live there. I will make sure the launch coordinates are accurate. Most of the time, I am only responsible for the cosmonauts when they are in space. But when I saw you out here, I thought: *It would be a shame to lose another man here.* I have already done so much math to plan the next voyage. But the path through the atmosphere and around the earth using the moon's gravity will not be valid forever. If you froze to death, my charts would be wasted. So you see I am somewhat selfish to come out here in the night." He stroked his long white beard. "You don't want to catch a pneumonia before you go to space. Your health is your most important possession." Here he coughed the sad hack of a man who has outlived his lungs. "I am not so healthy myself. But I promise you, if you stop sleeping outside, I will live long enough to see you into space and safely home."

The clouds blocked out the sunlight enough for me to see his face clearly. I extended my hand to him.

"Ilya Zamyatin."

"Viktoravich," he said. "Come inside. I will show you the route I have planned for you."

He ambled off without waiting to see if I would follow. Where else could I go? I stood and brushed myself off, then followed him into the space tower.

Looking back, it seems unfair that I entered that sanctum instead of Evgeny. He had so much more in common with Old Viktarovich, with his love of astrophysics. Still, we cannot choose our parents, and parents cannot choose their children. I ended up being his favorite of the cosmonauts. When he got sick, I took him to the medical clinic for tests. When he made new discoveries about possible future trajectories, he told me in excitement. Old Viktoravich was plotting courses from the Soviet Union for missions he knew he would never live to see.

He had mapped out courses for the next decade. The world would keep spinning and the planets would not change their orbit, so the work was sound. But what he hadn't considered was that the surface of the earth could change so mightily. That the borders of a country could give way, were as delicate as the dance steps of an asteroid tugged this way and that by passing bodies. His calculations were sound, except that they started from a patch of land that would soon belong to a country that could not afford to launch multiple costly space missions. His books of rocket maps are probably gathering dust somewhere now.

About paths through the night sky he was never wrong, that Old Viktoravich. The October Squad's first mission went like clockwork. We were nervous, to be sure, but the tasks were so easy that our fear was not a factor. After the demise of our precursors, the shadow space program needed a success to bolster morale, so they gave us a manageable workload. We did not even go to space. Instead, we operated a high altitude airplane to test the possibility of launching low orbiting spy satellites without the use of rockets. This would be ideal, if it was effective, because you could launch a plane in secret more easily than you could launch a rocket.

The four of us were in the back of a jet plane that arced high over the sky of the world. These are the same airplanes they use to train astronauts or to make Tom Hanks look like he is floating, for which he receives credit as an actor. We had already trained in these airplanes, to prepare for our time in space without gravity. But now, rather than floating around and laughing, we were required to eject several prototype low orbit satellites. They could not merely be released like bombs, as they were too fragile to travel on the outside of the airplane. Instead, we prepared them in the cargo bay and then launched them through the rear of the plane. The plane could not stay at the same altitude for too long, so it would coast down to a lower orbit between each satellite release.

Now it may sound simple to eject four satellites from a plane, but these were multi-million-ruble devices, a costly payload whose accidental destruction would not please Moscow. So we were nervous, strapped into the seats of the plane as it taxied down the runway and launched into the blue skies. Only two pilots and four October men were on board. All of us cosmonauts had received rudimentary training in flying the jet in case something happened to the pilots. The military would mourn the loss of two able men, but even more it would be devastated by the loss of this high altitude jet. I have said this mission was easy – and it was compared to an actual space trip. Nevertheless, it was a nerve-racking experience, unlike your typical airline flight.

Instead of a stewardess serving you drinks, you had to smuggle your own flask of vodka aboard. But you could not risk enjoying a sip until after the mission was done because you needed all your faculties for the satellite launch. And once it was safe to drink, the vomit-inducing zero-G forces would make you puke up the liquor like a drunk college student who is on their way to witness sex crimes at a fraternity.

Instead of an in-flight movie, there was only the window beside you, offering a view of the desolate North Russian landscape. Given a choice, I would prefer to watch even a horrible movie rather than stare at the frozen wilderness and its mind numbing repetition. Even a *Star Wars* prequel would be preferable to the misery of the view I had.

Instead of a secret rendezvous with the stewardess in the bathroom to join the mile-high club, there are five other men on the plane. I suppose, if you were inclined to join clubs, you could masturbate in the lavatory and induct yourself into the club. But if you've ever jerked off into a stainless steel bowl full of blue liquid you know that it induces more shame than pleasure. Whenever I hear tales of airplanes accidentally dropping toilet waste from the sky, I am first revolted, like you, by the thought of all that fecal matter landing on a house somewhere. Later, though, I am saddened to think of some poor teenager's sperm, having been squeezed into an airplane toilet, suddenly plummeting to its death without ever having a chance to enter a woman. Along those lines, if I was ever in a plane that broke up in mid air, and I had time to consider my impending doom as I plummeted to my death, I wonder if I would pleasure myself on the way down. What else can you do in that short span of time? You cannot tell your loved ones goodbye, or write a message to them, or do anything useful. Why not give yourself one last moment of bliss before you perish? The only drawback I can think of is that the Hazmat suited rescue workers will find your corpse in a field somewhere, or floating in the ocean, with your pants pulled down and your hand around your throbbing cock head. Although it will probably be pulverized beyond recognition anyway.

But I was talking about the difference between my high-altitude mission and a regular airplane trip. I suppose there some similarities as well. If you fly on a commercial airline, you are sometimes given captain's wings as a souvenir. We would receive medals of commendation if our trip was successful.

So we were airborne, rocketing towards the limits of the atmosphere and the horizon of breathable air. We were nervous but excited to be completing our first mission. And if these satellites we launched were successful, we would become a regular part of the great Soviet spy network. Even in the last dying lights of the Cold War, we could see that the space program was fading from its former triumphs – not yet in Russia, but in America, where space tragedies and disinterest were pushing NASA out of the glory seat. If America abandoned its space program, then it would not be long before the U.S.S.R. did also. Landing on the moon was an expendable goal, but spying on the U.S. would always be important even without the space program. We were becoming cosmonauts, but there was a surer future in espionage.

In the great history of mankind, spying came early. Imagine some caveman who has tamed fire and keeps a torch in his cave. A neighboring cave must have sent primitive spies to find out about his technology. Or a neolithic spy master recruited cave-women to sleep with the torch-owning caveman and steal his secrets. Perhaps one caveman spy was clubbed on the head with a rock and woke later with no recollection of his past but an arsenal of fighting skills that he used to hunt down the caveman who had killed his girlfriend. This caveman probably looked like Matt Damon.

The point is that it was important for us to complete this mission, both to get a success under our belt and to secure our future in the Soviet spy organization's good graces. We knew spies would always run the country. As we crested through layer after layer of clouds, our pilot called back that we should pre-pare to launch the first satellite. We had no intercom in the airplane, so he yelled into a megaphone pointed back towards us. Then he reattached his oxygen mask so he could open the back bay and risk depressurizing the cabin. We left our seats and locked ourselves into place with steel cables. In theory, they would keep us from flying out the back of the plane in the event of an accident. But for utility's sake, the cords were too long to offer much safety. If sucked out the rear, we'd be caught so far out that it would take all three comrades to haul us back in, something they could only do if they abandoned the satellite launching. Most likely, in an accident, our lifeless corpses would sail behind the jet and, assuming it landed safely, be dragged along the ground, past recognition, until we were hunks of hamburger meat in shredded jumpsuits. We would be better off releasing the cords and working unrestrained, accepting a quick death as the punishment for any errors. Too many questions, however, would be raised by the body of a janitor plummeting to the earth and landing in a potato field outside Kursk.

We quickly unloaded the first satellite from its moorings and moved it to the launch position. Evgeny took all the measurements to see that it was properly aimed for launch. Lev checked our airspace via a radar screen near the back of the cockpit. Fedor and I armed the heavy catapult arm that would jettison it into low orbit. We all had oxygen masks strapped to our faces.

Lev began the countdown and we all took our positions as the plane rose higher and gravity failed us. At the top of our parabolic arc we were in near space and as soon as the downward arc began we launched the satellite straight out behind us and into the daytime night sky behind us.

I should point out here that I recently saw a video of some amateur hobbyists launching a comparable camera into near space using balloons and cell-phone equipment. Just as space travel now belongs to tourists, the demanding missions of cosmonauts like me from the 1980s are now the weekend activities of American nerds. At the time, though, such powerful cameras could only be delivered to high altitudes with a lot of jet or rocket fuel as the camera machinery was too heavy.

The first satellite launched without incident.

The airplane flew down and we floated around, experiencing

our first true weightlessness, laughing and swallowing the vomit that lurched up inside us. Then the trajectory flattened out and we prepared the next satellite. The first had been spherical. The next was conical, with solar wings that would extend soon after we launched it. This, too, we launched without incident, although the stomach fluttering was starting to affect us. We began laughing dizzily as we prepared the final satellite, a long tube with flat wings. It looked like the science project of a child with disinterested parents: shoddily produced and doubtful. Our humor increased as we looked at this device.

"Time to take out the trash," Fedor laughed, preparing the catapult arm which was gently tossing these devices into the air behind our jet.

"I hope we don't get charged with space littering by the United Nations," Lev said. Then he began the countdown and we propelled the sad final satellite into low space, successfully completing our mission. The pilot gave us several more parabolic arcs into the upper reaches of the atmosphere to give us more weightless experiences. Evgeny tried to smoke a cigarette but could not get it lit as the flame dispersed in all directions. I performed several somersaults. Lev opened a bag of small candies and watched them float around. (They landed on top of Fedor when the airplane bottomed out of its final arc.)

We landed and returned to our base.

From what I understand, none of the satellites was able to maintain a successful orbit. Perhaps they all crashed to the ground while we were still in the air. In the Soviet Union's reckoning, however, we could still chalk it up as a success even if the mission's ultimate goal was a failure. We had done our part without incident.

* * *

It was time to go to space.

The men who died immediately before us had many missions planned for them. Next on the calendar was a one-man trip in a capsule designed for a specific cosmonaut who had been lost. When you're trying to launch something into space, every saved ounce helps. So the engineers had cut every corner possible, creating a hatch optimum for the vanished man, whose name was Lieutenant Grigor. I did not know it at the time and only discovered it after the Soviet Union's archives opened, but I will do him the honor of using his name at this point in the narrative anyway. All of Grigor's measurements were taken into account when the capsule was built. The angle of the seat built for the distance from his skull to his ass. The length of his thighs factored into length of the chair. Even his feet played a part. Not a centimeter was wasted. I do not wish to speak ill of the man, but I assume he had a small set of balls, because mine were always cramped when I was in the capsule. If he'd been a heartier man with a bigger sack, they would have left a little more room.

I did not know I was selected for the mission merely because of the measurements of my body. Instead, I was told that I had performed more admirably than my peers. I was not sure I believed this, but wondered if Vulkov had pulled some strings on my behalf, to make me the first of my class in space. Pretending I had earned the spot served two purposes – it disguised the fact that I was replacing a vanished corpse, and it created rivalry among the October men. Never doubt the Soviet Union when it comes to setting one man against another. Luckily the rivalry always remained cordial among my unit. But we did work harder in order to obtain the next advantage. We ran faster around the launch platform during drills. We cleaned more vigorously when on latrine duty. We ate borscht with more feigned enthusiasm than our table mates. We had been giving our all before this. Now we gave even more. We were tricked into our labors!

The next few weeks are a blur in my memory. I must have been preparing for the flight. I was too nervous to create any strong recollection, aside from my meetings with Viktoravich. Soon enough it was the night before my launch. I wrote a letter to Natasha. I knew it would never be delivered, but I had to put into writings my feelings for her and my shame at keeping the truth from her. Maybe if I perished, the letter would one day find her. I cried as I finished the note, and tried to distract myself by running through my equipment check again and again. I knew I couldn't get through my mission with Natasha on my mind, so I decided to head into the night and make love to one of the many women I'd pleasured since the announcement of my mission. They were not Natasha, but a woman's company and vagina are sources of pleasure even without true love. Plus I had a space boner and knew the only cure for that was pre-mission sex. So I left the airfield and went to a bar.

12 / THE DOWNWARD SPIRAL

S o that is how I found myself stranded in space, and how a
man like Vulkov felt he owed me the favor of bringing
me safely home.

Once my story was on the front page of *The Washington Post*,
a serious effort was made to bring me back to Earth. Some of
the technology involved is still classified, so I cannot tell you
whether lasers were involved, or if the United States has a collection of missile-deterring satellites that can hit targets in space
with great precision. All I am allowed to say is that my satellite's course was soon altered and I began dropping down to the
surface.

I was not out of the woods yet, however. My capsule was
spinning lower and lower in its orbit, but the craft did not know
it was returning to earth. So the parachutes that would slow my
descent to a reasonable speed did not know to deploy after I
burned through the atmosphere and reentered. In fact, they
were specifically configured not to operate if the security of the
capsule had been breached. That way, any Soviet secrets would

plummet towards the ground and be destroyed instantly on impact before they could fall into the hands of the Americans.

Through a series of Morse code messages, I was informed that I must reactivate my craft's parachute. I did this in a harrowing period of suspenseful action that should be of interest to any investors considering a purchase of the film rights to my story. Imagine the best moments of *Apollo 13*, but then replace soft pudgy Tom Hanks with a chiseled actor like Dolph Lundgren or Viggo Mortensen, and you will have a sense of the box office success that awaits the movie adaptation of this tale.

Incidentally, I realize that the two men I named are not actually Russian. But Mr. Lundgren is an honorary Russian for his work in the film *Rocky IV*. He does not know it, but he was secretly given a commendation by the Communist Party for his efforts to highlight Soviet superiority in defeating both Apollo Creed and Rocky Balboa. Those of you who are film fans are probably confused right now, as you are not familiar with the Russian editors' cut of *Rocky IV*, in which Ivan Drago first kills Apollo Creed, then beats Rocky Balboa to death. He punches his head open – and here, Soviet censors used a clip from the David Cronenberg film *Scanners* to depict Stallone's head bursting apart after a left hook from Drago. It is considered a great film! Of course, the follow up movies, *Rocky V* and *Rocky Balboa*, both fared poorly at the Russian box office, as audiences were perplexed by the Lazarus-style resurrection of a character who had been previously killed. As for Viggo Mortensen, you probably know him best for his work in the fantasy classic *A Perfect Murder* or the jingoistic feminist propaganda piece *G.I. Jane*. In our country, though, he is most esteemed for his work in *Eastern Promises*. In that film, directed by Mr. Cronenberg of *Rocky IV* head explosion fame, Mortensen plays a Russian agent who is attacked, while naked, in a bathhouse by men with razor blades. Now, I'm not sure if you've ever been naked in a steam room, but it is terrifying enough on its own. You are exposed to the world, and unless you have a giant horse cock like me, you are probably sad as the men around see your tiny penis. Imagine, on top of that, being chased by thugs with cutting tools! Yet Mortensen defeats his enemies, which convinces audiences that he is a tough Russian badass. So, while his penis is smaller than mine, he would still make a convincing version of me in the film of *Human Satellite*.

So anyway during this thrilling sequence in which I defuse the security devices, my capsule burns through the atmosphere, glowing with a white hot intensity that is hard to describe. Imagine being punched the head, then thrown into a tanning bed while you are trying to connect your HD television to a DVD player using one hand. That is how difficult my situation was. All around me, I could hear the heat burning away my protective shell as I struggled to disconnect and reconnect tiny wires using a set of tweezers.

And if it was not hard enough to do this while the atmosphere blazed around me, I soon passed through that barrier and into the upper reaches of the sky. Now I was no longer seeing white heat, but blue sky and clouds and I could feel how fast I was falling. I had unplugged the correct wires and was now soldering connections to use my camera batteries in order to fire the landing parachute. This is like driving your car at 100 miles per hour and then opening up the hood and attempting to change the radio station while reaching through the engine with a pair of barbecue tongs. Again, incredibly exciting from a cinematic standpoint. But also nerve-wracking when you consider how long I had been in space, hallucinating and considering my doom. Here I had a chance to save myself! It was no easy task. Many attempts failed as the metal connections broke before I could fire the parachute. As I considered the earth racing up towards me, I realized I had only one more chance to do it correctly. Out of my peripheral vision, I could make out the grid of a city as I made electric connections in my ship's mechanic hatch. I finished my work and entered the commands on my console that told the camera to take a spy photo. I held my breath. If it didn't fire, I'd have less than a minute to say goodbye before I splattered on the continental shelf. The metal was screaming around me and I couldn't hear. But I could feel it when I pressed the camera trigger. There was a barely tangible click as the hatches blew outside my craft. Then, two or three seconds later, I felt like I was tackled by a bear. When the chutes broke free and caught the rising air, my capsule slowed so quickly my whole body was bruised by the change in momentum. Yes, so imagine that the bear who tackled me was made of metal! *Krash!* My capsule slammed up against me and stopped my fall. But barely in time. My metal cocoon was still swaying wildly with gravity's reckoning when it smashed through the trees and dangled towards the Earth. The parachute had slowed it enough to keep me alive, but not enough to take me anywhere near the neighborhood of a comfortable landing. Instead, I was smashed into the dashboard of my craft and left swaying from overtaxed parachute cords in mighty trees hundreds of feet from the ground. The viewing hatch gave me a look at the distant soil. It would not have surprised me to travel this far only to die dangling from the trees. Such was my luck. I closed my eyes. Having grown up in an abandoned silo, I was used to sleeping at this height.

Now, I was only hanging there for an hour before the Soviet army arrived to retrieve me. Yet I was so taxed by the journey that I managed to fall asleep deeply. The next thing I remember was the sound of whistling and electric guitar. Vulkov had commanded the rescue party to wake me up with a new Scorpions song called "Wind of Change." I heard the soothing sound and saw the arc of electricity outside as welders clawed open my ship. A secret military construction crane had been driven into the forrest to give men access to my ship. First they cut through the outer shell. Then a bomb crew deactivated all the security explosives. Then I heard a wonderful hissing noise, the sound of new air entering my ship for the first time since I left the Earth. The door dropped out and plummeted to the Earth, badly denting itself and giving me a slight glimpse of what would have happened if I had failed to ignite my parachute triggers. The door fell only a few hundred feet, and it was destroyed. I would have fallen straight from space. Then I heard a dull thump. Then another. And another. Then Vulkov's rubber hand swung up into my ship. He had been swinging it towards the door with his neck and the noise I heard was it thumping against the frame. When it swung into view I immediately grabbed it. It was like the hand of God or a father. It was reaching out to pull me back to safety. And happiness.

I was back on Earth. I was home.

And I would soon be forgotten like so many veterans of Russia's century-long war with itself. There was first the ecstatic bliss of freedom, the great orgy of newfound thrills embraced by a generation of revelers who had never known life without the Iron Curtain. We danced in the street, as such children do. We marveled that there were no tanks bearing down on us. We hammered at statues with great sledge hammers. We melted them for scrap or sold them to eccentric millionaire collectors. You in America grow easily tired of teenagers with guitars playing folk music, but in Russia this was something new! The folk music movement had passed by us and so we never really knew Bob Dylan and John Denver and James Taylor. Even pimple faced nerds could learn to play a few chords and then sit in a town square, sing "All Along the Watchtower" and be assured of sleeping with a sexy rebellious lady that night. We lived your decades of upheaval, turmoil and unrest in just a few years, like cramming all in one night for a final exam in Turbulent American Studies at some liberal arts college where the pipe-smoking professor wears sandals and his wife is a lesbian.

And then we failed the exam.

Capitalism was a harsh woman. In America, you have a saying for when you wake up next to a woman so ugly that you would rather chew your leg off like a coyote caught in a bear trap than continue sleeping with your leg under her body. You call her "coyote ugly" because you would rather have sex with a coyote than with her. Well, capitalism was coyote ugly.[1]

The gangsters saw a vacuum and filled the void that the Secret Police had left behind. While scared citizens poured through their KGB files in the Soviet archive, the mob sprang up and imposed their own order on the streets of Moscow. They are fueled by tattoos, violence, oil money, sex trafficking, mink farms, and the nuclear black market. I wish I could say I fought valiantly against them, but I did not. I cashed in.

I bummed around the abandoned space port for a month in a drunken stupor, wallowing in self pity. I had missed the best days of the revolution because I was in space! And then I thought about all I'd given up for the space program – Natasha! – and how it had fallen apart after only one trip. My October comrades had not even gotten their one trip into space. They were long gone from the base by the time I made it back. I thought there would be a welcome party, perhaps some training for my next mission, or a path towards some future career. But there was only the chaos of a hasty departure. Papers strewn all about, because everyone had raced to make sure they weren't the last ones to leave this wretched secret sinking ship. Anyone associated with the secrecy of the U.S.S.R. was suspect. They tried to go straight, and failed, or they went deeper under ground and bided their time until they could rise back and take power from drunken old Boris Yeltsin. I considered trying to find my Natasha, but what could I tell her? *I gave up her love and lied to her for one lousy trip to space? And now I had nothing to show for it?* She was probably married to some rich performer like Yakov Smirnov. I was just a bum. I drank old bottles of vodka I found hidden around the space port. People had been in such a hurry to leave they had not even made sure to clean out their stashes of liquor. I found an old motorcycle and raced across the tarmac and towards the trees. I had a bit of a death wish. If my life were a movie, there would be a long montage here of me driving more and more recklessly as my beard grows longer and I find fewer and fewer sources of vodka to numb my existence. Towards the end of the montage, while the Scorpions' "Wind of Change" plays ironically, and my scenes are intercut with stock footage of post-Cold War Soviet life, I resort to drinking mouthwash as the guitar solo starts, and, the blue green liquid spilling down my chin and neck, I take a swig and throw the bottle out behind me as I drive a Soviet army jeep headlong towards a launch platform, crashing into the great iron structure, and overturning the jeep on the tarmac, spilling myself onto the pavement with a painful thud in the shadow of the great towering structure long since abandoned. Blood seeps from my head and mixes with drool on the cracked concrete as my eyes begin to close. The intercut news footage is now in slow motion, showing the coup attempts, Boris Yeltsin's fall from grace, the start of war with Chechnya and terrorist violence on the streets of Russia. The invading tanks in Chechnya remind viewers of my time in Afghanistan. I cough up some blood and close my eyes. I am not dead, not physically, but I have spiritually died. The music fades out and the screen fades to black.

13 / NOTES FROM THE UNDERGROUND

> "We are encircled not by invincible armies, but by superior economies."
>
> —Mikhail Gorbachev

I am a sick man. I am intolerable. I don't want you to sympathize with me, reader. All happy people are alike, according to Tolstoy, but every unhappy soul is unhappy in his own way. My distinct miserable condition was: having made a trip to space, I had trouble adjusting to life on earth. It didn't help that the ground was shifting beneath my feet due to the collapse of the Soviet Empire. So I struggled. I scraped along as best I could and tried not sink any further down. So here are the notes from my underground years.

I woke up on the tarmac of the secret space facility and found myself staring at a pair of snakeskin boots, so shiny and expensive, the most amazing apparel I had seen since that Moscow Music and Peace Festival concert in 1989. These were the sort of boots worn by rock stars. And yet, when I looked up from the boots, I did not see a leather-clad guitar player. I saw a man in a suit. I am going to give this man a fake name in my book. It is not because I am myself afraid, dear reader, but because I fear for your safety. If I gave his actual name, I could not promise that he would not hunt down every owner of my autobiography and kill them because they knew too much about him. Thus, for now let's call him Ivan Cesterosky. *Ivan* because it is a common Russian name, and *Cesterosky* because it is the name of a guy who always stole my rations in the army.

So: I looked up from the boots into the blinding light of the sun and saw Ivan, decked out in an Armani suit, wearing Gucci sunglasses, and smiling at my shriveled, scab-covered corpse.

"Comrade," he said, "you look like a man in need."

"Fuck off," I told him.

He kicked me in the crotch.

"Fuck off," I said again.

"I am only trying to help a sad, broken man I see on the ground."

"You can help me by finding me a drink."

Instead he reached down and offered me a hand.

I took it. I had no choice.

He pulled me up and we faced each other in the harsh glare of the Siberian sun.

"You are angry and beaten down," he said. "That I understand. I want to offer you an opportunity. I want to be your friend."

I wanted to say "Fuck Off" again, because I thought it would be even funnier if I said it a third time. But I also wanted to hear what he had to offer, so I remained quiet.

"I run a camp for children. In America, such establishments are very successful among the middle class. Russia will soon have a middle class matriculating in this school-for-the-blind of a country and I want to teach them how to read Braille. Metaphorically, of course. I want to offer a popular summer camp for Russia's new middle class. From my research, I have learned that America's two most popular summer camps are Meatballs and Space Camp. I don't know what a meatball is, so I must offer a Space Camp. And you are a veteran of space travel. I want you to be the face of my summer camp."

"Will you teach these kids how to go to space?" I asked.

"I will teach these children how to convince their parents to send me more money," he said. Here he spit on the ground in front of me. I was about to tell him to "Fuck off" once again, when he handed me an American beer. Had it been in his briefcase? Who knows, and who cares. Having lived on Russian piss my whole life, it was a real treat. The deliciously smooth taste of Milwaukee's Best beer won me over: I would help this sharp-dressed asshole.

"I think that your endeavor is about to blast off," I said. (I think this was a pretty clever quip, considering that I was lying on pavement and drunk when I said it. In case you don't get it, "endeavor" is the name of an American space craft and "blast off" is the technical term for a ship launching towards an orbit.)

"I'm about to countdown your ass," he said. I think we can all agree that his quip was far less clever than mine.

In any case, we shook hands, and I became the face of Russian teenage space camp.

For a pittance the Space Discovery Theme Park, as it was called, purchased from the government the unwanted plot of land that had hosted my secret space program. Our rusty economy could barely afford one space program. Keeping a second space program alive was out of the question. But finding a buyer for the launch pad of an orbital space program is not as easy as it might seem. You can't just make it smell like freshly baked chocolate chip cookies and let the buyers waltz in. Sure, there are countries with space ambitions of their own. But they do not want to lease space on the turf of a competing sovereign entity. They will build their own space program first. So your choices are to raze the facility and treat it merely as real estate (fat chance in this Russian wasteland) or make an asset out of the existing space travel equipment. Ivan chose the latter, and we opened the Space Discovery Theme Park, the only space camp which allowed its children access to functioning space travel equipment without adult supervision. We viewed this as an asset, although some parents considered it a liability.

Perhaps you saw my advertisements on television or in the regulated newspapers. After preliminary footage of a shuttle launching, you saw my face as I gave a thumbs up and said "It's time to blast off towards summer adventure. If you want to orbit Planet Fun, then you better get in your space capsule today! Tell your parents that Mission Control wants their non-refundable payment of $600 by March 31 in order for you to not become a maladjusted space-crazy teenager."[1]

And that is how I made my first million. Most citizens could not afford to send their children to Space Discovery. But the oligarchs could, the pigs growing fat on oil and gas money, the mobsters with their criminal wallets – and what's more, they could afford to send their children's friends to the camp too. So someone would fill a Learjet up with teenagers and fly them out to my concrete wasteland, a place that by all rights should have been forgotten by time. The kids loved space, or liked space, or didn't give a shit about space but had run out of things to do in Moscow, or were likely to get in real trouble if they stayed in the city: all told, we had a collection of nerds and future criminals or politicians. And guess who was there to greet them at the gates of the camp?

Me. At least, that is what I've been able to piece together

from looking at the pictures in the archive. To be honest, I was drinking heavily through most of this period. If I'd been anywhere near a city, I'd have burned through my money in a heartbeat and been left a pauper in the new Russian economy. Thank goodness for isolation – your Warren G. Zevon calls it "splendid isolation."[2] I drank like a fish, but it was all cut-rate vodka, or free booze provided by Cesterosky and his minions. They knew if I was drunk enough I wouldn't leave, and they wouldn't have to explain to some pissed off camper why there was no real cosmonaut at the Space Discovery Theme Park.

Again, according to the brochures and a few videotapes I've found, I was at the gate to greet all the campers. Sometimes I'd go on rides with them. Cesterosky had produced an interesting array of equipment. Junked airplanes and helicopters, refurbished gunships from the Afghan war (I refused to go near those bastard machines), bungee cords to jump off the launch tower, and trampolines. As someone who has spent a significant amount of time in space, I can tell you that a trampoline is completely useless as preparation. Also, it is hell if you try to jump on it with a hangover. But it was fun for the younger kids. Every summer there was talk of reopening one of the underground launch silos as a deep pool to train in semi-weightless conditions. Of course, that would have been a deathtrap. And thank god they never went through with it, as the old silos were a prime place for fucking.

Two years into the camp's existence, facing a shortage of campers, Cesterosky opened the Space Discovery to young women. I don't know if the young ladies learned anything useful about space travel, but about fucking they learned a thing or two. Before you go condemning me and the other camp counselors, let me say this. Many Russian teenage girls end up as sex slaves. If you have ever downloaded pornography from the internet, there's a good chance you have taken advantage of a poor young lady, you have stroked your cock or clitoris while looking at a peasant from St. Petersburg. You pervert and exploitative ass! Who are you to judge us? We had consensual sex with wealthy Russian young women, 18 and older. They wanted to learn their way around the bedroom before they went home and made love to their teenage boyfriends. And when I say bedroom, I mean it figuratively because we did it all over the camp site, but very rarely in the bedrooms, which were still the cramped dormitory residences of the space program.

How do I know this if I was too drunk to recall the period? Well, for one, I can look at the brochures of the camp from the coeducational years of its existence. In some pictures, I have my arms around campers, seeming to show them the ways of space exploration, but I know what's really going on. And also, I have the letters they wrote to thank me for the "most important summers" of their lives. "I learned and grew so much," they say. "I really discovered something about myself at Space Discovery camp!" That last line was so good we put it on the brochure for the next summer, although the thing she discovered about herself, no doubt, was that she could have multiple orgasms in the cockpit of a Cold War helicopter.

I feel I should tell you that one woman who attended the camp is now a cosmonaut, who has visited the international space station. I feel proud that she attended Space Discovery, and I hope that she looks fondly on her time with us. But it is possible that she went to space to get as far away from us as she could! If there's one thing you could say about those of us who worked at the Space Discovery camp, it was that we were the least likely people to ever go to space. Me, because I had been stranded there and had no desire to return. The others? Well, they were hooligans and misfits, drunks and sex fiends, the kind of people who fail any test you give them – in short, they were camp counselors.

What did I do the rest of the year? After all, this was only a summer camp. Sometimes I would travel with Cesterosky on his yacht in Lake Baikal or in the Mediterranean. He enjoyed showing me off as a sort of trophy – many people own yachts, but how many have their own cosmonaut? In these seasons, my memories grow a little clearer. When I was not surrounded by angry and horny teenagers, I did not need to drink so much to blur out the misery of my existence. So I remember things like the basketball game Cesterosky and I played against Larry Ellison and Shaquille O'Neal. Ellison, the Oracle owner, had a basketball court on the deck of his yacht (Cesterosky envied it so) as well as a smaller power boat that trailed behind to pick up the basketball whenever it went overboard. I should add, however, that Cesterosky's boat had a half-sized ice hockey rink below decks. His yacht was a converted fishing cruiser with an unparalleled and seldom used ice-making capability. But Ellison declined a hockey challenge and suggested instead a two-on-two game of hoops. Now, Russian men are not known for their prowess on the court. But we are also not cowards, so we accepted the challenge and played against Ellison and the large professional who was a guest on his yacht. Shaquille and I were in the same boat, literally and figuratively. National heroes taking advantage of the wealth and good will of our country men. Shaq did not want to play basketball any more than I wanted to return to space. Well, perhaps that is unfair. I believe Shaq enjoys playing basketball, as he has never been trapped in a basketball court for 14 months. But in any case, we were both on vacation, nudged into the brink of sportsmanship by our hosts, who wished to use basketball to determine which of them had the larger penis – although I can tell you that Shaq and I had larger manhoods than either millionaire. So we played, and I lost, but I would beat Shaq in a game of space travel.

Another time, Cesterosky took me on a camel trip in the Saudi desert. We were guided by nomads in the rich tourists' version of adventure. As you can tell from the way he ran Camp Discovery, he was not one of those millionaires who hung his hat on authenticity – it was enough to journey through the oil-rich dunes in what seemed like an old fashion caravan. But he still had his satellite telephone and we were followed by an air-plane in case we should run into trouble. Cesterosky was a survivor, yes, but he was not a survivalist. The camel ride was quite pleasant, as enjoyable as a night can be without women. Of course most of the men with us were impressed by the night sky. Out in the sands, far from the light pollution of a city, you could see far more stars than anywhere else on the planet. Some nights you could even see the clouds of galaxies against the black of space, and you would know where the Milky Way got its name. As for me, the stars were dimmer than I'd seen them in space, and a reminder of that horrible time, so I stayed in the tent with the cooks and tour guides. They taught me to make Afghan bread, and how to roast coffee beans in a frying pan. Their thick murky blend tasted far more burnt than the coffee I get at the Starbucks near my current home.

We also went on a safari in Africa. Cesterosky was intent on shooting a gazelle, again, without caring much for authenticity. When a few days of hunting provided no target, he purchased one from a wildlife refuge, released it in front of our jeep, where it stumbled, dazed and confused from its recent trip hanging from a helicopter, and he shot it down moments later. A few days afterward, we stumbled upon a wild gazelle. I impressed everyone by shooting it at a distance while it ran through the fields. They had begun thinking of me as the cosmonaut camp counselor; they forgot I had served in the army. My gazelle was bigger than Cesterosky's, so he took it for his own. We ate the small beast he had shot earlier and he had mine taken to a taxidermist. I believe it is still on display in the gaudy library of his dacha.

Once he threw an opulent Great Gatsby themed party at this bungalow. As a newly rich Russian, he was fascinated by *The Great Gatsby*, although I am not sure if he has actually read the book. Perhaps he was merely enchanted by the dazzling light show on its cover and the sad, naked-woman eyes staring out at you. In Russia, the book was called *Late Millionaire on the Ash Heap* for a long time. Only after Glastnost did we find its true title. As I said, I doubt Cesterosky actually read the book, because he could not have enjoyed its ending: the profoundly reborn rich man shot and killed in his own pool. Still: he loved the fashions of the Jazz Age, the secret liquor and ragtime piano, the catered Long Island parties, the carnival of orgiastic desires and city life. I had become one of the sideshows in his traveling carnival, and I was certainly on display. He asked me to wear my old cosmonaut's uniform, the secret outfit I had hidden in the closet for so many years. I found it easily, as my room on the base was still where it had been. I took it out of the dusty bag and tried to put it on, but could not. Here, you think, I have stopped to consider my life and am staring at a uniform I can not put on! But no, I mean only that I could not put it on because it no longer fit. I had gained weight in these years on earth. Gravity had done its work, as well as an abundance of food in my new life as a celebrity spokesman. I had become fat and lazy, like an American. Luckily for me, Cesterosky had a tailor who altered it to fit. So I was able to wander about this party amidst the faux flappers and fake philosophers, eating appetizers and drinking mint juleps as I paraded my uniform like a greatcoat of peacock glory. Piano players romped through old American standards. Women threw themselves at party guests (they had been paid to do so). We walked beneath a patchwork of small Christmas lights strung up over our heads as if they were stars we could reach up and grab if we were just a bit taller or could jump just a bit higher ... the entire universe seemed within our grasp that night, although it was precarious, and if you did wrap your hands around one, you would bring the entire canopy crashing down around you. We were surrounded by symbols and imagery at that party, the sorts of things literature teachers love to analyze. But the next day they were gone, taken away by the party planners and dream realizers, and all that was left was a bill for Cesterosky to pay. He wrote a check, and we moved on to the next party.

I was not the only man lost in the madness of the post-Revolution. Think, Americans, of your 1970s, your disco and sex parties, your STDs and nylon suits. In the wake of The Sixties, you let yourself go. We were no different. And the tragedy is that nobody was minding the store. Boris Yeltsin evolved from a spirited opposition fighter to a drunken dancing fool, a walking joke – the kind of man who, when he finally died, you were surprised to learn he hadn't already died years before. Worse still than the shenanigans at the top were the power-grabbing rats gathering in the sewers, the vermin that had gone into hiding in the light of Glasnost, now free to rifle through the trash once more, to spread their disease of doubt and distrust like a Black Plague from crowded house to overpacked tenement. Like Gatsby, the KGB rechristened itself the FSB and befriended the newly rich gangsters – once mortal enemies, they were now joined in friendship as they battled against freedom and accountability. "We can make it safe," the Secret Policeman whispered to the Mobster. "We can let your business flourish if you let us take control." No one needs protection when everyone is safe; only in a dangerous world do you pay for safety.

If I had not been sleeping and drunk for these years, I might be able to tell you more about how the deals went down. Instead, my memories from those years fade in and out, a decadent montage of thugs, whores, and unctuous millionaires, watching women in a hotel room fuck, fight, piss – whatever turned them on – blissfully unaware of the all-seeing camera behind the mirror. Whenever I see a Russian gangster on the news, or a high-ranking former KGB officer in the papers, I recognize their faces from the menagerie of power brokers Cesterosky gathered in the years when I was his guest, a passenger on his great ship of commerce. Did I play a part? Did I offer him some legitimacy with the people, as a champion of the Space Race? I hope I did not; but I fear that I did.

As we suffered through the hangover of Perestroika and the millennium approached us, people began to consolidate their power, to collect their wits about them in preparation for the dawn of the next century. Unlike the United States, we were not worried about the Y2K problem in Russia: we did not have enough computers or networks wired into the infrastructure of our world.

Around this time, Cesterosky decided to get out of the summer camp business. It was still making money, but he saw a chance to make even more money. That is what separates an ordinary businessman from a millionaire: a true entrepreneur will crush the feeble bird in his hand if it helps him buy the two birds in the bush. The remnants and remainders of the Soviet space program were getting old but were still far ahead of the technology owned by any of the satellite republics now forced to make their own way in the wake of the broken U.S.S.R. They had very little but the land beneath their feet. Sadly, that is what Cesterosky wanted. He began making deals for gas and oil and even for land across which he could lay his pipelines. Some people use "laying pipe" as a euphemism for sex; in this case it was exactly correct, because Cesterosky truly fucked these tiny Eastern European countries. He gave them old relics of a super power's space program, enough for them to build their own fledgling programs, and they let him do what he wanted with them. I would like to criticize him, but I had done the same thing before he did, having my way with women on the basis of my position as a cosmonaut.

I could feel things winding down, even in my drunken washed out state. You know how you wake up when a train is slowing down or a car is pulling into your driveway? Before anyone touches your shoulder or the alarm goes off, you have that sense that one leg of your journey has come to an end. Maybe there were specific signs I noticed sub-consciously. The disappearance of a rocket here; the absence of an airlock there. In any case, I started to sober up against my wishes. I saw the foundations my lifestyle starting to crumble. I needed to make plans for the future.

It was December 1999, when Cesterosky was planning his big millennial bash. He decided the pull one last hurrah out of the cooling embers of the once hot Space Discovery camp. Cleared of most of its valuable technology, it was now a great black canvas upon which he could paint a Dionysian orgy that he would never have to clean. It was remote, too, which offered some comfort to the paranoid end-of-the-worlders – if the cities descended into madness and urban crowds rioted in the streets, those of us in the distant woods could be safe, we had weapons and supplies and would have enough warning to fortify our defenses while eating left over cheese and crackers, finishing the last of the champagne, and listening to the last songs before the apocalypse. Security was on Cesterosky's mind, and I feel I might have been invited to the party even if it hadn't been held at the launch center and he didn't need a cosmonaut for decoration. He had not forgotten my marksmanship on the African safari, and he knew I could fight when it was required or when I was sober... if both situations overlapped, then I could take all comers.

So the preparations began. By now, petro-dollars had civilized the hordes of the wilds, and instead of flying in every camper and supply we needed, Cesterosky could now save money by using trucks. Rapidly, all the functioning machines disappeared, sold at bargain basement prices in order to make room; Cesterosky converted his earnings into gold just in case things went to hell. But the doomsday planning was just a hedge against his main bet, that Russia would continue to prosper, as would the world, and a rich reveler would not be forgotten by his party guests. Tents arrived. Prefabricated buildings arrived. Trailers and port-a-pots came too. An orchestra in tuxedos arrived from the backwaters of Siberia. C-list rock bands flew in on rented jet planes. Exotic animals growled in the cargo bays of approaching semi-trailers. Carnival side-show performers appeared and made themselves at home at the Uncle Sasha's, which was converted from its last dormant state into a fully functioning bar. Cesterosky even shelled out the extra money to fly in American microbrews by the keg. Alaskan king crab came across the Bering Strait and made its way to us. God knows how, but a harp player and his instrument showed up and began playing near the swimming pool that had been built for the summer camp. Hundreds of Chinese laborers arrived with trucks full of fireworks. Soon there were cattle grazing on the asphalt tarmac, eating the small bits of grass that slipped through the cracks. Fresh meat, Cesterosky's chef said, tasted better than frozen steaks and ribs. At one point, Warren G. Zevon arrived. Cesterosky flew him in to see if he would be interested in playing a concert. He demurred, sadly, so I never got to see him perform an entire concert live. I did see him play a song on the poolside piano, however, accompanied by the harpist and another itinerant musician. I may be one of only eight people on the planet to have seen a version of "Roland the Headless Thompson Gunner" performed on piano, harp, and balalaika. He seemed to be having fun.

As the month of December waned, I started making connections. I knew I'd need something to keep myself busy in the new millennium. That was how I began a conversation with Mr. Zevon about possible careers in music. After he finished at the piano, I took him on a tour of the facilities and told him my life story. He told me my life had been rough, but that the saddest part was my break-up with Natasha. I told him I had actually written a song about it and asked if he would like to hear it. He told me he would not, as life was too short. I was insulted at the time, but later, when I discovered how he had died of cancer, I was glad I had not wasted his time.

In this period, I also sought out other successful business men and tried to determine how I could make my way in the world. I had enough money to live for a while, as I had not spent much of my savings from my years with the Space Discovery camp. But a satisfying income does not necessarily represent a satisfying life. How was I to fill the days? I had lived in space but did not know how to live in the space of my own life. I dreaded becoming an old man in my youth, muttering to passing strangers about how great I had once been.

My desire to find a new calling could not have come at a

better time – I was shaking hands with captains of industry, artists of renown, and caterers of some note. These were the best and the brightest. At one point I began a conversation with a world-famous self-help guru with gigantic white teeth.

"How can I live to my true potential?" I asked him as we sampled guacamole out of an upside down cosmonaut's helmet.

"By visualizing your one path to success," he said.

"That is fucking nonsense," I said and walked away. He was so full of shit that I was willing to forego eating more of that delicious guacamole in order to avoid him.

But the people who had actually done something with their lives were more useful.

A famous American painter told me to act like a genius, because eventually people would start to accept that I was one, even if it was not true.

A banker told me not to save money, because only suckers tried to save. "Spend as much as you can," he said to me after we played badminton.

"But you have so much money! I can't believe you don't save! Magazines say you are one of the richest men in the world!"

"I try to spend it all, my friend, but I earn it so fast that I cannot keep up. I've even married five different women so they could help me get rid of it, and I hardly made a dent."

"I can help you spend it, perhaps," I offered.

"No, no. You must gain and spend your own money for it to mean anything. Spending other people's money is a form of theft," he said as he plucked from a basket of truffle french fries.

Eventually I had to choose another occupation, and I decided to become a writer. Of all the celebrities I met in those days, the writers were the most likely to have long full beards. I don't mean to suggest that I picked my life path because of facial hair. But a long full beard is a sign of rest and relaxation, is it not? Who grows long beards aside from great old novelists and prisoners? Both sets of men live a comfortable life in which everything they need is provided and they need not worry about their looks. (True, some great beards are grown by women at the carnival, but that was not a career path I seriously considered.)

Once I decided to become a novelist, I felt some comfort and purpose and was able to fully enjoy the remaining days of the year 1999. In fact, I looked with some excitement towards the future. I imagined my books on all the shelves of Moscow homes. I would write about detectives and lawyers, or doctors and bank robbers. I began writing down titles and plots. It would be a shame, I realized, if the world ended with the new year. Readers would be deprived of my literary genius, their flesh being melted away by fire or eaten by zombies before I got the chance to put pen to paper.

And then the day arrived. December 31, 1999. You probably have your own memories of what you did that night. Perhaps you drove to a friend's house, or watched the celebration on television, or drank too much champagne and threw up on a blanket your grandmother knitted for you before she died. Of course, while we were drinking and dancing, the Twentieth Century made a last gasp, burping up a few significant events that would cast a pall across the new millennium. For Americans, I suppose, the foiled terror attacks provided a vicious hint of things to come, of bombs and hijackings that would dominate the landscape of crumbled buildings and smoke-filled skylines in 2001. You may not have noticed, really, the news reports of men who planned to bomb the Los Angeles airport or to destroy a U.S. Navy gunship called *The Sullivans*. But, looking back, you should have been happy to live without terror for another year. And the threat of violence in peacetime played a part in the big Russian news of the day as well – we were caught off guard when Boris Yeltsin resigned the presidency at noon, handing the reigns of the country over to Vladimir Putin so the powerful thug could wage war against the Chechnyan separatists who my or may have not destroyed four apartment blocks in a September bombing.

The eye of history is sharper than the pupils of the present. I wish I could say I saw the historic significance of these events as they happened, but they were mostly just noise against the soundtrack of the party. Cesterosky's telephone rang urgently, of course, as we were dropping fireworks from a helicopter onto the crowd. He answered it and listened to the news non-chalantly. He disconnected the phone and said to an assistant, "Yeltsin is out. Putin is in."

"That Putin, he is..." The thought went unfinished.

"Yes, he is," Cestersoky answered. "But we can work with him nonetheless. Time for us to use our K.G.B. connections." He turned to me. "I'm sorry, Ilya, but I must leave you here for the time being."

He tapped the pilot on the shoulder and had the helicopter land near the party site. I jumped out and he shouted instructions to his staff.

"Good luck, Comrade!" he shouted to me. "I hope you enjoyed the ride."

"What about the party?" I screamed.

"Have a good time, so you can tell me about it later."

"When will I see you again?"

But the helicopter had lifted up into the sky, and I was left standing with the drunk and the wasted guests, the citizens who had time to celebrate, the men who were not busy planning for the next thousand years.

We got drunk. We fired rockets. We trashed the place. And then it was next year.

14 / WRITE IT LIKE DISASTER

January 1, 2000. Noon. It was to be the last morning I woke up hungover on the tarmac of the secret space facility. This time there was no one to cover me with blankets or offer me a beer. I was truly alone in the world. The powerful men were departing in their limousines and private jets. The caterers and musicians in their vans and buses. No one wanted to be left behind to clean up the mess we had made. The most vigorous party-goers were still asleep, covered in mud and whiskey, hidden behind stages or rolled up in carpets. I pushed myself up off the ground and realized I was getting old – it was the first time a push up had caused me pain since I had done 70 of them in a mad competition with Vulkov in my army recruit days. My knees ached. I made old man noises as I squinted into the weary gray horizon. I heard engines and walked towards them, hoping to get a ride towards Moscow, away from this dying beast of a town. On the ground I saw a black cowboy hat with silver trim. I picked it up and placed it on my head. It fit perfectly; I decided that anyone who would lose such a hat did not deserve it. I left it on my head and jogged towards the vehicles hoping the hat's owner did not see me make my getaway.

Who was left in my life? Vulkov. We had drifted apart after I returned to earth. Not that we had any disagreement or falling out. But he was getting older, a difficult life now took its toll. Getting me back down from space had been a struggle that took a lot out of him. He retired to a small country home and stayed out of the spotlight. He had not wanted me to visit too much. As he saw his days ending, he knew I must learn to fend for myself in the world. And I had been busy with the Space Discovery Theme Park summer camp.

Now I had time on my hands. I decided to visit him, to say goodbye in case my path should lead away from his door long enough that he might die before I saw him again. But first there was the matter of getting back to the West.

I found semi-trailers being loaded by giant men with beards and faded t-shirts. They were roadies in America, they told me, hired by Cesterosky's underlings to help with the lights and music for his great party. It paid well and they'd never been to Russia before.

"How do you like it here?" I asked them.

"Not so well," said the oldest, a man with white hair and an Allman Brothers T-shirt beneath a Harley Davidson jacket.

"You would not come back?"

"Only for the money," he laughed. Then he looked around. "I don't know how you people do it. How could anyone live in this country for no money?"

Another man laughed and said "Hell, it's no worse than Ohio. Remember that load out in Cleveland where we got mugged? Some young kids pulled guns on us and took our wallets. We told 'em this equipment was worth more than anything in our wallets. They said, *How we gonna disappear with five guitars and a soundboard?* Then they disappeared with our money."

"If you were closer to the city, someone would rob you," I told them, feeling the need to defend my country's criminals. "Are you flying back from Moscow?"

"I think so," said a man wrapping cables around his forearm. "But Robby would know for sure. Hey Robby!"

A younger, less burly man headed in our direction. He had long hair but no beard.

"What's up?" said this Robby.

"Ivan the cowboy here," he said, pointing at me, "wants to know if we're flying from Moscow."

"Yeah, convoy back to civilization, then home. Of course, Cesterosky took the armored cars when he left, so we're driving by ourselves."

"I've been through those woods when I was in the space program," I said. "I would be happy to travel with you and offer my services to keep you safe in return for a ride home."

"I can't promise you a seat, but if you can find space in a truck, you're welcome to it. I don't think anyone will mess with us."

"You never know," I said. "This is wild country. Of course, with any luck the savages are too hungover to cause much trouble."

I helped them load the gear into the back of the rig and they made some space and rolled out a protective drop cloth for me to use as a mattress. I made sure they knew to wake me up if the convoy needed to stop along the road. They had radios to communicate between trucks.

"Enjoy your sleep – we got big fuel tanks, comrade," laughed the man with the white hair and beards. "And we can switch drivers without pulling over. Remember, we're professionals."

He handed me a flashlight, a few bags of potato chips, a six pack of beer, and a gallon of water. I had trouble carrying them to the back of the truck with only two arms. How did that man carry all those things at once so easily? I guess he carried things for a living.

"Wait a moment," I said before getting into the truck.

Quickly I ran towards the catering area, where I liberated a block full of cooking knives from a prep table. Never get caught in the back of a truck without a knife or two.

They rigged the back door to close with ropes tied on the inside, so I could open the hatch if I needed air or ran into an emergency. Just before we sealed the truck, Robby handed me seven empty vodka bottles.

"That's your commode. Don't piss on any of the equipment!"

Then the door slammed shut, I pulled a square knot tight and felt my way to the makeshift bed of guitar cases. I fell asleep before the truck moved.

The smell of shit woke me up. At first I feared I had crapped myself in the truck, but I checked my ass and mercifully discovered it to be dry. The smell was overwhelming. Soon I could recognize it as cow shit. The trucks were passing a cattle farm. I didn't remember any ranches along the road, but it had been a long time since I arrived via the highway. In the heyday of the Space Discovery Theme Park, I had always flown in from the distant cities of the Mother Country.

In the dark, almost perfect black, I could sense only the ominous presence of giant crates and other shapes surrounding me. It was even blacker than the nights I spent in space. This was true darkness, like a musty open womb from which I hoped to be reborn. I sweated out the previous night's whiskey and beer. Potato chips stumbled towards my mouth by the greasy blind handful. I thought again about my life. Maybe the crazy drunken years as a camp spokesman had been a needed taste of the wasteful life, of laziness and leisure, something to tell me what I had missed out on during my life of regiment and labor. The haze over my memories told me that unencumbered living was not for me. Some people require hard work to keep them alive, it is their fuel. You hear stories of men who worked in factories their entire adulthood, until bumping up against the age of retirement. One week off of the factory floor and they drop dead. In some ways I might have been a true child of the Soviet Union – raised for labor's sake, a working boy who became a working man. Had my parents been around, I might have become a more fully formed human. Instead I was a ward of industry, grown to maturity in a grain silo by the state. How could I have been anything but a worker, meant to unite with all the other workers of the world?

It was time to return to the nation of the workers. I would leave yachts and private jets behind and earn an honest day's pay once more. I decided to write novels about space travel and soldiers, the things I knew best. All the way back to the city, I plotted out stories about Russian heroes. My fictional adventures lacked all sadness and heartbreak that I had known in life. They were, truly, fantasies – not the kind with wizards and elves, but the kind that present life as a place of wonder and magic where evil is a force constantly beaten back by good. *Escapist fiction.* I make no claim otherwise. But what else does a man or woman want at the end of the day? Solzhenitsyen's depressing epics may have served a purpose as rebel fiction goes, but surely a country of free souls in bondage only to the time clock deserve a lighter fare at the end of the day, the literary equivalent of the pint of beer enjoyed by British working class punters, no?

All the stories were conceived by the time the trucks rolled to a stop. Fourteen sci-fi tales and nine espionage novels. I just had to find the time to actually write them down.

But first, a detour. The equipment truck lurched towards a stop and then began moving again. We were in Moscow, paying bribes to gangsters and tolls to modern trolls. I suppose it is never terribly pleasant being in the back of a shipping truck, but some cities make it worse than others. The heat of the American south is pretty bad, and the cattle slaughter and shit smells of the American Midwest must be no special treat either. In both those cases, however, one is at least moving along at a pretty good clip, making progress. I felt no such momentum once the truck slowed from the rural roads on which we had approached the city. We would move a few yards, and then stop again. We made countless turns. Maybe the driver was lost. I banged my knee against a guitar, my head against an amplifier. If I had spent the trip from New Year's recovering my wits and health, I almost lost them once more in the great Russian city. I even felt a hint of motion sickness – me who had ridden a rocket into space and conquered life without gravity. Finally, hours later, we stopped for good. The engine shut down and one of the roadies banged his hand against the back of the truck, signaling me to open the door. I expected to be at an airport or shipping depot, but we were along a city street, staring at the ugly architecture of Communism.

"We're unloading some of this junk for a recording session," Robby told me.

I helped tote a few guitars into a newly constructed modern recording facility.

"They're trying to get Paul McCartney to record his new album here," Robby said. "You know, 'Back in the U.S.S.R.' and all that."

"Do you really think it is possible?"

"Between you and me and the wall, not a shit ball's chance. These guys are used to bribing people until they get their way. That works with most Russians, who haven't seen anything valuable in 50 years." He turned to me and patted my arm. "No offense. But you know what I mean."

"You can bribe Westerners too, can't you?"

"Sure, the normal ones. But not one of *The Beatles*. Those guys could wallpaper their house with hundred dollar bills, the royalty checks they get."

I was so thankful for the ride to Moscow that I didn't correct Robby about Paul McCartney actually being in The Monkees and not The Beatles. Of course, even if they weren't as successful as The Monkees, members of The Beatles would be hard to bribe too. After all, I read in a Russian newspaper that one of their mothers had invented paper clips.[1]

After we unloaded all the equipment, I went out for lunch with Robby and the other roadies. Russia had been home to a McDonald's for nine years at that point, but they said they wanted to try a last meal of Russian food, so I took them to Luba's and ordered the famous potato platter.

"I'd love to invite you along with us, but we don't have extra visas," Robby told me.

"Thank you for the offer, but I need to stay here in Moscow anyway. I have some old friends to visit and business, always business."

The white-haired roady finished his fried potato pancake and spoke.

"I don't give a lot of advice, you know. Christ, look at me. I ain't no model citizen myself. But I've been to some bad parties in my time and been to scenes that were on the verge of disaster. I was at Altamont. But shit, this place..." He waved his hand around to suggest the whole city. "... this place has some rough days ahead, my friend. There's a reckoning after every great party. The rock stars know when to get out of the hotel room. You don't want to be around when they start turning over the mattresses and finding dead bodies in the bathtubs. So take care of your business. But make sure you get out before it's too late."

"Sure, that New Year's party was pretty extraordinary, but it was damn messy," Robby said.

"I ain't just talking about that party," the old man said. "I mean Moscow too. I know I ain't been here long, but all my life I been going from city to city, sometimes less than a night before getting back on the road. I know how to read a town quickly. This town is about to wake up from its terrible orgy. I saw a French guy on TV late one night during a Stones tour near Paris. He was asking, 'What do we do now that the orgy is over?'[2] The dark, dirty truth is that you get in the shower and wash your dick like you've never washed it before. *That's what you do after an orgy.* Moscow is fucking people and getting fucked by people. So be sure you pull out and wash yourself so you can go home and get on with your life, before the afterglow fades."

We continued chewing on the rough ragged breakfast, the only meal Moscow knew how to serve. He was right, this old road soldier, about everything, about the misery to come, about the trashing of the hotel room that was the newly free Russia. And he was right, too, about the dead bodies, about how misfortune cuts short the lives of even the great and beautiful, leaving nothing but a corpse in a bathtub. All dead bodies are alike, it is only the living ones that are unique in their own way. The father I never knew caught his death in a cold tub, because he had the audacity to complain about it. He merely wanted warm water to bathe. But even when you are trying to make yourself clean, death will create a mess.

Robby paid for the bill and we walked back to their truck. I shook their hands and walked back into the recording studio. Nobody stopped me. I was famous enough to pass for somebody worth letting in – not that their standards were too high. They were hoping to record a famous musician one day, but for now, any famous person would do.

I found the studio technicians setting up the equipment we had delivered. The walls of the place were covered in carpet and foam. Between that and the numerous wires and computers, it reminded me of a cosmonaut training facility. Nobody paid any mind to me as they focused on their own tasks.

I stumbled back out into the recording studio's lobby. A lot of money had gone into decorating it – modern furniture everywhere. A steel lamp curved out of a marble block and shined onto a thick glass coffee table. Leather and steel chairs surrounded the three-inch glass slab. Noguchi. Eames. I recognized the luxury pieces from rooms I'd visited with Cesterosky. Standing in the middle of the table was a balalaika. It was as if Russian folk musicians had conquered a New York furniture store. That was probably what the designer intended – to remind you that you were in a Russian recording studio. It was doubtful that any of the Western superstars they wanted to record here would know how to play the instrument. I barely did myself, and I was entirely a child of Russia. I picked up the instrument and began strumming it. I soon found that I was playing Natasha's song, the tragic blues ballad I had composed on the lake right after she left me. I fell into the song and began singing as well. When I finished I saw that I had an audience. A technician was staring at me.

"You're a musician?" he asked.

"No, I'm a space traveler," I said. I must have sounded like David Bowie for a moment. "But I also write songs."

"Good. We need somebody to sing something in the studio, make sure all the equipment's working before Mick Fleetwood or Jagger shows up."

"Are these me coming?"

"Who knows?" he said. "But if they do come, I damn sure want to know that the equipment works. Bring your little guitar in here."

He disappeared into the studio and I followed.

A Japanese man put a large set of earphones on my head. Then I heard a voice through them.

"This is the booth. Give me a thumbs up if you can hear me."

I saw a small man with a small beard watching me from the soundproof booth.

I gave him the finger. We all laughed.

"It's like mission control," I yelled.

I saw him wince through the glass.

"You don't need to yell. The microphone is right in front of you."

"Sorry," I said softly.

The Japanese man brought another microphone towards me and aimed it at the front of the balalaika.

"Play a few notes," said the voice in my earphones.

I struggled a bit. Then I found the beginning notes of "Glory Days" by Bruce Springsteen.

"Alright," the voice told me. "Levels are good. Sing us a song."

And so I sang. And I played. And I could see some of the men in the booth tearing up. Some others stood impassively, but they probably did not understand Russian and could not make sense of my sad song. By the end, even those strong men were broken by the sadness of my plight.

"What is that song?" the man in the booth finally asked.

"That's Natasha's Song," I said. "For Natasha."

He wrote it down on the label, and that's how "Natasha's Song (for Natasha)" came to be.

Of course, it was not released right away.

After I finished performing the song for them, I was so heartbroken that I could not stay. I knew I needed to find Vulkov and say goodbye. I couldn't let another loved one slip away as I had that day on the lake. I would tell him how much he meant to me, how he was like my father. I had lost one father already without getting to say goodbye. I would not lose another. I set the balalaika on the fancy table in the lobby.

I walked away from the studio into the cold Russian city air. Moscow is a city constantly reminding you both that you are alive, and that you are struggling to remain alive. Every time you breathe, you see your breath, the exhaled moisture like steam fighting against the cold. You don't need a mirror to find out if someone has taken their last breath here. The people of the city are like a series of power plants. When smoke stacks puff their last cloud of exhaust, you know work has ceased. It is the same with people.

My breath clung to my face, crystallizing around my mouth and nostrils. I began running to keep warm. I was heading north out of the city.

A communist country should have one thing going for it – well designed cities, the result of a central planning committee that can destroy a whole village because someone wants a highway there. And yet Russia did not have even that going for it. The roads did not go where I wanted them to go; we were certainly not a Utopia, but we were not even a dystopia. You know those science-fiction movies where the city is so orderly and well-maintained that it is boring? Well, we did not have that problem. Moscow was always exciting.

Eventually I tired of running and hitched a ride north in a small car.

"You should not stop for strangers," I told the driver. "What if I was dangerous?"

"Ha! You're not dangerous!" he said, as he puffed on a cigarette and pulled back into traffic. "You're famous. You're the cosmonaut."

"You know me!" I said happily. "But who are you?"

"Nobody famous like you. I'm just a newspaper editor."

"That sounds fun."

"It is, now. I only started doing it recently. In the old days, it was shitty job for apparatchiks. Then one day there was freedom, and we could actually write things and publish them. We were like Redford and Bernstein, the famous American reporters who brought down their own President.[3] Although this new president scares me. He is former KGB, you know. I don't think he likes freedom."

"What paper do you work for? Maybe I have read it."

"Doubtful, in the circles you travel in."

"What?"

"I've seen you, my friend. On Cesterosky's yacht. At his space camp. He does not read my paper. *Novaya Gazeta* is too critical. He prefers the glossy version of events, which overlooks criminal pasts, dark secrets, and closeted skeletons. *We* want to find out where the bodies are buried. *We* are not as easily distracted by topless women as some other newspapers. *We* will keep digging through the distractions."

"You think he has buried bodies?"

"It's a figure of speech," he said. "But, if you want to know, *yes*. I'm sure he has been responsible for a death or two."

"And you think he hides his sins with topless women?"

"Sure. He knows many tabloids will abandon a story about, say, embezzlement, if they get a better story about a topless orgy."

I snorted. All orgies are topless. And bottomless. This editor knew his way around the newsroom, but not the bedroom.

"It's true!" he said. He had thought my snort signaled disbelief. "Here in Russia our news coverage is so shallow. Not like America. They don't care about c-list celebrities showing their skin when there's actual news to cover."

I laugh, now, thinking back. America's newspapers may have been different in 1999, I suppose, but as a current resident of the country, I am bombarded by headlines about an actress's lack of underwear in a limousine while two simultaneous wars with Mid-Eastern countries are relegated to the back pages. What is more important, a gash in the fragile peace of the Holy Lands, or a gash between the thighs of a starlet's legs?

"Ahh," I said to the editor in the car, back in January of 2000. "At least here in Russia you have important history to cover. America is boring, but in Russia we have controversial Presidential handovers, oligarchs controlling the media, and wars on terror. If you were in America, you would not have any of that stuff to write about."

"I suppose you are right," he said, gesturing to the landscape of Moscow receding behind us in the snowy distance. "It's like that Jesus Jones song said, we have more to sing about than Bob Dylan did."

I had no idea what he was talking about, but I nodded my head.

"You know, we have a reporter in Chechnya. You wouldn't

believe the horrors of that war. She says that Yeltsin really screwed the pooch there, and Putin will only make matters worse. He is like a young Stalin, she says." He turned and leveled his gaze at me. "What do you think about Stalin?" he asked.

"He killed my parents."

"Yes," he said. "He was a horrible man. And this Putin is like him, she says. Sadly, there are people in Russia who would welcome Stalin back. They miss the firm steel fist." He coughed, then rolled down his window and spit out of it. "Did you know this Vladimir Putin is a judo champion? That means he excels at grabbing people by the lapels and throwing them down on the ground. Is that who we want running our country?"

He pressed on the gas pedal, as if to speed away after making this point. But, it was a Russian-made car, so we went no faster. The buildings slipped behind us at the same pace they had before.

A little while later, he turned on a tape recorder. I agreed that he could interview me in exchange for a ride all the way to Vulkov's dacha. As I ended up remaining in the northern town for many months while my song recording was released and became a big Russian hit, this was the only press interview I did during the height of my music career. The editor didn't publish it right away, as I was not terribly famous or interesting at the time. Still, he had the writer's instinct to record every insignificant detail in the hopes that something important might one day emerge from the noise and other detritus collected in years of notebooks and other journals. When my song topped the charts, and I became famous, he dug it out and published it as a rare interview with the reclusive *ex-cosmonaut* turned *camp entrepreneur* turned *musician*:

Another Journey in a Life of Journeys:
Talking with Ilya Zamyatin
Novaya Gazeta Exclusive
(reprinted by permission)[4]

January 2, 2000 - On the road north of Moscow.

The cosmonaut/musician spoke with our reporter while traveling out of the city at the beginning of the year, shortly after he recorded his hit song, "Natasha's Song (for Natasha)."

Q: Do you ever miss outer space?
A: No, never! (Laughs) I've had my share of it. If I miss anything about the experience, it was the time alone. But you can spend time alone anywhere. It's like asking a felon if he misses prison.

Q: Well, some of them do, right?
A: None that I've ever met.

Q: In America, they do. Or so I've heard.
A: Space is not like an American prison. It is cold and unforgiving like a gulag.

Q: Are you still running the Space Discovery summer camp?
A: No. That time is behind me. Cesterosky sold most of the facilities, in any case. There's not much left there after New Year's. I enjoyed my time there, and I enjoyed sharing my experiences as a cosmonaut with the children. Very few people get to travel beyond the atmosphere. I was lucky enough to do so - shouldn't I share it with my fellow countrymen, or their children?

Q: **For a price.**
A: It's not a charity! (Laughs)

Q: **Looking back on the last year, the last 100 years, what is your general impression?**
A: I'm not that old! I remember the last year, not the last century! But I suppose I know what you mean. This was a hard time for Russia. Harder than usual. Maybe the future will be brighter. We can hope, can't we? Perhaps what we need is some optimism to melt the ice that has frozen us in place since the 1900s.

Q: **Do you feel frozen?**
A: Look at this car. It's stuck in the past, no? I've been to the West. They are not frozen in time.

Q: **Where are you headed?**
A: I'd rather not say. I'm visiting an old friend. No, that's not quite true. I'm visiting family.

Q: **Are you close to your family?**
A: No. My parents were taken away when I was young. I never got to say goodbye to them. Then I was married, but it ended. I had the chance to say goodbye to my wife, but... I found it hard. I have one family member left. An uncle who is like a father to me. He is getting old. I want to be sure I say goodbye to him.

Q: **That can be hard.**
A: Yes, I know. (pause) Yes.

Q: **If you're no longer in the Space Discovery Theme Park business, what is next for you?**
A: I was thinking I'd become a novelist.

Q: That is not easy!
A: It's easier than saying goodbye, isn't it? Writing allows you to create your own world, to control the fates of the people in your life. You can keep them around if you want them around, and you never have to say goodbye unless you are ready.

Q: Have you written a novel before?
A: No. But how hard can it be? Look at some of the idiots writing novels. I may not be the next Leo Tolstoy or Ivan Grisham, but I can tell a story as good as the next fellow. Mind you, I've bedded many a woman with my ability to tell stories and my dashing good looks. So I figure I will tell some stories and be sure to put my picture on the cover of my book, and readers, like women, will be seduced by my charms.

Q: You fought in Afghanistan.
A: (Silence)

Q: What do you think about the war in Chechnya?
A: I don't know too much about it, but...

Q: But what?
A: Listen, I am proud of almost everything I did in a uniform. Out of a uniform, my record is mixed. But in a uniform, I behaved honorably almost all the time. It was my duty. Did I fuck some women while wearing a uniform? Sure! I am a man! But I did it honorably. I guess it comes down to saying goodbye. That's always the hardest thing. Letting someone walk away from your life is hard. Making someone walk away from their life is harder. You are the one taking away their chance to say goodbye to their friends and family and countrymen. It's a lot to

```
take away from a man. You better have a good
reason if you're going to kill a man.
```

Q: You don't think we have a good reason in Chechnya?
```
A: (Silence)
```

Q: Do you feel we should get out of Chechnya?
```
A: Take this exit up ahead.
```

Soon enough we were at the dacha. The editor asked if I was sure it was the place I wanted to be. Should he wait in the car, he wondered, until I found out if my friend was inside? But I told him not to bother. If this was not Vulkov's home, I had nowhere else to go. The wrong place was as right as any other place.

He pulled away in his pitiful car, the machine choking and coughing into the late afternoon until I was left in the silence of the sun and the snow. I walked towards the door, my feet crunching along the unbroken cold ground. I could see only one set of footprints towards and away from the door. The door, once painted red, was mostly brown as the paint had peeled away with the rotting wood.

"Hello!" I called out, and then rapped against the doorframe for good measure.

There was no reply.

"Is anyone home?" I asked again, even louder than before.

Finally a voice responded.

"I'm not expecting anyone." It was Vulkov's voice, quieter and weaker than I had ever known it before.

"I am not expected, that is true. But I'm hoping to visit any- way. My name is Ilya Zamyatin, and I believe I once served under you in the military of a great power."

"Ilya! Much has changed since those days. Come in!"

I opened the door and made my way towards the back of the house, where I had heard his voice.

"I am an old man," he said. "I am afraid you will be sad to see me, but I wish to see you nonetheless."

I found him in a bed. Next to his head was a contraption that allowed him to grab the things he needed – a stick with a claw at one end and controls for his teeth at the other.

Vulkov was so small. He had already lost most of his body once before. Now he had shrunk again, the way old men do. It was striking to see the way even the trunk of a man can waste away with time.

"Do you need anything?" I asked. All along the mattress, where a normal man's arms and legs would be, were a variety of things he might need – food, water, tissues, and a bedpan.

"I can reach anything I need," he said. "The only thing I really need is company."

"How do you manage?"

"A friendly neighbor, Madina, comes twice a day to check on me and bring supplies. Plus, she is kind enough to take away my shit and piss."

I snorted.

"You've never heard me talk this way. Well, old age brings a bluntness. I have no time to be polite and coy. So: *she takes away my shit and piss.*"

"She sounds like a good woman."

"Sure. Sure. She is good. But not a saint. What is remarkable, truly, is that she is just a woman. She is grumpy and full of complaints. Yet she will help a cripple in the dacha next door. She is a Russian! With people like this in our land, I have faith in Russia still."

"There are not enough people like her in the world these

days."

"That may be so. I do not travel like I once did. And she is old. Maybe your generation will not care for its neighbors."

"My generation does not even trust its neighbors," I said, "much less care for them. And the one after mine would kill them in order to take their apartments and have an extra bedroom. The country has been poisoned by too many years of lies and disappearing men. Trust cannot grow in a salted earth."

He nodded his head. I looked around for a chair, but could not find one. I guess he had no need for furniture other than his bed. Since I could not sit, I began walking around the room, straightening things up. Soon I found myself in the kitchen, washing dishes. After that I fed the stove, then went outside to chop some more wood from the lumber pile.

I wanted to say, "Thank you for taking care of me my whole life. Now I'll take care of you." But I found it hard to say for some reason. So I just worked. I replaced his front door with a sturdier one made from the wall of an abandoned shed. I washed his floors. I cleaned his windows. I made his house into a nice place. I stayed up all night with these projects.

In the morning, as I was falling asleep on the floor of his bedroom, Madina entered the front door and woke me up.

She was younger than I expected. I had pictured a hag or great round old woman. But she was young, an innocent, jittery girl from the country with small teeth and large round eyes that darted from left to right. I knew I could not stay in Vulkov's dacha with Madina as a neighbor and not make love to her. And yet I knew I could not leave Vulkov. So it was simple math that we would end up fucking. But that would come later.

"I thank you with all my heart for caring about old Vulkov," I said, standing up to greet her.

"I was pleased to help my neighbor," she said, smiling.

I wanted to think of the kind charities she had done, but she bent over to help roll up my blanket and I saw her breasts. It is hard to think of goodwill when you are face to face with the beautiful chest of a woman. Still, I restrained myself from grabbing her in front of Vulkov. Instead I helped roll up my makeshift mattress.

"No longer tired?" Vulkov whispered from the bed. He may have been old, but he was not blind. He knew what I was thinking about. "Ilya here was about to go to sleep when you arrived."

"Oh!" Madina said, covering her hand with her mouth. "I'm sorry. Please, go to sleep. I'm sorry to have disturbed you ... Ilya."

"Ilya Zamyatin," I said, holding out my hand.

"Madina Rublev." She curtsied slightly, and then shook my hand.

"I am no longer tired," I said. "Perhaps you can show me around the village and we can pick up some supplies for Vulkov."

She nodded.

"Are you one of his children?" she asked.

"Yes," I said.

"My father died some years ago." She looked down at the floor.

I took her arm and we walked out to the front of the house.

"I'll be staying with him for a while," I said. "So I'll need to pick up some things for myself. I can tell you keep the house stocked well for him. That is kind of you."

"I don't take any money from him."

"I know. He probably doesn't have much money to give."

We walked out into the morning.

"Vulkov was never a rich man," I said, "as far as money was

concerned. His wealth was power and knowledge, but the market for his wealth collapsed with the Soviet Union. The men who owed him favors no longer have favors to spare. The secrets he kept are being forced into the light. He gave his life to a country that is no more."

"He was a powerful man, then? That explains the visitors. Every few months, a big black car will arrive from Moscow and some old men will visit with him. I'm not sure what they talk about, but in a day or two, some new gift will arrive at my house. We turn the gifts all away."

"You could keep them. If you don't take them, the delivery men probably sell them on the black market."

"The gifts all seem tainted. I have never told Vulkov that we send the gifts away. He probably thinks I am enjoying the washing machine and the refrigerator and television."

"He probably knows you decline them and respects you the more for it. Very little gets by our friend Vulkov."

"I am glad you consider him a friend. I used to worry for him. I could tell he had a strong heart and a giving nature, and yet here he was alone. And what if something should happen to me? He could not fend for himself very easily."

"He usually finds a way, despite the odds."

We were walking arm in arm along the road. I could see smoke from chimneys up ahead, and small radio towers. This must have been a village frequented by Soviet leaders who needed to remain in contact with the Kremlin. Not the most powerful men, as there were no cellular phone towers and satellite dishes. The top ranking men would have built such devices near their vacation homes so they could stay on their vacation and still conduct private business. The radio towers here suggested high level functionaries who could be recalled to capital by their bosses, to handle the dirty work while their superiors remained in the comfort of a country dacha. In many cases, our former leaders intentionally went on vacation when they knew dirty work was on the horizon. It was so much easier to call for a rash of executions if you didn't have to face the men's families and neighbors on the streets.

It began snowing slightly just as Madina and I reached the small village with its exhausted store fronts and long-abandoned supply depots. She led me to a small grocery. It still had the shelves and posters of the Soviet Era. Modern price and product information had been painted over top of the previous labels. Behind the counter were more expensive items like radios, razors, and Coca-Cola. In the city, of course, Coca-Cola was everywhere, but here in the country it was still an exotic treat, like champagne or toilet paper.

Traveling around the world with Cesterosky, I'd seen the cornucopia that modern society has presented to man. As children, we Russians were taught to disdain the capitalistic greed of the West, but only the most brainwashed, mindless souls will look at a shelf full of toothpaste varieties and not smile at the abundance. How many different kinds of mint there are! Green mint, spearmint, blue mint, cinnamon mint, citrus mint! And then the whitening paste, the whitening gel, the whitening powder, the whitening strips! There are as many varieties of toothpaste as there are flavors of ice cream, almost as if they are armies facing each other across a battlefield of teeth, one good and one evil. It would take a fool or a hippy to see anything but beauty in the array of dental products on a modern day grocery shelf. What surer sign of civilization's greatness is there?

That was not the case here in the small Russian grocery where I walked the aisles with Madina. Most products only had one variety. Want batteries? You'd have to settle for the Red Voltage brand. Looking for potato chips? You're in luck if you want to purchase Strong Ivan brand plain potato chips. Don't bother looking for sour cream and onion flavored chips, or, God forbid, barbecue. You're lucky to find even salted potato chips in a place like this! In just a few departments, there were options. Other than the expensive American brands behind the counter, the closest we had to Western groceries were modern knock-offs. So, if you were looking to buy a bottle of Vodka, you could choose between White Bear brand, the state option, or Starry Stripe brand, *the Choice of U.S. Men and Musicians*, which was made in St. Petersburg. If you wanted to buy a box of matches, you could choose between Soviet Imperial Matches and Mickey Mouse Eagle Rushmore matches (from the Ukraine). For soap, there was either Odessa Soap or New York California Clean City Soap. The more American references in a products name, the further its origin was from the U.S.A. In this store, for instance, there was a locally produced candlestick called Uncle Sam's Red White and Blue Thomas Jefferson Candlestick for 1776 Style Lighting with Hollywood Finish and Television Friendly Base. The irony of a candlestick purporting to be the choice of Americans was lost on the customers in this store. Or so I smugly thought at the time – picturing the poor Amish as the only Americans who would actually buy a candlestick. (Nowadays, nestled in my Manhattan home, I am bombarded by catalogues from *Pottery Barn* and *Crate and Barrel*, who must know of my humble origins, as they continually try to sell me candlesticks, barn house furniture, and rustic bookcases that I should fill with bales of hay, according to the pictures.)

In many of your American movies, young couples experience the bliss of new love while walking the aisles of grocery stores. But amidst the stark, almost bare shelves of this market, Madina and I had trouble smiling with the quirky grace of a pair of movie stars. We simply found the items we needed, the food for me, the medical products for Vulkov, and then paid our bill. Our first glimpse at romance did not come until we decided to stop for lunch at Thin Olga's, a borscht house near the grocery store.

"I'm hungry," I told Madina as we left the store.

"Let's get a bite at Thin Olga's," she said.

When we entered, we were greeted by a monumentally fat woman.

"It must be under new management," I joked quietly to Madina.

"No, that's Thin Olga's mother," she said as we sat down.

"Where is Thin Olga?"

"She couldn't get enough to eat as a child, and she died. During a Five Year Plan." Madina frowned. "Her mother named the restaurant after her."

"I'm sorry. I didn't mean anything."

We sat in silence for a while.

Then Madina let out a great whooping laugh. Some loud laughs are more annoying than anything else, but hers was not like that – it was so pure that it made you love her.

"I'm sorry. I was teasing you. Thin Olga is alive and well. She moved to Moscow and works as a model. She sent her mother the money to open the restaurant, so Mama named it in her honor. Although, from what I hear, she could have named the restaurant *Cocaine-Addicted Olga's*."

Olga's mother arrived to take our order. I had a borscht without lamb. Madina had a borscht without shrimp. We shared a bottle of vodka.

"Good thing we don't have to drive home," Madina said.

"Yes," I agreed.

"Actually, I don't know how to drive," she said. "I've only

been in a car two times. Once when my mother died, and once when my father died."

"I learned to drive trucks in the army. But I've never had my own vehicle."

"I hear that, in America, everyone gets a car when they turn 15. Can you imagine? Where do they put all those cars?"

"They have skyscrapers built just for cars."

"No!"

"Yes. I once traveled in a limousine that drove to the fourth floor of a shopping mall parking lot."

"A car on the fourth floor... you are pulling my tit."

"I'm not pulling your tit, it's true."

Like many restaurants in a world without reliable electricity, Thin Olga's closed at sundown. So in the romantic half light of the falling sun, we finished our meals. Olga's mother came by to explain that she had a generator, purchased by her daughter, but generally only turned it on for big events like weddings and wakes. We told her we did not mind and settled our tab. We sailed forth, two human ships that had been drifting through uncharted waters for too long.

"Where are we going?" she asked me, her arm around my waist.

"Home."

"Do you know where that is?"

"I'm not sure, but I hope I'm going in the right direction."

Soon enough I realized we were indeed on the correct road back to Vulkov's house. Then, as the dark blue night began to fade into the treetops and obliterate the horizon with night, she pulled at me.

"Turn here," she said.

"This is not the way to Vulkov's house."

"I know." She began tugging at me more urgently, pulling at

my shirt until it came undone. Soon she was almost running, with me behind her, as we found our way to her small home. It was a stone structure, covered with peat moss for a roof. It looked like the leftover portion of a large castle, except that there was no stately manor anywhere near.

"This is where I live," she said.

Through her door, through the halls, into the back of the building, we stumbled into her bed and grasped at each other's clothes.

"I have only Russian condoms," I said. Like Russian cars, they were not trustworthy.

"I have no condoms at all," she frowned and burrowed her head into my chest.

"Don't be sad. I would be more alarmed if you had a large supply of American condoms."

"Do they even use condoms in America?" she asked, sincerely.

"Of course they do. But they have so much money, they throw them away after one use."

We hugged each other tightly and rolled around on the bedspread.

"We can do things without actually making love," she said.

And so we groped and rubbed and grabbed each other for an hour or so, swearing that we would find protection some day soon and insert ourselves into each other. And then we were tired and sweaty in the rough Russian sheets, remembering that we should return home to Vulkov.

"Where did you learn all those techniques?" I asked her. After all, I had traveled to Afghanistan and outer space, but she had grown up in the Russian wilderness.

"Other girls in town taught me a few tricks." I could not tell if she meant they had told her about things to do with a man, or that they had shown her. I chose to believe they had shown her, and became so aroused fantasizing about her and other women that I became excited enough to make another run at things. This time, wet with desire and sweat, she opened up to me and we dangerously intertwined ourselves without protection. I have traveled beyond the atmosphere on a rocket, readers, but this was one of the most dangerous things I've ever done. She did not seem like a loose woman, make no mistake, but perhaps she had been ravaged and taken against her will by a K.G.B. member or a secret policeman. And even if neither of us carried any reminders of affairs past, there was the risk of pregnancy. And yet... in the face of Vulkov's all-too-real mortality, there seemed some small comfort to both of us in this affirmation of life and immediacy through abandon.

I awoke some time later, alone in her bed. I was disoriented. It was a common feeling for me then, since I had no regular bed. Opening your eyes to the unexpected is always a shock: *Who knitted this comforter? Why is this pillow less scratchy than my own? Where am I?* I rolled from my side onto my back and stared at the ceiling. It was comprised of muddy clumps of hay. I worried that a clump of dirt would fall onto me. I turned over and faced the wall again. It was like a guilty yoga. I stretched one way and then another, but could never relax. I was tangled up in anguish and sex.

What of Vulkov? I had come back to care for him, and less than a day later was in some woman's bed. But I could tell from the moment she had entered his dacha that she cared for him as much as me. Did that mean that she cared for him greatly? Or that I did not care for him as much as I should?

I rolled out of the bed and found my clothes on the floor around it. I got dressed and looked out her bedroom window into the night. My breath fogged up the glass. It felt like Christmas. I could see only the stars and, faintly, the caustic light of the village far towards the invisible horizon. I put on my shoes.

I pulled my coat close to me and left to find Vulkov again.

On the road, I could hear my foot steps in a way I never had. The crisp frozen ground cracked under each step and the lack of city life or military action was a new kind of silence to me. All of the world I had known was filled with the hum of electricity, the anticipation of something. Here there was only silence. No expectations, no threat of violence or friendship. Just the great black night and blanket of calm.

Vulkov was no fool. He could tell from the look on my face that I'd been having sex, and it was not much of a leap to figure out who my partner had been.

"Listen," he said, after I had tried unsuccessfully to sneak into his room without waking him, "I won't give you some sermon about taking care of her and making an honest man of yourself. I only ask you not to chase her away. I need her. I suspect that you do as well. Now I'm going to sleep! You kept me up all night! I was worried."

He threw his head back onto the pillow and closed his eyes. I must hand it to Vulkov – he could gesture and animate his body with the best of them, despite having so little to work with at this point. I rolled my bedding out on the floor and went to sleep, my first peaceful night in quite a while. Not the all-encompassing peace of a man at ease with his life and position, mind you, but the slight glimpse of peace that comes when you know where you are sleeping and who will be there when you wake and your bed is not moving or shaking or traveling through the night.

In movies, men are always trying to escape from the cud-
dling and spooning of their women, as if they wish to be
constantly moving. I am not sure this is true. Some women,
true, you do not want resting on top of your arm. But others are
a fine night's company. What men do not like is a woman calling the shots. If you want to give her your arm, then she might
be the woman for your. If she sneaks your arm and holds it
against your struggling, then she may be a judo master, a
wrestler that you would be wise to avoid. Those who practice
judo would use your clothes against you, grabbing you by the
collar and throwing you to the ground. What kind of civilized
behavior is that? Clothes should separate us from the animals,
not provide us opportunities to show how much like them we
still are.[5]

If you're wondering whether I might fall in love with
Madina here, I should be more clear. I liked and enjoyed her.
Many people find mates they like and enjoy. But I knew I
would not love her with a lifetime's unbridled heart. I have a
type; most men do. Sometimes, in conversation with a man,
you will ask him to describe his type and he will describe
someone unlike his wife or girlfriend. "I like short-haired
brunettes with glasses," he will say, while his long-blond-haired
wife is in the bathroom. Or, if you live in an American
Republican state, you might meet a man who is clearly gay but
has married himself to a woman and become a politician. These
are men who have compromised; made a negotiation with
reality and decided to settle. I don't mean that in a negative
way. Settling is important. Our great cities and countries were
founded by settlers. You can wander through the wilderness for
centuries and millennia and never find a good night's sleep, or
you can plant your seeds in the best patch of land you have
found. A true optimist is always single and does not own a

home. A pragmatist is married and pays a mortgage. The optimist is looking for something better. The pragmatist is happy with a vagina that his half full rather than half empty (the vagina is half-full because he is on his way in; it is half empty when a pessimist is pulling out).

Which is a roundabout way of telling you of some other women I have known. They were not the great lost loves of my life, and I have not yet mentioned them because they did not play a great role in defining the arc of my life. And I have no wish for this book to be a mere list of my sexual conquests (as long and impressive as such a list may be). But when I think about the women now, I fear that it does them a disservice not to mention them at all. They were important. So here, with certain essential biographical facts disguised or removed, is a list of some women I knew intimately after Natasha but have yet to mention:

— *The environmentalist folk singer.* Passionate about restoring and atoning for Chernobyl, she had a few minor hits on Russian radio. She was truly beautiful, with eyes that seemed almost clairvoyant in the way they searched to the truth of everyone in front of her. If she did not have such a strong conviction of character, she might have been a successful sexpot. But she knew better, and disguised her sensual figure with men's shirts, so that the focus of her audience was on her lyrics and ecological message. She made love as if we were the last two people on earth, responsible for repopulating the planet, and our chances of doing so depended on the sheer force of our coupling.

— *The Bulgarian dancer I met at an embassy party.* As Tolstoy once said, there is nothing sexier than Bulgarian folk dance.

– *The girl who looked like a boy.* Sometimes a woman will cut her hair short and dress like a man while still retaining the graceful jaw of a lady. When I meet such a woman, I feel compelled to become her lover because I am attracted to the rebellion inherent in such a choice.

– *The angry red-haired woman.* The passion of an angry woman is something to behold! Why was she angry? She could not afford an apartment with a bathroom and often had to urinate in trash cans. You would be angry, too, would you not?

– *The woman with the dogs.* She kept two small terriers in her apartment and had them trained to do their business on newspapers on the floor of her bathroom. I did not know this, and, naked in the nighttime, almost stepped in a pile of dog shit while going to the bathroom after she pleasured me. Normally I would have pleasured her in return, but the dog shit I almost stepped in killed the mood, and I crept away into the night. I apologize!

– *[name of famous actress redacted].* She was quite muscular and did most of the work.

When the harsh Russian morning breathed into Vulkov's room, I woke up and did something I had rarely done in my life – I stayed in bed. It was not a proper bed, but nevertheless, I stayed where I woke. I was, I guess, content. Previously, I had woken up with hangovers and remained in bed on account of them. But this new feeling of enjoyment, being in bed alone, was new. Even at my happiest in the past, I had trouble remaining in bed. Or, say I woke up next to a beautiful woman – I would be happy, but not satisfied to just lie there, because why not wake her up and have another go at her? So here, this, now... this was new. Waking alone and feeling the urge to stay in bed.

I suppose I was not actually alone. Vulkov was there. As a child, I had rarely known what it was like to wake up in a home with a loving parent. That is the kind of experience that makes you wish you could remain in bed forever.

I thought I about the improbable events of my life so far. The odds were against me surviving childhood and war. The odds were certainly against me going into space (statistically, maybe one in 100 billion people go to space). The numbers were there to back up my feeling of uniqueness and individuality. This may seem like some pathetic realization – those readers raised in America where every child is taught they are special must wonder that it took me so long to discover this about myself. *I am somebody*, I thought as I let the morning fill up the room. *I am a survivor of the great train wreck that was Russia's twentieth century.* And I crawled out of the devastating crash, over broken locomotive parts, through the charred human remains to find myself in a better position than when I had boarded the railroad car in the first place. That must count for something.

This realization did not change my plans for the future. Instead, it gave me a sense of peace. I suppose this is the solace some find in religion, the understanding that God created you and made you a special being. Everyone wants to be the main character in the story of their life.

I hugged myself, not because I sexually desired the attractive man that I was. But I hugged myself to give myself the love I now knew I deserved. Vulkov might have hugged me if he was awake or had arms. If you are reading this book at night, in bed, set the book on your nightstand and hug yourself to make sure you know you are loved. Unless you are in prison, in which case you should not put the book down – you might need it to protect yourself from being stabbed by your cellmate who has fashioned a shiv out of a toothbrush and some stolen copper wiring. A book is a good defense against violence.

After hugging myself, I still did not get up and begin my day. I stayed there and imagined where I would be in ten years. The image of me floated into my head and I decided to have a conversation with this future me. I entered the vision and flagged down the convertible I was driving across a hover bridge.

"It's me," I told myself. "I'm you from 10 years ago."

"I know," my future self said. "I remember being you and imagining this conversation."

"I have so much to ask you."

"Well, I cannot just stop here on the hover bridge. I'll get a robo-ticket from the traffic processing machine. You better hop in; we can chat while I drive."

And so I climbed into the convertible, sitting next to myself.

"What do you want to know about the future?" I asked myself.

"Not too much. I want it to be a surprise. But I want to know if there's anything that's important that I don't realize. Or if there's something insignificant that I am putting too much emotional stock in; really, I want to know what changes I should make in my life."

"Drink less," I told myself.

Then we both laughed and laughed.

"I know you don't want bullshit like that," my future self said. "You want the *Oprah* version. The quick life changing inspiration."

"Oh God. Do I watch *Oprah* ten years from now? What a

wimp I will become!"

"Hey, don't judge me. I only started watching now because it's her final season."

"What? *Oprah* will go off the air? The future seems so sad," I said.

"Ten years from now is no big deal. Worry about what will happen two years from now. Except don't. You shouldn't really worry too much. That's what Oprah would say if you could ask her. You can't control the future any more than you can control the past. All you can do is live in the present. Life is a gift to you. That's why today is called the present."

I almost threw up in this imaginary convertible. Such treacly pronouncements! And from myself, no less.

"Live in the moment? What garbage! Are you offering me advice or trying to sell me soft drinks?"

"Listen. If I told you where you would be in ten years, and what your life would be like, you wouldn't believe me. Suffice it to say that things get worse before they get better. And, also, they don't get better. So really, things just get worse."

"But the future can't be that bad... What about this sweet convertible you're driving?"

"It gets horrible gas mileage," he said. "And the roof leaks when it rains."

That reminded me of a song by Leonard Cohen, which I mentioned to my future self, about there being cracks in all things, but that it was okay because cracks let the light in.

He laughed at me. "Who told you that nonsense? If there's a crack in something, that's where the rain gets in."

And then we just drove for a while, rolling across the high-ways of the imaginary future, me wondering how bad things would get, and my future self driving in silence, happy to have made a few vague pronouncements about the bleak times ahead.

Of course I know why he didn't tell me something more specific – he did not know. He was only a figment of my imagination, a creation of my subconscious. Soon, our journey took us to the Atlantic Crossing Bridge and we engaged our solar thrusters to power our vehicle across the oceanic canyon between Europe and America. The dream disintegrated in my mind's eye while we were driving across the bridge, great mile-high pylons passing off to the side in a hypnotic rhythm.

Back in the present, comfortable in my bed, I wondered if any of this future would come true. I remembered hearing once that a wish spoken aloud won't come true, so I considered telling Vulkov what I worried about the future. It wasn't a wish, I understand, but it was a premonition, and perhaps those were controlled by the same rules as wishes? Yet I remained silent. Why burden a dying old stump of a man in his last days with needless concerns about a future he would not live to see? The burden was mine alone to carry.

Speaking of being alone, where was Madina? Was it rude to have left her bed? But she had left me first. I presumed she had something important to do. Maybe she had just gone to the bathroom, or gone to fetch some firewood? Now I felt guilty about failing to leave a note to explain myself. And so I buried my head in the pillow to drown out the voice asking how I could have treated her so thoughtfully. Here was a woman taking care of my father figure and I had bedded and abandoned her within a few hours of meeting her.

I suppose no one can treat everybody decently all the time. But is virtue measured by how badly you feel after mistreating someone or by how infrequently you do it? I had mistreated many people in my life. I rarely felt bad about it before now. The last time I felt this badly was when I lied to Natasha. It seems like mistreating women causes the most guilt. And yet it also gets the most results. Treat a woman poorly and she might hate you, but treat a women right and she will forget that you exist. Unless she had the careless heart of a man, Madina would wonder and worry about where I had gone when she returned to her bed and found it empty.

Later, she turned up at Vulkov's house and did not mention why she had left in the night, or the fact that I had been gone if and when she returned to her bed. We shared the chores as the morning grew into afternoon. I changed and cleaned Vulkov while she prepared us a pleasant lunch. She roasted some turnips for herself and me, and then mashed up some vegetables for Vulkov. Usually he preferred to eat mashed food which he could handle by himself with a straw. When he felt like celebrating and trusted his friends, he allowed himself to be spoon fed like a toddler. The experience of chewing food and allowing the flavors to break across your tongue is not something you give up idly. We took our meal out into a spot in the yard here the sun poured down and kept us mildly warm. We used tree stumps for chairs. Madina and I put our asses on them, while Vulkov leaned against one.

"What a funny picture we make," Vulkov said as we chased the last few morsels of food around our plates. "It's like Tolstoy says, 'All normal families are alike. Abnormal families are each abnormal in their own way.'"[6]

"Tell us of your adventures," Madina prodded me.

"Yes, yes," Vulkov said. "You are an international traveler! Surely you brought back some stories from your travels."

I thought back to my years of wandering drunkenly with Cesterosky. Few of my stories were polite enough for mixed companies. I did not dream of telling Madina about some exotic foreign woman I'd bedded in the guest cabin of a rich man's yacht. But then I remembered one night where I did nothing a gentleman would not do. So I told them the story:

"In the sands of northern Egypt, we joined a caravan. Our heavy machines fell in line behind their camels, which seemed graceful by comparison. The sands were dark gray and brown, sloping around us as the night was approaching. We became aware of the violent noise of our jeeps and decided to travel by other means. A few flares of our headlights signaled the riders, who turned to negotiate with us. Not business, so much, as a hospitable offer of some extra animals for us to ride. They worried about our machines, but we promised to send someone for them using Cesterosky's satellite phone. I was not part of the discussion, so I cannot be sure whether we slipped them a few gold coins for their troubles or if they shared with us out of the samaritan spirit of nomads through ancient times. More camels were produced, and makeshift saddles. A mild sense of urgency fell upon us as we tried to mount the beasts before complete dark. We almost made it, but the last few riders took to the camels by torch light.

"Then we were stalking through the sands on the backs of camels, keeping time with the riders ahead. We had abandoned the modern world for the oldest journey in the land. It was so exhilarating that we hardly noticed the smell of the creatures or the strange noises they made. Only after we settled for the night and could still hear and smell the pack animals did we realize what rough beasts they would be in any other setting. At first ride, though, it was like crawling back through the millennia into the undeveloped heart of civilization. We saw more stars than we are accustomed to in the world lit by lightning. I had seen such star-filled skies in Afghanistan and outer space, and did not share the thrill of the natural universe or the joy of my traveling companions who had not yet experienced this unadulterated view of the night sky. There was a kind of music in their view, aided by the percussion of small bells and jangles on the wrists and feet our our caravan leaders. The galaxies fell all the way to the horizon, with no cities or forests to obscure the view. We did not need to look up to see the constellations – they appeared straight ahead, reaching up from behind the endless plain of dark sand ahead.

"Using some ancient art of timekeeping or geography, the caravan found its own resting place and we halted in a cradle of sand. As the Russians found each other and shared our amazement at the night, our hosts set up camp and began cooking their spiced meats and throwing dough against angry pots in the fire to make bread. They called us when it was ready and we dined in the glow of the cooking fire, a circle of men living the oldest ways of civilization. Further back in time we would have been forced to find a cave and eat raw meat. We complimented the food honestly and gave the men our blessings and best wishes. One of the men smiled and opened a bag of green coffee beans, which he proceeded to roast in a pan over the popping embers of the last fire. When they were heated to the dark brown we know as coffee, he transferred them to a great bowl and crushed them with a stone mortar and pestle.

"Then he boiled them and served us the thickest cups of coffee we had ever had. It kept us awake all through the night, which was desirable as we could watch the stars in their endless parade across the heavens. Such a night makes you curious about man's progress and whether it has really made life better for us. I say this as a man who has taken advantage of the greatest technological leaps of the 20th Century. I went to *space*, for Christ's sake. And yet it led to so much misery. I doubted whether these nomads had ever known the fear and sadness I'd known. Perhaps the only advancement mankind has made is finding new ways to become miserable. We had grown accustomed to our forefathers' ways of sadness and were forced to throw our inventiveness into discovering modern depression. The atomic bomb. Trench warfare. Chemotherapy. Tell me truly, does the greatest invention of our times equal the pain of such things? A car phone? A walkman? No, these nomads in the sands of history knew the ancient ways, the best ways.

"Even here, now. This cold hard life of the Russian winter is no match for the weary life of a Chernobyl family with mangled children and ghost towns where villages once stood. We have each other."

I grabbed Madina's waist. Enough of such seriousness!

"I have this fine woman! I will ride her all night like a sexy camel. I will find her oasis with my great big caravan. Oh, my caravan can't wait to enter the oasis."

Vulkov laughed.

"Traveler," he said, "be careful not to get any sand in the waters of the oasis."

"And," Madina said, smiling, "don't be so sure the oasis will open its gates to your caravan."

"But surely a weary traveler such as myself can find solace and welcome!"

We tumbled along the cold ground together until Vulkov cleared his throat loudly.

"I grow cold out here," he said. "I can't make myself warm the way you two can." Here he winked at us. "If you would be kind enough to take me inside, I might take a nap."

We took him inside and put him in bed. Then Madina and I trudged into the woods to make love once more. I don't wish to boast too much or be indiscreet. I merely tell you this story because it is the truth. And, perhaps, in our constant lovemaking you will find some definition of the loneliness we had endured in the past year. We were selfish and both had our own reasons for plunging into each other like we did. I found my spirit to live inside her, in the way her breasts splayed across her chests when she leaned back. In the sheen of sweat along her thighs when I reached down between her legs. In the feel of her worn stockings under my hand. And she found the warmth of another body which was hard to hold onto in the distant rural forests outside the great cities of the Mother Country. Sometimes we fuck to prove we are alive.

In the woods, she found great broken branches and smashed them against my bare back like the proprietor of a bathhouse. She stuffed great balls of snow and ice into my mouth. She even tickled my asshole with soft round icicles. I shivered and felt my whole body tightening beneath her touch. For my part I used my tongue and fingers and pulled her hair and lightly bit her as she wished. Our skin was raw and chapped and our faces flush with life by the time we rolled into each other's arms, spent, and huddled together beneath the trees for a few minutes, catching our breath before returning to the warmth of the house. We carried the broken branches we had used in our lovemaking and put them in the stove for kindling.

I swear that they made the shack warmer than any other wood burnt before.

Madina, I discovered, also cared for a variety of elders in distant dachas. None required as much attention as Vulkov, but with me there to help him, she was free to make her rounds of the other aging spirits of the cold villages and towns. This left me time to visit with the old man, who could not muster more than a few hours of life and conversation per day. In the remaining hours, I wrote my novels, the ones I had mapped out in the back of the rock band's truck. I found gray sheets of paper in the town store and expensive imported ink. I wrote each page once in my head before I began typing, in order to conserve the precious supplies of my trade.

Every two or three days, Madina returned and told me of some other old widow or veteran she had helped. Upon returning, her sexual appetite was always greater than it had been. Caring the for the sick and the elderly made her lust for life even more. She would wrap her thighs around my torso and squeeze almost all the life of me. "Fuck me like you're alive," she'd whisper into my ear. "Squeeze my tits and let me feel your dick inside me!" Already being inside her, I was sometimes at a loss for what else I could do. Did she think I could control it like my fingers or make it longer somehow? Still her enthusiasm was exciting even at its most confusing.

And then the next morning, after a sunrise coupling, she would pack her small bag of medicine and food and begin the journey to another nearby town to care for some other old soul. She was, truly, like an angel to those octogenarians, and I confess that it was exciting to make love to such an angel. Who among us would not like to rip the heavenly robes from some white-light bathed seraph? Throw her harp down from the sky, and lay her bare angel's body against the cloudy mattress of Paradise! If there is truly no disappointment in heaven, the mind boggles when it considers what fucking is like up there. And do not try to tell me there is no mating in heaven, for what is heaven if not a place where we fuck and kiss and love women and/or men for eternity?

While I was writing and Madina was taking care of the old men and women of Russia, my song was climbing up the Russian charts. For the sake of imagery, it would be nice to say it was rocketing up the chart like I had rocketed into space, but that would be inaccurate. "Natasha's Song (for Natasha)" was released by a minor record label without much fanfare. It might have disappeared into the dustbin of history along with so many Lenin statues and Trabants were it not for a strange coincidence. The song had been placed on a promotional CD put together by the record studio. They sent it the great rock bands and musicians of Russia in the hopes that they would begin using the studio instead of whatever makeshift gear they had cobbled together behind the Iron Curtain. Of course, all the serious bands found studios in the west. But a few of them listened to the CD. And one of these bands, Most Finland Station, liked the song enough to play it at a few small club dates when they grew tired of playing their big hits like "Mustang Auto Baby" and "Volga Vulva Volcano." At one of these shows at The Warsaw, which was in a hip part of Moscow, a television producer heard the song and asked about it. Most Finland Station give him the CD and he began using the song as the love theme for his game show, *Hammer For Cash*. When a husband won money for his wife's surgery, or gained enough winnings to be reunited with the wife he had sold into the sex market, they would play my song to express the joy and tragedy of modern love.

Viewers loved the song and began clamoring for it. Since *Hammer For Cash* was the most popular game show on the air that year, producers eventually marketed a soundtrack, which featured my song, the game show's main theme, and a bunch of other crappy songs and excerpts of dialogue from famous moments on the show. (The most famous being the couple taking the marriage survey. The host asks a woman to name a place where her husband wants to make love. He has guessed she would answer "In a sports car." But she replies, "My wet pussy!")

Of course, the myth of Ilya Zamyatin, the space hero and songwriting genius, was only stoked further by the fact that I could not be found. The record company made a big show of putting my royalty money in an account for the day when I showed up, assuming I had not died. Nobody could remember seeing me after the big New Year's Eve party at the Space Discovery camp, and it was assumed that I had been left behind there, possibly killed by the savage Russian natives who overran the campus once Cesterosky departed. Many great newspapers and newsmagazines pegged expose pieces to my disappearance. I was the face of the forgotten Russian hero, swept aside like so many crippled veterans after the wars. A famous poster showed my face and asked HAVE YOU SEEN THIS MAN? It was so famous that the record studio used it as a cover for my first solo album, which was merely my version of "Natasha's Song" along with my half-way completed version of "Glory Days." The rest of the album was horrible techno songs that used sound clips of interviews with me or promotional recordings I'd made for Space Discovery as lyrics on top of insipid rhythm and bass lines. Although you can bet Cesterosky made sure to get his cut of the money from anything associated with his summer camp.

It was one of the posters of me that first drew my attention to my nascent musical career. I had gone to the grocery store with Madina to buy supplies for her various dependents. As I picked up some loaves of dark rye, I heard her laughing. I looked up and saw her with her head propped on her hand and tilted at a rakish angle. She was describing me to the clerk who turned to me with an astounded look that made her mouth into the letter "o" with an umlaut (because of her nostrils). Then she jumped up and down and let out a manly shriek.

"It's you! I never knew!"

"Who am I?" I asked.

"Don't you know who you are?"

"I thought I did, but now I am no longer sure. Who am I?"

"You're the lost cosmonaut! The man who wrote 'Natasha's Song'!"

As I brought the loaf toward the counter, she explained how my song had been featured on television and the almost-frantic search for me that had ensued. It sounded a bit like the hunt for Dr. Livingstone in the dark heart of Africa, except that my story was not invented by the newspapers.

I laughed heartily as I did not believe her story. I knew, of course, that I had written and recorded a wonderful song for Natasha. But the string of events leading to its success and my fame seemed unbelievable. More likely this was a prank of some sort. And then she turned on the small hand-crank radio behind the counter.

"Just wait," she whispered over the music we heard. "They play it so often we're sure to hear it."

Sure enough, in a few minutes, the DJ announced that he would play my song.

And as it played I noticed some light change come over Madina. I had agreed with the clerk that I had once written this song for Natasha. And now Madina realized, I suppose, that I was still in love with this woman I had lost. I enjoyed Madina, and we had made no efforts to pretend we loved one another. Still, it was hard labor to be confronted with the brutal fact of my true soul mate's existence. She did not begin hating me or grow angry, but we lost something in that moment, perched over the counter of a pathetic Russian grocery. It was like accidentally seeing the clown without his makeup – you knew his face is not so white, his hair not so red, his handkerchief so long, and yet it was startling and shocking to see him as a normal man nonetheless. So it was, I believe, with Madina. With a chart-topping hit to make my other love clear, it was impossible to go on pretending we had a future together. And, just as we did with our groceries, she began to check out in that moment. It was not instantaneous, but it was irreparable. We would go our separate ways.

Vulkov was dying slowly. Each day he was weaker than the day before. Soon we knew he would not be strong enough to continue breathing. We asked if he wanted to go to a hospital.

"No, my son," he told me. "I shall die here in my bed where it's comfortable."

"You're not dying," I told him.

"I am. And you know it. Let me die here. And bury me out in the yard. My fondest memories from childhood are watching my father work in the field. It seemed so much easier to do an honest day's labor back then. Now there are so many machines. You'd have to be a fool not to take advantage of technology, so only idiots work hard any more. Idiots will take over the world when we all grow too weak to take care of ourselves." He laughed a little, weakly, then smiled at the small sounds he made instead of larger ones.

"I used to have a powerful voice," he said.

"I remember. When we arrived at basic training..."

"I had arms then. And legs. Make sure I am not remembered as a cripple."

"I will tell the world about you as I knew you. I will sing of *arms* and *the man*."

"Oh, dear, wearing such a fancy pants. Just speak of me simply. And take care of Madina."

"I'll try," I said.

"You don't have to love her or marry her. Just make sure she has enough money. She'll go on taking care of the other old people. It's in her nature. But when they're all gone, if she doesn't take up new charges, I want her to enjoy life. There's been a famine of enjoyment out here in the country. Tell me you'll take care of her."

I promised him I would. I assumed I would get some money from my hit song. And when my books were published, she would have some of that money.

We let the silence fill the room. I thought of all he had given me, the life for which he had been my steward. I began to cry.

"Stop that," he said softly. "I will not die today. I have a few days left in me."

"Tell me, old man," I said. "Was it you who called the press to let them know I was trapped in that space capsule, who alerted the world to my dilemma?"

"Me? That is a good notion," he said and then he smiled. "But how could I have dialed the phone?"

Madina and I began to make love more furiously in these days, perhaps because we saw the end coming. Who knew how long it would be until we found new partners? There was little question we would part ways after Vulkov died.

"I'm glad we found each other," she told me one night over potatoes at Thin Olga's.

"Me too."

"Even if it wasn't meant to last, it was nice to have someone these last few weeks."

"Months!"

"It's been months? The time has passed so easily," she said.

We played with our food, moving carbohydrates one way and another with our forks.

"Do you want to talk about it?" I asked finally.

"That woman? No. Not now. If she makes you happy, you should be with her."

"I hope you'll find someone to make you happy."

"In some ways, I don't ask for much. I live a simple life. But perhaps that is a lot to ask these days."

"Everyone is looking for complications. We call them advancements – cars, boats, spaceships, computers, telephones, walkmen, solar wristwatches, calculators, remote controls, laser pointers, food processors, microwaves – but they are complications."

"Do you think you could be happy living off the land? A secluded simple life?"

"No. I could not. At least, not my whole life. Maybe when I'm older and I've accomplished more, I'll feel ready to retire to the country."

She laughed at this. It made me feel better to hear her laugh.

"You want to do more?" she asked through a smile. "You've done more than anyone I know. You've been to outer space!"

"I know. But I can't help looking for new worlds. I would like to spend some time in America."

Her face flinched. We both laughed. We had been programmed to hate the United States from birth.

"What do they have there?" she asked.

"I'm not sure, but I intend to find out."

We finished our potatoes and ate a dry, hard cake for dessert. Then we went back to her place and threw our bodies against each other like wrestlers. It was sweaty and violent and we raised each other's arms in triumph when we were done.

"I would like to go to America some day too," she said.

"You want to climb the Empire State Building? Or walk across the Golden Gate Bridge?"

"I would like to hear Mandy Patinkin sing some folk songs

of Russia. I hear the man has a terrific voice and a real gift for capturing the emotion of our people."

And she was right: a great singer is worth crossing oceans for. A great poet worth traveling to the underworld, worth scouring the afterlife in search of.

Vulkov died on a Wednesday. Or maybe a Thursday. Or a Saturday? Who the fuck knows. Novelists will give you this sort of detail, but I cannot. It's unimportant and hard to remember. He died all the same.

I was at his side. Madina too. He breathed and breathed and breathed and then stopped breathing.

It was silent in the room as we held our own breath.

"What do we do now?" I asked.

"I am not sure," Madina said.

We both began laughing. In the face of death, laughter is an affirmation of life. And, really, we didn't know what else to do.

"I've seen many elders die," she said. "But I've always been alone with them."

I took his rubber hand from the nightstand.

"Do you think we should bury him with this?"

"He told me once he did want to wear it with him to the afterlife. He hoped to be reunited with his limbs in heaven, he said. But just in case they weren't there, he wanted the hand in his grave somewhere. He was worried his real hands would go to hell for all the sins they'd committed."

We buried him in the fields, beneath a sturdy oak tree. I played a Bruce Springsteen song on a walkman. Madina and I each took one ear phone and listened. The earth was so frozen I had to use an ax to open his grave. It was as if the earth did not believe he was dead and was not prepared to take his corpse. I dug six feet down out of respect for our service. I would have felt like a roustabout private if I did any less. The hole felt entirely too large for his shrunken tree trunk of a body.

Despite the cold, Madina had found some flowers, which she laid on top of his grave. I filled in the dirt and we stood by his side until the moon rose above the dark night.

He was the first parent I buried, though I had lost my mother and father already. Madina rested her head on my shoulder. I felt like I should cry but no tears came. Even the sadness was not in attendance. It would come later.

She came inside with me but we knew we could not spend the night together in his house.

She cooked a fine meal, stewed meats and carrots. I played songs on a Jew's harp. We didn't know what to do with ourselves. We adjusted our legs, crossed and uncrossed our arms, played with our hair all night. What else is there to do?

I thought of all the years since he lost his limbs in that cave. I wondered if he was happy he had lived through the fire. He made the best of it, but I wondered still. And then, inexplicably, I wondered about the women he had been with in those years. He must have used his tongue to pleasure them. And then I felt guilty for thinking about such things. I tried to think only solemn thoughts. For one brief moment, I admit, I thought of how I had lost Natasha when he convinced me to join the secret space program. Was it his fault I had lost her? And had I stayed away from her out of respect for him? As if it would repudiate his decisions to find her and be with her and acknowledge it had been a mistake to lie to her and lose her to the Star City underground.

And I wondered where she was that night.

And I knew I had to find her.

I would write letters.

I would make telephone calls.

She was the only connection I had to my earlier life, to the time before everything went crazy. Natasha could point me in the right direction. Vulkov could no longer tell me where to go. But Natasha could guide me to happiness and peace. She was my lodestar.

15 / LODESTAR

"There are only two things now,
The great black night scooped out
And this fire-glow."
                    –D.H. Lawrence, "New Year's Eve"[1]

Most of my life, it seems, has been made up of orphan journeys: Put a few meagre possessions into a bag and head out on the road with no place to call home.

This time I loaded my typed manuscripts, wrapped in plastic to keep them dry, into one of Vulkov's suitcases. That was it. I had the clothes I was wearing.

"I hope to hear from you," Madina said.

"I have your address. I will write to you."

"You will find this Natasha. She must be looking for you, too. Any woman would find the man who had written such a song for her."

It was early morning in front of Vulkov's home. I promised to check in with her every three months, even if I found Natasha and settled down with her.

She handed me some baked potatoes.

"A hungry man cannot walk far," she said with a smile. And then she turned away, presumably so I would not see her crying.

My hand reached out and stroked the side of her face.

"Sweet Madina," I whispered. "You are too good for the men of Russia."

"This is my home. What other men are there but Russians?" She kicked at the ground. "Now get going! It is too cold for tears. They will become icicles on my face."

"Farewell," I said, and walked away, south towards Moscow.

It was early enough that the sun would catch me out on the highway, providing me some warmth if I could not catch a ride with some trucker. In American movies, they romanticize the great expanse of black top and the hitchhiker's world. Nothing is more miserable, though, than the scent of gasoline and smoke, the grit in your eyes, and the constant sense of being passed by. No wonder so many hitchhikers turn out to be serial killers... they were probably normal men when they began hitchhiking, but a life of upturned thumbs and automotive rejection made them monsters.

Railroad hobos had it easier, emotionally. A train cannot stop to pick up strangers, so there is no feeling of failure when a great locomotive blasts by without a second glance for the ragged pedestrian. But on the highway, each passing car is another decision, another driver deciding not to stop, not to be a samaritan. Even Jesus would have snapped and strangled a few motorists if there were highways in Jerusalem.

But my walking days were not wasted; I used the time to figure out how I could win Natasha back and where I would find her. Hopefully she would realize I had been forced to lie to her about my occupation and let her walk away only because I cared so much about her. It would be like in *Casablanca*, when

Laszlo returns to Ilsa and she has no choice but to let him back into her heart, no matter how attractive her bar-owning boyfriend was. And by no means was that an easy decision! Rick could have provided her free drinks for life, while Laszlo could only offer fear and hiding and his scar face. Still, she went with Laszlo at the end. It was only sad that the Germans were so evil they shot down her plane at the end of the film. (I have heard that the American version of the film does not include this scene, which was useful helping incite the passions of Russia against the Germans in the middle of World War II. Of course, without that scene, *Casablanca* ends poorly, with just an improvised conversation between Rick and Renault. Poor Americans! You've been lied to about the fate of Ilsa and Laszlo, and also about the effectiveness of fighting against evil regimes. It always ends poorly, with planes crashing. It would take you almost 60 years to learn this lesson.)

So assuming I could not win Natasha back instantly, I would have my work cut out for me. Still, I was a famous songwriter and soon to be a famous novelist. And I knew that somewhere, back before the madness of the world interfered, she had loved me. She must be able to love me again!

But where to find her? She had not tracked me down during my days at Space Discovery. And I had been too foggy to find her. Maybe she had gone home? Doubtful. She would only be happy in the city. Therefore she must be in Moscow, or at least had passed through Moscow on her way to an even bigger city: Paris, London, New York. I would hunt for every trace of her.

Maybe I could find her artist friends, the ones I had met after the Moscow Music and Peace festival. My first stop would be her old apartment. Thinking back on the beautiful morning I'd spent there after reuniting with her, I felt a longing to unlive part of my life, to return to that simple morning, wrapped in a blanket, when I had walked the streets and discovered a country that had matured and changed while I fought in Afghanistan. You can't repeat the past, of course. *You just can't.*[2]

Whatever had changed, whatever debts had been accrued and lessons learned, I would take into account. But whatever the price, I would pay it.

The world is a large place, over 25,000 miles around. Getting lost is easy. Despite countless hours of training in navigation and astronomy, I had no idea where I was. Geographically, I knew. But geography is nothing when it comes to really mapping the world. Emotions are mountains, longing is an ocean, separation is a canyon. A hard cock is a peninsula, a welcoming vagina is a hot spring, and passionate sex is an earthquake. No GPS can tell you these things. If you ask your car's navigation device how to find true love, it is useless. Sure, it can find you a gas station, but it cannot pinpoint love, no matter how many mechanical satellites are dedicated to it.

Nor can you stop and ask for directions. Nobody else knows where your true love is. Do you really think the clerk at a gas station can tell you where your darling lies? He barely has the intelligence to sell you a bag of potato chips.

No, love is a crap shoot. Maybe, like a nomad starving in the desert, you'll stumble across the oasis of a caring woman. Or maybe you'll collapse into the sand, and your bones will sink under dunes.

Does it ruin my metaphor to call Natasha my lodestar and simultaneously decry modern navigational practices? What I mean to say, however, is that no star chart could have told me where to find my bright luminous angel in the ether of the sky. I simply knew when I saw her. Love is like pornography, in that sense: You know it when you see it.

A just world would provide everyone with a soulmate within walking distance. My Natasha grew up near me. I was lucky. But like seeds of a flower, we had spread to the distant winds.

No matter how many metaphors it took, I would find one that made sense, *and* I would find *her*.

No cargo truck stopped for me, but a small Toyota did. The driver was an American. He worked for an oil company and went to great lengths to tell me he was "not a typical suit" or a "9-to-5 cubicle monkey." Instead, he went out into the field and tried "to make things happen." He was working on a pipeline of some sort. I tuned him out after a while, but it did nothing to stop him from yammering on about synergy and strategic interests in the pan-European free market.

When the radio began playing "Natasha's Song (for Natasha)", he sang along in broken Russian, some sort of phonetic approximation he had picked up after hearing it repeatedly.

"I wrote that song," I told him.

"Sure you did, Drago!" he snorted.

He called me Drago in reference to the American version of the film *Rocky IV*, at the end of which an honorable American boxer defeats a ruthless Soviet giant. The joke was on him, however, as *Rocky IV* was not a good movie. I mean, really.

Still, he provided me a ride back to Moscow, burning the fuel he hoped to steal from Russia and sell to Americans in their sports utility vehicles. Twenty miles outside of the city, we passed a billboard with my face and the words "Have you seen this man?"

"Uh oh, Ivan, are you wanted by the law?"

"No," I told him. Then I explained the history of the song we'd heard earlier and he slammed on the brakes.

"Shit, man! You're famous! Maybe you can help me with the Ministry of the Interior."

I opened the door and got out of the car. I would rather walk 20 miles than continue talking with this asshole.

"I can't help you. I am trying to find the woman I love. Also, you're a sack of shit." Then I repeated it in my best English. "You are being quite a bag of feces," I screamed.

I pulled my suitcase out of the back seat, turned my collar up, and began the long march to the city.

If you've never sought out a missing person, or tracked down a lost love, then you have no appreciation for the task at hand. You may assume that I will find Natasha as quickly as it takes you to read a paragraph or two. But remember that this was before the internet had widely spread across Russia, and my love had one of the most common names in the country. I knew where to start, perhaps, but I could not type her name into a web browser and find an address or a picture from her social network.

So I began at the old building I had known as hers. It had not been in great shape when I first visited; now it was barely the memory of a scrap heap. Rats had free reign. Thin drywall gave way to apartments and broken water lines stained the walls with blossoms of mildew. Pictures of haunted houses never do justice to the ravages of time and moisture. Yes, holes appear and cracks spread across the ceiling, but more tragic is the growth of fungus and green spores. The living world attacks a home more ferociously than dust.

I could scarcely believe that anyone still lived in the high rise, but for the trash bags at its base and mail overflowing from its slots. In the era of communist rule, mail slots had been built to tiny specifications as there was no junk mail, very few official correspondences, and personal mail was too expensive for all but the wealthiest and most corrupt apparatchiks. Once the floodgates of capitalism were opened, however, we were deluged with direct mail, questionable overtures, and credit card offers, which overtaxed the slender mail slots which had previously been sufficient.

As for the trash on the street – it was not that our people were messier than others, but merely that collection was sporadic and undisciplined now that the free market controlled it. Like American health insurance, Russian garbage was too much for the private sector to manage.

In the low shadows of this mess, I entered the building's lobby, hoping that my Natasha no longer lived here, as it would be too sad to find her among the ruins. I climbed the stairwell, ignoring the broken alarms and failing locks, and found myself on her old floor, an uninvited ghost in the hallway. My footsteps sank into the soft moldy carpet of the corridor. I was thankful when I saw that her apartment had been separated into four rooms, the tenants' names carved into the door, none of which was hers. She no longer lived in this abandoned mess.

Of course, that left the mighty question of where to find her.

I immediately considered seeking out our home town, finding the old silo and asking if anyone knew where she was. But as I thought about it, I realized that would be a great waste of time and travel. Natasha wanted to live in the city, and probably did not have the means to own a permanent address. If she returned home, she would not tell them where she lived, since she would not know how long she would be there. They, on the other hand, were not going anywhere, and she could always contact them if needed. At most, they might have her most recent return address, but that was unlikely to point me to her current location, and would swallow weeks of time in between.

In the modern world, I felt sure, a landlord would not know or be willing to share the current address of a former occupant. So I was on my own.

I decided to use my fame to my advantage.

But not before I stupidly walked around Moscow on my own, hoping to see her in restaurant windows, or opposite sidewalks.

Eventually, though, I smartened up and walked into the broadcast studios of Russia's biggest broadcaster. The receptionist recognized me immediately.

"You're Ilya Zamyatin!" she shrieked.

"Yes," I said calmly. "I would enjoy being interviewed by your station."

"I'll see what I can do," she said, as cooly as she could. But this was undercut by the words I overheard from her next conversation, with a producer. "Ilya Zamyatin is here in the lobby. He wants an interview! Of course we should grant him one, right?"

I smiled as if I could not hear her and bided my time.

Eventually, a famous reporter appeared in the lobby, flanked by two assistants. I assume they were there to yell and curse the receptionist if I had not been who she claimed, for, as soon as he saw me, he waved them away and approached me directly.

"You are Ilya Zamyatin," he confirmed.

"That's what I've been told my whole life," I said jokingly.

"Why would you be told anything else?" he asked.

I realized I was dealing with a moron.

"There is no reason."

"So you are Ilya Zamyatin?"

"Yes."

"Cosmonaut?"

"Indeed."

"Songwriter?"

"Of course."

"Hero of the Soviet Republic?"

"That I cannot comment upon or deny."

"And you wish to be interviewed on television?" he asked.

"More than anything."

With that, he ushered me into the inner sanctum of the television studio. An ugly woman applied make-up to my face. A producer barraged me with questions to determine what I would say. I explained that I was looking for Natasha, the woman who had inspired my hit song. They ate it up like a starving child eats grubs and maggots.

"And I have a message for her," I said, "which I hope to deliver on your airways. Sort of an exclusive," I added, as I was no dummy.

"We always have time for an exclusive message," the producer said.

And thus I made my way onto Russian television, delivering my heartfelt message of love and loss and truth. "If you are watching," I said to my dear Natasha,

...then you are probably feeling angry. Despite the vows we made to each other on our wedding day and our long history as friends, I lied to you. It does little good to say that I lied to protect you. To tell you that I couldn't tell you the truth without risking your life. And I know that it's unfair to put you in this position now, where you have left a cosmonaut because you didn't know he was one. All of that does not matter. The years fall away behind us. I can ask only for your forgiveness. I can hope that you will find it within you to look past the lies and deceit, to embrace instead the hopeful future like so many of our countrymen.

If I could go back in time, I would have said no to the space pro-gram. I would have stayed in Moscow with you happily. But I did not know of the secrets involved, and it seemed like my only choice was to go along with the lie. Anything else would have threatened you. Think back, Natasha, to that time when we feared the state. The secret police had taken away my parents. I couldn't let them take you away. It killed me inside to let you walk away, but it was better that I should die than you.

What I say now is hello. *I greet you, older than I once was. Sad-der and beaten down by life, although more prosperous than before. But the money does nothing for me. Only you can make me happy. So I ask you to call me. Send me some message about you. How are you doing, Natasha, and what is your life like?*

Perhaps you have found someone. I will learn to live with that if he makes you happy. I will shake his hand and offer him my best wishes. It will hurt, but I will wish you the best in your life together.

Or maybe you are alone and wish to remain that way. I would understand that as well. Loving me brought you only misery and deception.

But tell me at least that you are alive and that you know I love you, have always loved you and did my best never to hurt you. I tried to shield you from the state. I promise you I will never do that again. I will be honest in all things because the truth is that I love you, and that truth is more powerful than any dictator, any tyrant, any regime.

Natasha, that is all. I hope you do not mind that I have shared this message with the whole country. It may embarrass you, but I do not care how many people know I love you. And if it helped my voice reach you, I would take over every television station, radio tower and internet connection on the planet. I had to tell you this once, in case we should never meet again. I have loved you when we were together and loved you more dearly when we were apart. We are apart now, but I still love you, and I will love you until I die. Or until you die. Because only death can end this love.

I said it once, on our wedding day, and I say it again, Natasha. I am yours until death. I hope you will be mine.

Here I turned to the interviewer.

"Can I ask her to contact me here at the station?"

"Sure!" he smiled into the camera. "An exclusive ... our channel is the only home to correspondence regarding Ilya Zamyatin's true love. Contact us by telephone at the number below, or on our website..."

I removed my microphone so that my tears would not damage the electronics. I was crying. I grabbed my suitcase and somehow I made it down the stairwell, through the television studio's lobby and into the street. Great rock walls of buildings looked down upon me and did not care.

Concrete is the coldest material on earth. Snow eventually melts. Metal grows cold in the winter, but warm in the summer. Concrete never offers solace. It is barren, and the Soviet buildings crafted from it were as lifeless as the policies they embodied. They shed no tears for me.

But though I was crying, I felt a little better. I had tried to find Natasha. That was something, was it not?

Great black cars sped by, ushering Russia's new businessmen to meetings and parties. I was far from the part of town where poor orphans huddled and took comfort in their mutual loneliness. Here the city moved to fast to pause for sadness. A siren wailed somewhere in the distance. It was spring of 2001 and the long Soviet winter was still struggling as it gave way to the thaw of the Twentieth Century. Most of the people were drowning in meltwater.

A street musician ran by me, a host of policemen behind him. It was dangerous to be poor in the wealthy neighborhoods. I walked in the direction of the chase, thinking the guitar player would be headed someplace a man like me would feel safer and more at home. Sure enough, he led the officers down a few alleys which gave way to a great street market. As I lurched from one table of goods to the next, I began to notice looks of recognition as eyes recognized me. In the middle of the market-place, some vendor had erected a pyramid of old televisions for sale. Cheaper than the LCD modernities at the electronics stores, these old tube boxes were all tinted green and could handle limited numbers of channels. Still, they revealed moving pictures, flickering images that excite some primal feeling in man, some recognition of cave drawings come magically to life. On every screen, beneath a thin layer of static, was my face, my crying eyes as I asked Natasha to come find me. The station was replaying my interview, as were competing networks – there was no intellectual copyright to keep one channel's interview exclusive. On some smaller networks, you could see three different station logos on the bottom of the screen as one channel had recorded the footage from another channel that had recorded it from the original broadcast.

The TV salesman smiled and began yelling, "Come buy televisions from me! I have the stars around me!" He patted me on the back and eagerly pushed me on the shoppers as if I, too, was for sale. Taking charge, I stood on top of my suitcase and yelled even louder.

"Countrymen! I was a poor orphan, and now I have done well for myself. But I have spent the last few months caring for a dear old man in the country, and as a result have no money in my pockets. If any of you can buy me a drink, I will be sure to pay you back once I find the bank that has my music royalties!"

The crowd roared, and I followed a newly formed mob towards a great beer hall, left standing from the days of Soviet/German cooperation. The East German diplomats had built their own little Berlin in Moscow. While most of the specialty shops and German-language bookstores had disappeared when the Berlin Wall fell, the Beer Hall that had taken root remained. While our politics may vary from decade to decade, our Russian love of drink and drinking houses is more powerful than diplomatic considerations. True, we prefer vodka to beer, but we are not so set in our ways that we cannot appreciate the craft of a fine beer hall.

It was to this multi-floored establishment that we went, as I was hoisted on the shoulders of the crowd. They had some love for me, sure, but they also knew I was a ticket to free drinks for the poorest of them. The taps began flowing and those who could afford it picked up the tabs for the celebration. It was a pure evocation of the communist ideals. Each man paid to his own ability, and each man drank to his best ability. If the population had more payers and fewer drinkers, perhaps our empire would still be standing!

On a small TV screen behind the bar, we watched my interview over and over. It was not the last time a video would endlessly loop across the TV screens at the turn of the century.

After a bit of carousing, I was encouraged to give a toast.

At this point, they lifted me on the bar. I raised my pitcher (having abandoned glasses earlier) and shouted my second great address of the day.

Brothers! Countrymen! Survivors of the cruel Twentieth Century! Thank you for bringing me here! Thank you for helping out a comrade in need! While the fortunes of a nation may teeter this way and that...

(here I swayed back and forth on the bar, precariously)

... one thing is constant. That is the giving hearts of the Russian people! Have we not given up almost everything these past 80 years? We gave our children to the war, and our freedom to Stalin, and our economy to the Cold War. And now we give everything to the pack of wolves in the Kremlin, everything but our hope for a better future. So let's drink to that hope!

(here I drank half of my pitcher and everyone joined me and drank from their glasses)

I hope to find my Natasha. For those of you who already know where your Natasha is, I hope that you never lose her. If you have yet to meet your Natasha, I hope you meet her soon. My fondest wish is that every Russian man find and keep his darling Natasha, that he be faithful and true, and that no lie should tear them asunder. Would that the world were a fair enough place for this to come true!

The crowd cheered and drank and lifted me on its shoulders and we danced and moved until things became cloudy and, like Natasha, the whole night disappeared into the fog.

16 / A NEW DAY

Each night we go to sleep, assuming the world will still be there in the morning – and this terrifies us so much that we drink ourselves to oblivion. Look at the men and women in airport lounges. Put them in pajamas and you'd see them as they are each night, taking a drink to steady their nerve as they embark upon a perilous journey.

What of all the opportunities lost if we were never to awaken? We might never learn how that mystery novel on the nightstand ends, might never tell our parents we love them (*we should have done it years ago*), might never learn to dance, might never again see the women and men we love. When you're sleeping, they say, and dreaming of falling, you must be sure to wake up before you land. Sleeping is falling dangerously.

So it is a minor miracle to wake up. To be given another chance. Yet we are blind to the miracle of the morning when we are hung over. Oh well. We need the spirits to help us sleep, but they keep us from appreciating the waking.

All of this is just to say that I woke up with a massive

headache, crusty flakes of saliva on the sides of my mouth, and the smell of old beer climbing up my nose and clawing at the back of my throat. I had none of the thoughts of life and sleep that I described above in that moment, but I feel that too many chapters of my life so far have started with me waking up in strange places after falling down drunk, so I buried the lede.

My pillow that morning was a stack of newspapers. They were that day's papers, so I knew I had stayed out carousing late enough for the morning edition to be flung like a bag full of dead cats toward the newsstand under which I'd taken shelter. Then I'd laid my head upon it, my weary face upon a bleary ink-smeared halftone picture of my face, for the top story of his publication was my televised plea to Natasha. I struggled to lift myself, found my forearms too weak to lift me, and felt sad that Vulkov was gone and now neither of us could seemingly do a push up. I rolled over onto my back and rocked myself forward until I could sit up.

It was a morning in the city and I thought of the morning after the concert, when I'd promised Natasha in her bathtub never to leave her. How much I had fucked up things, broken promises and wasted my days. In all the passing years, what had I learned, aside from how to put on pants in the morning and not to shit in an alley. I found my pants, hanging from the low tin roof of the news stand. I leave it to scientists to figure out why they were up there. My hypothesis: I was worried about being robbed as I slept, and so threw them up there as one would put valuable food in a tree to prevent it from being eaten by bears when camping in the woods.

I pulled up my cold denim pants and rubbed my eyes. Another man was sleeping on the curb at my feet, his head on my suitcase. He was not known to me, but I nudged him with my foot and we wordlessly agreed to seek breakfast together. In the streets, we passed the embarrassed red faces of lovers returning home. We brushed the sleeping husks of homeless men and gypsies. Soon we were near a branch of the famous *McDonald's* which had spread the joyous capitalist treasure of Big Macs as a peace offering and reward for the mere price of a month's wages and the submission of our brave country to the greedy eagle of America. I had eaten a hamburger from this place and not been greatly impressed. Still, it was open, and I found my pockets mysteriously stuffed with cash – hopefully I had been gifted the sums by fellow drinkers at the Beer Hall and had not robbed a bunch of peasants sometime in the night.

Scraping my tongue across the roof of my mouth a few times, I prepared to talk.

"I'm Ilya," I said.

"Colin," he said.

"Russian?"

He shrugged.

Entering the bright white palace, we shielded our eyes. Wondrous smells greeted us: grease, beef tallow, salt, eggs, milkshakes, coffee. As our eyes had yet to adjust to their duties, we were forced to order by pointing vaguely at colored squares on the counter top, the geometric grid representing an array of choices. The clerk had to repeat the total a number of times before I could comprehend. He tried Russian first, then English, until I waved him back and he repeated in Russian. Peeling off the bills, I looked at him after each one until he nodded and took the small pile from me. It was more than I could handle to look at him and then down at the money and back up. Moving my head was trouble.

Then Colin and I sat on some hard plastic tables. Was it possible we were the only customers in this place? How quickly the shine wears off a golden arch, I thought.

All my negative thoughts about the establishment disappeared, however, when I bit into the salty velvet Egg McMuffin. In quick succession, I devoured the crunchy hash brown wafer, and swallowed the contents of an orange juice container. Only the coffee was a disappointment, but the rest of the meal was a revelation. No wonder America had won the Cold War! They were fighting for Egg McMuffins. I would conquer a legion of giants for this breakfast. And it provides motivation to a country full of otherwise lazy fools, who must wake up before 10:30 AM in order to get this goldenrod breakfast treat.[1]

I ate three Egg McMuffins that day, and five hash brown wafers.

"Fuck me," I said to Colin.

"I would kill for one of these sandwiches."

I laughed and patted him on the back.

But weeks later, I saw on the television that he had, in fact, killed a couple outside the restaurant in order to take their McDonald's bag and its breakfast from them. And a little over two years later, the restaurant itself was the target of a car bomb which nearly destroyed it.[2]

After we parted, I found a humble park bench and sat to watch the day unfold. Moscow comes alive like a zombie, rising from the frigid vaults of a coroner's locker. First a finger twitches. Then a knee creaks to life. You're so busy watching each tiny detail that you fail to notice the brainless body lurching towards you with a taste for your brains. Many good people have been killed by the city. By the time Moscow was staggering at full pace, I had been recognized a few times. Many citizens wished me well in my quest to find Natasha.

Of course, I had no mobile telephone. Since New Year's, I

had been a vagrant and rural farmer with no fixed address. How was she to find me? Through the television studio was the only way, so that was where I eventually headed. I took my time, however. Anxious as I was to reunite with my soul mate, to hand her a poster with my face on it and say the words "I am your soul mate," I dreaded being forced to wait on the air, being strung along by the television station to goose their ratings. It seemed the best plan would be to wait until early evening. By then, she would most likely have contacted them, if she was ever going to, and when I showed up, they might force me on the air for an interview, but they would tell me what she said, or point me in her direction as they did so.

I decided to pass the day in Moscow like a tourist, taking in the many sites I had missed in my abbreviated childhood and civilian life. Marching around Red Square in uniform is no way to experience hundreds of years of culture. With only one day to spend, it seemed a poor use of time to stand in line for hours to see Lenin's Tomb, so I skipped that particular attraction, despite all the historical weight of it and the tremendous effect that man had on my life. Although, to be fair, Josef Stalin had a larger, more insidious hand in my upbringing, and I would not have gone to see his corpse even if there were no line and it was watched over by sexy blonde women with giant breasts and willing minds who encouraged visitors to kick the rotting carcass and spit on his grave for all the trouble he caused and orphans he created. So, no mausoleums for me that day.

Gorky Park. The Kremlin. The State Historical Museum. St. Basil's Cathedral. In these places, wrapped in the warm blankets of history, lying on a mattress of non-Russian tourists, I was able to forget myself and my troubles and merely enjoy the splendor of the country. The colorful spires ascended toward heaven like any great people wish their cities to do. The recent past may have been torture, but some magnificent artists had grown and prospered here, left these indelibly beautiful fingerprints, and then signed the great history books along side Czars and generals, popes and poets, saviors and madmen.

Luckily I had no camera, and so the memories of this day are all the more vivid. We eat more hungrily if we expect a drought, and we see more fully if we think we'll have no pictures to remind us later.

As the vendors broke down their stalls and folded up their blankets, I found my way back to the television studio where I hoped the news would be good. A few reporters snapped my picture as I entered the lobby and a great commotion broke out. I felt like a famous felon making his way from court, except that my only crime was letting love slip away.

An eager producer grabbed me by the elbow.

"Where have you been?!" he asked incredulously. "We want to get you on the air!"

He was from the generation that could not believe someone might pass up an opportunity to be on television. His hair was cropped closely, his glasses thin and dark, his turtleneck thick and the color of ash. An earpiece spoke garbled commands directly into his brain, leaving a hand free for his clipboard.

"I have been walking around this wonderful city of ours," I told him.

"That's great! Say that on the air. *You love Moscow.* People eat that kind of shit right up."

"I don't wish to be a chef making shit sandwiches."

"No, no, of course not. Just tell the truth."

"Have you heard from Natasha?"

"I, uh, I ... wait until you're on the air. I want your reaction to be real."

"What else could it be but real?"

"I'm going to put you in here. Someone else will come do your make-up and give you a headset."

"I don't want those things."

"Trust me, you'll need them. You can't be on TV without make-up."

And then he left me in a tiny room, sitting behind half of a desk, staring into a bright white light and a camera. It felt like getting an eye exam.

To be honest, it felt a bit like going to space as well. If you've ever been interviewed on television, then you know what I'm talking about: not a man on the street interview, but an in-studio encounter. That used to be an experience reserved for great minds, historical figures and the like. Now it is the domain of anybody willing to subject themselves to it. *Live in a house with complete strangers for a year, and then be interviewed on television!*

I kept waiting for someone to explain what was happening.

Finally I heard a voice.

"Ilya?"

"Yes."

I wasn't sure where to look.

"We understand you're waiting to hear back from your long lost love Natasha."

"Yes, I am."

There was static in my ear and a long pause.

"Hold for twenty seconds," a voice said.

"Are you talking to me?" I asked.

There was no answer.

Twenty seconds later, a new voice boomed into my ear: "We're talking now with Ilya Zamyatin, the famous cosmonaut and songwriter who last night made a televised plea to his childhood sweetheart Natasha Babel. But he does not know where she is."

I nodded. And then

A different voice whispered into my ear, "Why don't you smile?"

I didn't like being told what to do by a random voice, so I set my face into a scowl.

"Come on," the voice said. "Smile. You're on television."

"Excuse me," I said loudly. "Am I on television? I'm just sitting in the dark in a room where one of your producers put me. All I want to know is whether Natasha contacted the station to find me."

"Yes," the anchor's voice said cheerfully. "We're just getting to that."

"Hold for connection," said the quieter voice.

What was going on?

I guessed that I was hearing the audio feed of both the anchor and his producer, and that I was, at least some of this time, being shown on the air, sitting in a studio, doing my best not to smile.

"And now," said the anchor, "we have another guest, by telephone."

"Ilya?"

I couldn't help it. *I smiled.* It was Natasha. The producer got what he wanted, but, then, so did I.

"Natasha!" I jumped up as if she was walking into the room.

"Sit down," the voice in my ear said.

"Where are you?" I asked.

"I'm in..."

Suddenly her feed was cut.

"Whoa, not so fast," said the anchor's voice. "We're arranging for a surprise reunion, so we don't want Ilya to know exactly where she is."

I tore off my microphone and opened the door, letting myself into the hall.

I could still hear the voice of a producer in my ear.

"What are you doing? Get back to the camera! No one can see you!"

I stopped and turned around, then picked my old microphone from the floor. I screamed into it.

"Tell me where she is!"

I heard the producer yelp at the loud sound in his ear.

"Listen," I continued, "this isn't a game or a TV show. I'm a real person. She's a real person. We don't want to be part of your soap opera. We just want to talk to each other."

"But our viewers are entitled to see..."

I tapped on the microphone several times with my finger and the producer moaned again at the loud noise in his ear.

"Get back in that studio!" he cried. "Or you'll never see her again."

I laughed.

"I doubt that. You're a TV station, not the KGB. She knows I'm looking for her. I know she knows. We'll find each other. And I'll be sure to let some other TV station film our reunion, just to piss you off, you dog-penis taster."

I tore out my ear piece as well.

"No, wait!" I heard his voice growing quieter behind me as I stomped down the hall.

"Wait!" his voice again, but muffled now. He was yelling at me from behind a large window on the set of the broadcast.

I gave him the middle finger.

He urgently began scribbling a note on his clipboard. He turned it around and held it to the glass. It read:

SHE'S IN THE BUILDING!!

I stalked up to the window and pounded on it. He jumped back.

"Where!?" I screamed.

He looked at me and pointed down a hallway.

I ran. Suddenly I realized a camera man was trailing behind me, trying to keep up.

I opened every door in the hall.

Behind the first door, a man was applying make up as he looked at himself in a mirror.

Behind the next, a woman was viewing sports footage on a small television monitor while she smoked a cigarette. If I hadn't been in such a hurry to find my soulmate Natasha, I might have entered this room and made love to the woman.

Behind the next door, a cameraman was yelling into a telephone.

I passed a lobby and saw another hallway. It stretched into the distance. And offered many more doors.

Turning quickly, I grabbed the camera man's arm and asked him politely, "Which room is Natasha in?"

He pointed his camera at the floor and whispered softly.

"She's not in a room on this hall. She's upstairs in Studio G. They're trying to stall you while they set up camera equipment so they can get your reunion from every angle."

"Thanks," I said. There was an elevator in the lobby, but I couldn't wait for it. I opened the emergency exit door next to it and found myself in the stairwell. An alarm went off and began screaming its digital shrieks. I was up a flight of stairs before I noticed the noise. The door back into the hall was locked, so I stepped back and prepared to kick it.

"You might hurt yourself," warned the camera man coming up quick behind me.

"Love is a source of super powers," I said, and then kicked at the big steel door.

It swung open, setting off a second alarm, and series of flashing red lights down the hallway of the second floor.

A young man in the hallway was scared by my sudden violent entry from the stairwell and shrank back from the busted door.

"Which way to Studio G?" I asked.

He pointed in one direction and ran in the other.

I found the studio and opened the double doors leading into it.

A different producer yelled "Wait!" as I entered. I ignored him.

Bright lights glared in the center of this studio, and so I headed toward the light.

One giant camera turned to face me as I ran into the middle of Studio G.

Everyone backed away from a plush red chair and its occupant.

There she was.

Natasha.

17 / GORKY PARK

You probably saw the video. It was hard not to see it, as every station aired it repeatedly that night and throughout the week. She jumps up out of the chair and we embrace. We kiss. A reporter tries to ask us a question and we ignore him.

"Let's get out of here," I say.

"I'm with you," she says.

We run from the studio, and the camera sees only our backs through the hallway, down the stairs, through the lobby and out into the night.

The night which was ours.

"We found each other!" I screamed.

"Never let us walk away from each other again," she said.

And we kept running, through the streets, all the way to Gorky Park.

What happened next cannot really be described or explained, except perhaps to those of you reading this book in bed next to the person you love, if you ever lost that person and got them back. Whatever time is lost to the years is made up for by the certainty of the reunion. You know, now, completely, that you are bound together by the universe's desire. This does not go for every couple that parted ways and reunited to fuck every now and again, but only to the serious couples, the ones who conquered separation and strife, who stared down turmoil. Any country that survives a civil war comes back stronger. Most countries don't survive. Just as somebody who faces death and lives another day has a new appreciation for breathing and seeing, feeling and touching the world, so too did Natasha and I have a certainty and a sense of wonder about our embrace there in the cold snowy field of Gorky Park. We tumbled together and saw in each other's eyes the future and every tomorrow we would cherish, for the only future that mattered was the one where we were together.

Put another way, we became the kind of people who understand the widow banging her fists on the coffin of a dead husband and the man who visits his wife's grave every day and communes with her – those readers who have seen these things and laughed at them or questioned the emotions have never experienced love completely.

I wrapped my arms around her; she wrapped her legs around me. We had reunited before, in our dreams, and now that it was actually happening, our dreams seemed shallow depictions, mere sketches compared to the grand museum-ready masterpiece of the real thing. To the rest of the world, we probably looked like any other couple huddling together for warmth on a cold night. Witnesses cannot see love, cannot vouch for true connection.

It took a while for the cameras to catch up with us. And when they finally did, they gave us distance. We kissed on the ground, illuminated by the TV lights, our intermingling narrated by the anchormen standing in a circle around us, as if we were children rescued from a well or championship athletes. Truthfully, I was so lost in Natasha's presence that I did not notice them filming us. While it may have been uncivilized to make love there in the park, I did not intentionally have sex on television like some of my enemies later suggested. But after years of separation, after the uncertainty of space and the twentieth century, we were not going to be prevented in our coupling. We pulled each other's clothes open as much as we needed to, our genitals at once red hot and freezing in the Russian night, and then, as the videotape shows, we pounded each other raw with the animal power of great wild boards or frenzied elephants, only younger and skinnier. Was it violent? Perhaps. It was not angry, though. I felt her warm legs part and made my way inside. If you are reading this book as a bedtime story to your children, this may be a good point to stop reading. Not just because it will become graphic in its depiction of sex, but also because you must have been reading to your child for over eight hours at this point.

Wrapped in the comfort of her vagina, feeling her insides hug me tightly, I was like an insect willing – perfectly willing – to leave a part of me there forever, to be killed and eaten alive by her just for that one moment. I would be a praying mantis to her altar, a voluntary fly in her black widow's web, allowing myself to be eaten away by her venom. I screamed and sweated, she clung to me, and pounded on my back with her fists.

"Keep yourself inside me!" she yelled, a bit of dialogue that was broadcast across most of the networks of the time.

"I will never again pull out of you," I grunted.[1]

We sank deeper and deeper into the snow drift that was our mattress, the heat of our thrusting melting the ice around us as we disappeared from view.

The cameramen edged closer, like scientists on the edge of an active volcano, interested by the sight and majesty of nature, but cautious and worried about their own safety.

Eventually we hit dirt, and our fucking became a new art, a rhythmic attack, the slapping of skin and coats against each other, the percussive sex of pornography, so common in films and videos, yet rarely seen in the wild, in real life, now manifested itself before the eyes of the Russian people, something dangerous and beyond any known scale, like a Chernobyl of private parts, a sexual siege of her Stalingrad, an October uprising that covered her Odessa Steps with bodily fluids. I rammed my manhood into her just like the powerful railroad plowed through Anna Karenina in Leo Tolstoy's magnificent erotic novel. I uncled her vanya; she parted her wet seagull to take in my proud, firm *Chekov* of an erection. Her tightly guarded gulag rode my long, curved archipelago.

In short, reader, we had sex.

18 / IN THE YEAR 2000

Apartments were easy to come buy in those days. Construction and renovation ruled the streets as unregulated money flowed into Russia. Our country was like a starving man who finds himself at a great banquet – not believing his good luck, he gorges himself unhealthily, tasting every dish he dreamed of eating for years and years until his stomach bursts, and he dies there under the salad bar, a victim of his own feverish gluttony. China knew to introduce capitalism in small bites. Russia became a bloated mess.

Natasha and I took an apartment in a new glass tower in Moscow. The builders were happy to give us one of the first completed units so they could advertise our happy story's happy ending in their growing complex of suites and condominiums. We partook of the bounty of the West. Natasha had a modern kitchen installed. I bought the largest television available. We covered our place in fine upholstery, filled our closets with beautiful linens, built a wine room and stocked it with the best French vintages.

Perhaps we went overboard, but one of us was an orphan who had known mostly poverty and military life, and merely tasted the wealthy life through someone else's largess, and the other was an art student who had been sharing a small room with three other friends, rotating once a month to see whose turn it was to sleep under the broken wall where the rain fell into the room before freezing along the floor.

You might suspect that we installed an extravagant bathroom, too, with a bidet, but you would be wrong. We put in a simple workingman's toilet. If we wanted to spray water up our assholes, we could use the detachable shower head. As Plato said, things should go into a toilet, but nothing should come out of it.[1]

We settled into living. I had to correspond with a publisher about my novels, for which Natasha designed the covers. We built her an art studio next to my home office.

Describing happiness is generally boring, and you risk offending those readers who are not happy themselves. Still, I will attempt to put some account of our joy in these pages.

Perhaps it's best to include a passage from my runaway best-selling novel, *The Space Wife*:

In the dark chambers of the sky, Captain Stigorsky found something truly alien to him: love.

The beautiful Neptunian enchantress Sohshyre approached his starcraft in her voluptuously curved saucer. Her voice whispered into his intercom.

"Earthling," she called. "Follow my ship's trajectory. I can guide you from this dangerous meteor belt."

Stigorsky knew he would follow her anywhere. He engaged his Protshy Blasters and steered his ship expertly behind hers. Even the escaping force of her alien propulsion system complimented his ship's-- he could pull in tightly to her rear without risking his own ship. In fact, it was safer that way.

After twisting and turning through the stormy meteor field, they finally came together through the night and landed on the surface of her planet, Neptune. Her saucer glided down a crater and entered a space cave. Stigorsky followed.

Behind the icy rock wall he saw great metal blast shields protecting an airlock. The two of them passed through to safety behind the walls of the airlock. This was her home.

"What is your Earthling name?" she asked as she climbed from her saucer.

"My name is Stigorsky. I am from a place called Russia on the planet Earth. The third stone from the bright star we called the sun."

"I know this place," she said.

She helped him from his clunky ship's cockpit. He was startled to find her naked! Or at least he believed her to be naked. She was green, with soft skin unlike anything he expected to find on the cold surface of Neptune. Her nipples were a darker green than the rest of her, and a bush of brown hair covered the pink of her private spaces.

He blushed and turned away.

"Earthling, do not be ashamed," she told him, putting her hand on his shoulder.

"On my planet, we cover ourselves," he said quietly.

"But you are on my planet now," she said in a pleasant voice. "Please make yourself comfortable in our customary way."

She began removing his space suit. He gave

up his objections and let her strip him down to his space underwear.

She felt his form beneath it and smiled.

"I have been alone in space for quite some time," he said.

"You are alone no longer."

She tore his space underwear off and pushed him up against the smooth surface of her saucer, where they made space love for two minutes. (Remember that on Neptune, much further from the sun than Earth, two minutes is more like four hours, so that is quite impressive!)

The bliss was something beyond earth.

Stigorsky and Sohshyre settled into the cave and began working on new technologies. She was busy most of the day harvesting happiness.

"It grows like a plant here, beneath the surface," she told Stigorsky.

"Then all here must be happy?"

"Those who survive are happy. But often Neptunians become so enamored of harvesting happiness that they forget to take their protein meals. They waste away in a happy slumber."

"That happened on my planet. We were happy until 2021, and then we became so addicted to our ..." he choked up and could not finish the sentence. "Soon, it became difficult to survive. That's why men like me were sent into space, to find a new home."

"You can live with me here," she said. "I once loved a man just like you, and now here you are. It is truly like the Great Comet has answered my prazers."

"Your prazers?"

"They are like your human *prayers*."

While she was away in her harvesting module, he tinkered with her protein farms. Everything was grown hydroponically, with melted ice from the surface of the planet. Using time-tested Russian agricultural methods, he soon increased her output to record levels. With a large excess of food, he had time for other projects.

Stigorsky began growing flowers, using the seeds he carried in his spaceship's Ark Hatch. Taken from some of the world's last remaining grain preserves, the seeds had been sent along with the space explorers in the hopes of taming planets and making them hospitable. He grew roses and daises, tulips and lilies. Some chemical reaction in the Neptunian water caused the flowers to bloom more vividly than they ever had on Earth. Perhaps it was the happiness coursing like a mineral through the waters of the planet. Or maybe it was the tender care of Stigorsky's thumb. A plant tended with love, after all, spreads its petals and shows the true blossom of desire and care.

They were happy together.[2]

I will leave them there, in their perfectly described happiness, before the invading Plutonians appear on the black horizon one night to ravage and burn the planet's happiness fields. A fierce interplanetary war follows, as I'm sure you know, if you've seen the famous movie based on my book.

But that is for another time. Buy *The Space Wife* if you wish to know how it ends. For now, it is enough to consider the happiness they found together. I used that passage because it illustrates how our love isolated us like were living on another planet.

But no marooned hero can live forever on an island. Eventually the conquistadors pass by in great sailing ships and destroy the paradise. I was slow to notice the approaching gloom. At first it was just necessary parts of my life. As my books made money, I became a useful spokesperson for the Russian imagination. Great seminars invited me to sit on panels and opine about the new century and coming technological advances. I was full of shit. I knew no more about the future than a cheese sandwich does.

Still, it was great fun and paid for Natasha's extravagances, and mine as well. We collected guitars. She painted great canvases. I told people that space travel would never come to the common man. I engaged in a great public debate about space tourism and its economic feasibility as a potential savior of Russia. We had the rockets and the landing pads. *Could we not send billionaires to space*, people asked, *could we not launch former boy band singers into orbit?*

A few such trips could bring in rubles, maybe dollars. But once you've tapped the three or four courageous millionaires, I said, who will buy the next tickets? Space is no substitute for a vacation. It is cold, dark, bleary, and despite the expanse of open nothingness stretching into the night, you are forced to remain in a cramped quarters for warmth and safety. In short, space is Siberia. Try selling trips to Siberia, I proclaimed, and see how far that gets you!

For this I was roundly booed and disinvited from a few conferences. But I was going to be an honest man in Russia, even if it put me in the smallest of company. Lies had ripped Natasha and I apart before. This time, the truth would hold us together.

19 / PRAVDA MEANS TRUTH

An honest newspaper is a strong defense against tyranny. The weak press is a tool of a dictator. The comics pages are stupid either way, but *true*. Listen! One famous cartoon in Russia depicts an orange bear, lazy and sarcastic, named Garfikiev.[1] Is this bear punished for his listless ways? No! He is cared for by a sad sack of a man, Ivan, who talks to this animal because no one else will. This comic strip, while stupid, is the *truest* thing in the newspaper. The lazy, short-cut takers will always survive off the hard work of honest men, the cunning beasts learn to feign domestication so that they may lie down with humans, taking advantage of their kind nature and their lonely longing for happiness and companionship.

That deceitful orange bear is not merely fiction and drawing. He is a man named Vladimir Putin.

How hard it is to watch this villain take the stage of history as I look back at those years. He is a thug who hid in some dank sewer throughout the warming of Glastnost, waiting until it was safe for his cold blooded hide to return to the surface.

The KGB, like a tumor damaged by radiation, grew back, quietly and unchecked, to metastasize to Russia's fragile bones.

I have mixed metaphors because Putin is all these things: a bear, a sewer rat, and a cancer.

Also, I called him a "wart on the ass of the country" on live television. Perhaps you remember that? I discovered, pretty quickly, that my insults about Putin never made it into print because he controlled all of the major newspapers. Sure, I could criticize him in the small weeklies, but they only circulated in Paris and London, or were quoted in *The New York Review of Books*. But nobody read any of those things, they just piled them on the coffee tables of their cosmopolitan apartments to impress you with their intellect. Television, however, is the great direct connection with the people.

You can complain about reality television and cheap tawdry spectacles, but they offer a rare chance for celebrities to speak freely to the masses. Most of the time we don't care what celebrities say, because they are empty-headed bags of excrement. But for all their sins, they can speak to the world like preachers and prophets. So I took advantage of my celebrity status.

I appeared on a musical talent search show and compared every contestant to Putin: "You're awful, your voice makes my ears hurt, and you have no stage presence, but you don't offend me as much as Vladimir Putin!" or "You were so bad that whoever wrote that song is probably rolling over in his grave. The grave that Putin buried him in." or "You can't sing; Putin sucks!"

(I was not invited back to the *Moscow Music Hits Finder* program.)

Then there was the time I appeared on a televised round table discussing space travel.

"I would not go back to space for any reason," I told the interviewer after being asked about space tourism. "Except to get as far away as possible from Vladimir Putin."

While serving as emcee of a May Day parade, I told viewers, "Here comes a float representing the people's hardships. I assume it is a bust of Vladimir Putin."

After a while, I stopped getting invited onto any televised programs.

Fear sneaks up on you. The scariest part is that it makes you doubt yourself – are you paranoid, or is someone following you? Maybe someone *is* following you *and* you've become paranoid as well?

By December, I knew I was being investigated. Hundreds of Christmas cards poured in from my fans, but they didn't open properly. From my secret space program days, I recognized the crinkly feel of the envelopes having been steamed open and resealed. Someone was reading my mail! And think of the waste of government resources that entailed! Some beady eyed bureaucrat in a damp concrete basement perusing picture after picture of Christmas trees and mangers and ice skating scenes, looking, presumably, for secret coded messages to me – maybe this camel represents a command from CIA handlers ... maybe this candy can is actually a microfilm ... maybe you could rearrange the letters in "Christmas" to spell "CIA SR H MTS" meaning *CIA senior handler mountains* —that had been meticulously planted in one out of hundreds of holiday greetings. And this is one of the secrets of Putin's dark genius. In this day and age of electronic communication, nobody would risk sending hard copies of spy messages. But recruiting thousands of secret policemen and spies helps reduce unemployment, so it serves a purpose to pretend my mail must be read over and over by various apparatchiks. Politicians: put people to work and they will keep you in office!

And all of it was a glorious waste. I was not on anyone's payroll. I merely wanted people to know about Putin.

Natasha got the worst of it, though. She had remained relatively sheltered from the hardships of military life and covert operatives, leaving me at the foggy crossroads of my entry to the secret space program. Now she was rudely introduced to the state at its worst. Large men followed her and bumped into her. The first two times that happened, she chalked it up to a growing lack of civility in Moscow. Eventually she saw the pattern. When she drove into town, her car was ticketed or her tires were slashed. Telephone conversations with her friends were interrupted by clicking sounds.

"Are we in danger?" she asked me finally.

"Not so much," I told her.

We were drinking wine at the end of a quiet evening together.

"I don't feel safe here," she said.

"I am too famous for Putin to try to kill me."

"You think he wants to kill you?"

"No, no. I just meant my celebrity offers us some security. The people would turn on him if he came after us."

"'*Came after us?*'"

"Look. If things start to get bad, we can get out. At the first sign of real trouble, we'll move to Europe. Or New York."

"Where they say '*I love New York?*'"

"Yes. Everyone loves it there! That's where Batman lives."

We refilled our wine glasses and she sat back into my lap on the couch.

"Could we really move so easily?"

"Of course. If you want, we could move to Los Angeles and stay with my friend Shaquille O'Neal."

"And you won't insist on staying to fight the good fight?"

"Not a bit. I'm not like Rick from Casablanca. I'll get on the plane with you. Only this time, it won't be shot down." (Remember that we had only seen a version of the movie where Victor and Ilsa's airplane is shot down by the Germans.)

"Then I should start planning our new home. It's like planning for a baby!"

"We'll pack a suitcase and keep it by the door, just like pregnant women do."

She laughed. "We should come up with a secret signal! A code word so we'll know if it's time to leave Russia."

Natasha scratched her perfect head.

"Hmmm. Let's figure this out. It can't be something crazy, in case we need to say it in public. So it can't be 'florfgat' or 'zolfagar.' But it can't be a common word, or else we might use it accidentally. So it can't be 'dinner' or 'the.'"

"*The* would be an awful secret code word."

We laughed and fell back on the couch, saying "the" over and over again in simulated urgent tones.

"Pass 'THE' milk."

"Has 'THE' newspaper come yet?"

"Where's 'THE' beef?"

We kissed for a while. Eventually Natasha sat back up.

"I know! It should be two words, they can be common, but unlikely to occur in the same sentence. That way if one of us juxtaposes them, then we'll know trouble's afoot!"

"What about 'ramrod' and 'caterpillar'?"

"No, silly. That's too hard. Try to use them in a sentence!"

"That caterpillar looks pretty stiff. I'd say he's almost ramrod straight."

"Uck! That will not do, darling."

We kissed some more.

We thought for a while about the perfect words.

Then we spoke at the same time:

"*Shampoo*," I said.

"*Razor*," she said.

"*Shampoo razor!*" we chimed together.

"It's perfect," she said, laughing. "But only remember not to say them together accidentally."

"What if I have to go to the supermarket and buy shampoo and a razor?"

"You can't say that! Our secret code is only effective if we don't use it."

"Then I'll say, 'I'm going to the supermarket, but I cannot tell you what I will purchase there.'"

"That is fine. Just don't say 'shampoo' and 'razor' together or I will think we need to flee the country."

"Can I say them one more time now just to get them out of my system?"

"Of course," she laughed. "But then never again."

"Shampoo." I paused. "Razor."

"That's it. The next time one of us says those two words in the same sentence, then we'll leave Russia."

"I don't think it will come to that," I said, hugging her close.

"But it doesn't hurt to be safe."

"Promise me one thing," I said to her. "If I do use the signal, go without me. If I'm in jail or call you on the phone, or even if I shout it across a crowded plaza on a winter night ... don't wait to see me again, get on the next jet plane or locomotive or hitch a ride in a Volvo, but get out of the country as soon as you can."

"I will, if you promise the same thing."

"Sorry," I told her. "You'll have to live with the knowledge that you must leave me here in Russia, while I will never let you go again. I tried that once, and I didn't like it."

"I tried it too," she said.

We stopped talking and made love on the couch.

I wish I could tell you it was a tender and soulful moment, but really we went at it like furious hounds. Furious, but tasteful.

Natasha began working at a gallery. We didn't need money, but she enjoyed making contacts in the art world and interacting with other painters. At the same time, I consulted on the motion picture adaptation of my first novel, *The Space Orphan*. Set decorators, costume artists, make-up designers, production painters – all of them pelted me with questions:

"Are the homes on Jupiter angular or spherical?"

"What color belt does Major Stigorsky wear?"

"What do the Mercurians' shoulders look like?"

"What color is the moon?"

I answered the best I could, although one day I pulled the director aside and confessed that I did not really know the answers to these questions. I had made up the story in my head, and saw a few small details, but had not painted a giant canvas of the universe in my mind.

"For God's sake, man, don't tell them that!" the director said.

"I wouldn't tell them that! I'm too embarrassed."

"The producers of this movie were insistent that I follow your guidelines to the letter! And the public will insist on it too!"

"Well, as long as you know I'm making it up as I go along."

"Don't tell anyone else!"

"It will be our secret," I said.

And it was, until I wrote this book.

Not that I did a bad job. Looking back, when I watch the film today, I wonder if my depictions of the aliens and horrifying landscape of other planets were inspired by Afghanistan more than by my time in outer space. My choices, which were greatly enhanced and articulated by the filmmakers, touched a chord with the movie going public of Russia that spring. The film's success put me back on the cultural map. Slightly chastened by the previous winter's brush with state thuggishness, I kept a lower profile. In interviews, I talked about the movie, about space, about music, about anything but Putin. I resisted the questions that called on me to link Jupiter to Afghanistan to Chechnya.

"It's all just a story!" I said lightly. In fact, I said that particular phrase so many times that one entertainment magazine used it as the title of a profile of me linked to the release of my third novel, *The Space Wife*, in July.

Ilya Zamyatin: It's All Just a Story
(reprinted from the July 7, 2001 issue of *Comradez!* Magazine)

It's about six in the evening, and Ilya Zamyatin is eating dinner on the run.

After a meeting with his publisher, he is en route to his wife's office at Gallery NowSpace to pick her up for a benefit gala at the Heritage Museum.

So rather than sushi or delicate salad, this artistic soul is eating a sausage from a street vendor, and literally eating on the run as he tries to make it across lanes of traffic towards a taxi stand.

"Taxi!" he yells.

When one cab driver slows, but does not

stop, Zamyatin jokingly yells after it, "But you must stop – I'm famous!"

After spending much of his life in the army and the space program, Zamyatin seems well adjusted to his new role as public persona and as an unofficial Russian minister of the arts. (Unofficial because of his numerous disagreements with President Vladimir Putin.)

Zamyatin gained experience as a spokesperson during his years as the face of Space Discovery, a period he prefers not to talk about now.

"It's just something ... I mean, I'd rather focus on my books and music," he says with a shrug. "That was just a job."

As for where he spent the months between the end of Space Discovery and his return to the public eye, Zamyatin is keeping that a secret too.

"A little mystery never hurt anyone," he says devilishly.

Of course, now that he is back in Moscow, citizens are suddenly remembering having seen him during those lost months. A fish cleaner on a Bering Strait ship claims he worked as a crewman at sea. A former diplomat in Cuba claims Zamyatin spent the months enjoying a tropical holiday as a personal guest of Fidel Castro. A grocery clerk in the rural north claims he was a regular customer at her store, where he bought foodstuffs with a secret wife. Are any of these true?

"They all make good stories," Zamyatin says. "I'm not the only gifted storyteller in Russia. But if I give away all my secrets, what will I have left to write about next?"

Zamyatin's wife, Natasha, is also adjusting well to her celebrity status. The daughter of a schoolteacher, she grew up at the end of the Soviet Era and is now a first class citizen in the new century. When Zamyatin finally arrives at her art gallery, she offers him a hug and jokingly notes that he is late.

"I couldn't catch a cab," he tells her. This reporter backs up his story.

Zamyatin has never learned to drive a car.

"Military jeeps and rockets are all I know," he says, "and neither are useful in the city."

Together, they take a waiting limousine to the benefit for an orphanage in the city.

In the car, Zamyatin talks about his newest book.

"This novel is really about making a home, no matter where you are. Of course, it is also a thrilling story of interplanetary war, and will make a great movie!" He laughs, as the book is currently the subject of a bidding war between two rival studios. "But, truly, it is about finding home. Soldiers at war are always thinking of home ...."

He trails off here, perhaps wary of speaking further about Chechnya, a subject he has come under some scrutiny for discussing previously.

"Well, look at it this way," he says. "It's like *The Odyssey*. You have the Trojan War, a great epic conflict, but then the greatest work of art to come out of it is just the story of one man going home."

Is he comparing his new book to *The Odyssey*?

"Ha ha ha! Of course not! Mine is much better!"

Should fans of his earlier works, *The Space Orphan* and *The Space Farmer*, expect to see their favorite characters return?

"No," Zamyatin says. "Although the works are conceived as part of a larger whole, the people and stories of each stand alone." Aside from the artistic reasons for separating the books, Zamyatin stands to earn substantially more this way, since he can now sell the movie rights separately (if it was a sequel, Odessa Stepfilms would retain the rights to the characters, since it bought the rights to *The Space Orphan*). This matter is delicately brought to his attention.

"True! My orphanage didn't raise no fool!" he laughs heartily, before turning serious. Orphanages have been one of his favorite charities since his recent burst of good fortune. "Everyone expects their parents to help them out as children. Obviously, if your parents are rich, you have a head start in the world. But even if your parents are poor, at least you have them. But as an orphan, you have neither money nor parents. It makes you hard and hungry while you are still young. Orphans are not children for very long."

Zamyatin's own odyssey began when he left the children's home at St. Martyrsburg to join the army. He had little choice at the time. What's the next leg of the journey for this modern-day Homer?

"Now that I've found a home," he says, hugging Natasha tight, "I plan to hang up my walking shoes, take off my coat and stay a while."

In July, I attended a symposium of international space understanding in Houston, Texas. It was scheduled to coincide with the new Quest module of the International Space Station, which allowed for both American and Russian astronauts to exit the craft and walk in space. It was symbolic that neither country had won the space race – both astronaut and cosmonaut uniforms could be worn in this new airlock.

Of course, symbolism aside, Russia was the clear winner. We have a more durable and utilitarian space program. If an asteroid were ever heading for earth, it would be a Russian team of heroes that saves us, and they would politely take one American astronaut along for the ride, despite all the trouble he causes with his cowboy ways.

At this symposium, however, it was all hugs and kisses. We shook hands and posed for pictures. We held up flags of each other's countries. And then when the cameras weren't looking, we played drinking games. It was a rowdy night, but one of mutual understanding and cooperation: for example, when we kicked a keg of Budweiser beer, Alan Bean and Yuri Glazkov worked together to install the fresh keg. And when a party of Dallas Cowboy cheerleaders showed up to dance for us, we cooperated in order to help our fellow space travelers go home with the ones they liked. (I did not chase after any of these ladies, as I knew Natasha was waiting for me at home.)

President George W. Bush promised to show us Texas in the following week. At first I was excited, as I imagined that he knew where all the best bars were and who sold the best cocaine. But then I learned he had stopped having fun because he found Jesus or got married or something like that.

As the night wore on, after the press left, we began really competing with each other. First, it was running races across the ballroom. We piled the dinner tables in the corner for the races. Then there was a push-up contest, which I won, dedicating my victory to the spirit of old Vulkov and his magnificent, fully functioning arms. Soon we were too tired to stand and we pulled the tables back down to sit. After all, some of us were old men! Here the arm wrestling began, after some Texas country bar band began playing on the stage.

"This is how we settle arguments in Texas when we're too drunk to shoot straight," Bush told us. His wife shushed him.

We started with the old men – we wanted them to arm wrestle each other so they could amass some victories among themselves before the younger generation began clobbering them. John Glenn jumped out to an early lead among the elderly. He had returned from a second space trip a few years ago, which he kept boasting.

"I was the oldest man in space!" he yelled after every arm wrestling victory.

"You look like the oldest man on Earth, as well!" yelled some joker.

Glenn promptly beat him.

Pretty soon he was beating opponents half his age! And not just women like Sally Ride and Mae Jemison, but men too. You had to hand it to him, he was pretty impressive for an old man. Finally, Fedor stepped up to his table.

"I'm sorry, old man, but I must hand you a defeat."

Fedor rolled up his sleeve and flexed his impressive bicep.

"Oooh, boy, Glennie, that guy's arm is bigger than Tom Wolfe's ego!" said one of the Texans.

The Americans all hooted and hollered as a tiny sad man in a white tuxedo fled the ballroom.

Fedor sat down across from Glenn and they grabbed each other's hands. Veins popped on both men's arms. (Fedor's veins stood out because of his enormous musculature. Glenn's because of his age.)

"This one's for Sputnik!" Glenn shouted. "You may have beaten us to space, but at least we never burned any dogs alive!"

Fedor blinked once and suddenly looked lost.

"It's true, comrade. That dog was cooked soon after launch."

Although the truth of Laika's death came out in 2002, it was secret knowledge at the time of the symposium, and Fedor had not known it. But the steely resolve and earnest composure in Glenn's face told him it was true. The life slumped out of him, and as soon as the match began, Glenn slammed his hand to the table.

I was up next.

"Don't try to scare me with Laika's fate," I warned him. "I was abandoned to die in space too."

Rolling up my sleeve, I downed a shot of American bourbon and took his hand.

We faced off across the table like Rocky Balboa and his opponents did in the *Rocky* film sequel, *Over The Top*.[2]

"On your marks, get set, arm wrestle!"

So it began. We pushed our full strength against each other like test rockets fired into a concrete embankment, not worried about survivors as much as about the size of the impact. We pushed and pushed and our hands stayed dead set in the center of the table.

"You wrestle pretty good for an orphan," Glenn said to me.

"You're not so bad yourself," I said. "Plus, I really like your work with The Eagles."

"You're thinking of Glenn Frey," he said.

"Oh, my mistake. You're the 'Life's Been Good' guy!"

"No, that's Joe Walsh. I went to outer fucking space, I didn't play in some sad-sack light rock band from the Seventies."

"A thousand apologies. I am just a poor Russian veteran. Let us focus on our arm wrestling."

But no progress was made, despite all our taunts and mental attacks. This arm wrestling match was like a chess game: One where the knights had gotten off their horses and were engaged in an arm wrestling match in the middle of the board.

Sweat gleamed on his shiny head. My teeth gritted against each other in my mouth. Finally, I began crushing the joints at the bottom of his fingers in my hand. He tried to do the same. But my grip was stronger. While American space craft were luxuriously adorned with hydraulic power, Russian satellites and orbit craft had no such amenities. We grew up like teenagers before power steering, who still cling to the steering wheel for dear life while today's teenagers barely rest a single finger on the wheel as they simultaneously change the radio station, send text messages to their friends. Who is the better driver? Me, of course.

"Aghgghgh, my hand!" Glenn yelled out in old man's agony.

"'We will bury you!'" I replied, slamming his hand into the table.[3]

A great many astronauts and cosmonauts let out a whoop. The Russians were happy the American had finally been bested. The young Americans were happy that an old man had finally lost (probably they were worried about the mounting Medicare and Social Security costs of his generation if they refused to go silently and I had, at least, proved that they were vulnerable).

"My turn!" yelled a familiar voice behind me. I turned to see Evgeny standing at the table. "Comrade!" We hugged, and I was amazed by his massive arms, his upper torso.

"You look so different," I said.

"I stayed in science after the space program," he told me. "Now I make and sell nutritional supplements. I am as strong as a horse today." He let out the whinny sound of a giant stallion. "My muscles are probably 50 percent horse chemical."

He shoved John Glenn aside and took the seat opposite me. "Let's go!"

Evgeny beat me soundly, and then ran the table. While his body was now massive, his head was not misshapen like so many American baseball players and steroid users. Perhaps he had found a way to increase muscles without cutting off oxygen to the brain. When it was down to him and one last American astronaut, a hush came over the room and we all watched.

"We won the Cold War!" yelled the American.

"You think it's over?" asked Evgeny with a smile.

"You tore down the Berlin Wall!"

"But we kept our Nukes!"

The judge shouted, "On your marks, get set, arm wrestle!"

Evgeny toyed with the American for a while before finishing him off.

Once he'd slammed his opponents' hand to the table, he began rolling his sleeve back up.

"I guess Russia wins the 'arms' race," he laughed.

Amidst the laughter we heard a great slamming sound and turned to see a guitar smashed on stage, its ruined pieces being held by a ferocious white haired demon which proceeded to yell into the microphone.

"NOT SO FAST! I haven't had a turn yet."

It was a voice that made clear it would not be denied and would crush anyone who tried to stop its owner.

Technically, Barbara Bush had never been an astronaut and did not deserve to participate in the contest, but she was one of our hosts, and in addition to that, far too scary to interrupt.

She took the microphone stand and cracked it in two over her knee.

"You think you know *strength*? You think you're *men*?" She cackled. "I've got *wrinkles* tougher than you sissies."

She leapt from the stage to the ballroom floor, then held up her fist.

"Listen, Ivan, you might be full of steroids, but I'm powered by a burning hate, and I will destroy you."

She stalked across the floor, and a wind blew the fallen banners and menus across in front of her like tumbleweed. Where did the wind come from? Perhaps the fleeing busboys, who raced out the emergency exits, creating a draft in their wake. The echo of her orthopedic heels reverberated through the almost silent ballroom. The only other sound was the low hum of feedback from the microphone she'd left hanging lifeless from the stage.

All of us cleared a path for her to the table where Evegeny gulped.

"My husband's up in some hotel room reading *David Copperfield*, but I want to brawl," she said through gritted teeth. "Be careful not to break your glasses, boy."

Then she rolled up the sleeve of her pantsuit and extended her weathered, shriveled, mighty hand. Her smile was deadly. I've never known a smile to convey such venom and hate. Each glistening tooth seemed to say, "I'm surrounded by children, bad boys who must be disciplined."

Evgeny tried to appear confident.

"Pardon me, Ma'am," he said with a quiver. "I'd hate to defeat a woman."

"You won't defeat me. Do you know how powerful I am? I've had *two* Presidents inside me."

She sat down, grabbed his hand, and smiled again.

"Whenever you're ready," she said.

Her glare was so intense and unblinking that I would have thought she was a robot except that nobody would make a robot so wrinkly and old.

"On your marks, get set, arm wrestle!"

There was never any question. From the start, Evgeny's hand

fell slowly backward, with him struggling valiantly, then nervously pretending that he was letting her win. For his sake, we all pretended that was the case, that this was a good natured lark rather than the unadulterated whipping that it was. When she had touched his hand to the table, she released him and sat back in her chair smiling. We all continued our pretend merriment until she stood up, knocking her chair over with an exclamation point and opening her mouth to speak. Everyone quieted to listen.

Without raising her voice, she looked at all of us and muttered: "Your best days are behind you. All of you."

Then she spit on the floor and strode out into the Texas night like a whirlwind or a stampede or a horde of locusts.

The next night, there was a public dinner party for the most famous of us space folks and politicians. John Glenn. Neil Armstrong. Myself. President George W. Bush. Vladimir Putin. Tom Hanks. William Shatner. We spent the day touring the city. We had barbecue, rode horses, and received free coffee mugs at Enron's headquarters. We met Chuck Norris and rode in one of ZZ Top's old-lady cars. If you could put all of Texas into a single day and give it to someone, that's what we got, although why anybody would want that is beyond me.

Finally, the limos dropped us off at the hotel to prepare for the big banquet. I dressed in my military uniform, since it was more comfortable than a tuxedo. It was not my original uniform – I'd had a new one tailored after my first novel was released and I needed to attend publishing events at modern, clean restaurants. Looking at myself in the hotel mirror, I thought, *There's a handsome man. If he didn't have a loving woman at home, he could get in real trouble.* I would not be unfaithful, even though they say "What happens in Texas stays in Texas." Thinking that I might have a lot to drink that night, I decided to pack up my things. In the morning, I'd only need to change into my civilian clothes and catch a ride to the airport.

The elevator was made of glass, with bright white bulbs running up and down its shell. Taking a leisurely descent from the upper reaches of the skyscraping hotel, I thought about how far I had come, from my days in the orphans' silo, climbing down ladders every morning, to the present, being shuttled around in luxury, whisked up and down entire buildings in a matter of moments. In the razor black glass of the car I saw my reflection. My face was older, my hair a bit gray. Shadows crawled all across the surface. As the car sank further, the lights of the lobby filled in the darkness and my sunken eyes seemed a bit more clear. Perhaps it had just been illusion, the damage all the years had done to me.

With a hush of air, the doors opened and I headed towards the ballroom for dinner. The American cameramen mostly ignored me, but a few international reporters recognized me and lobbed a few questions at me as I entered. Waving, nodding, smiling, I answered briefly and found my way inside, where a woman with enormous hair smiled and handed me a name tag. She walked me up to the head table, where I sat on the Russian side, just next to Putin, and one seat away from George W. Bush. It seemed I was the most famous Russian space veteran at dinner. It was like a wedding reception, with some poor organizer trying to group together people with similar interests and a common language. On my other side was an aging veteran, who I can only assume was the oldest living cosmonaut, or at least the oldest cosmonaut healthy enough to make the trip across the Atlantic. He was not much of a conversationalist, and spent most of the evening tearing off small pieces of a dinner roll and gumming them down to a swallow-able size in his soft toothless mouth. I thought he had a distinguished mustache, but I later discovered that it was just an untamed patch of hair growing out of his nostrils.

Given the old man's semi-comatose state, I was forced to engage in conversation with Putin while he wasn't nodding politely at the sports trivia Bush was sharing with him.

"I used to own the Texas Rangers," Bush said. "That's a sports team! They play baseball." He spoke slowly and deliber-ately, in the voice one uses to talk to a feeble minded person. Neither of us could tell whether this was due to the language barrier, or if Bush always spoke that way, perhaps as a result of the fact that people always spoke to him in that voice.

"I am a judo champion," Putin said.

"That's something. That's wrestling with togas on, right?"

Putin turned to me and said, in Russian, "I don't understand how we lost the Cold War."

He expected me to laugh at his joke, but instead I answered him: "Foreign wars against ghosts in the mountains is how we lost the Cold War. With your war in Chechnya, perhaps you can lose the Cold War a second time!"

This did not make him smile. Instead, he deliberately picked up his steak knife and forcefully cut a piece of the filet in front of him. Then he lifted it up on his fork and stared at me. "You should learn to whisper. The loudest mouse is first to be killed by the cat." Putin thrust the hunk of meat into his mouth and chewed it up.

"If all the mice remain silent, no one will know the cat is killing them," I said.

"I suppose we have different notions of the fate of vermin," he said. Then he turned away from me and motioned one of his security guards to the table and whispered something into his

ear. The guard nodded and left. Putin smiled at me, the smile of
a cat.

I was about to ask him what made him smile when he stood
up and offered a toast to the entire room.

"I would like to thank our excellent hosts for their
hospitality," he said, as a translator repeated his words for the
English-speakers in the crowd. Of course, as a KGB agent,
Putin knew the language of America, but he preferred to keep
the barrier of translation like an Iron Curtain of meaning
dividing East and West.

"We have come here to celebrate the union of former enemies in the skies above. Russia is happy to cooperate with the
United States for the benefit of all mankind. While we have
been competitors in the past, we have always had much in common. Since the beginning of both country's space programs, we
have had one sad thing in common – the loss of brave men and
women who gave their lives in the name of science and exploration. So let us, tonight, remember our fallen comrades, the
pilots and teachers, the soldiers and engineers, the angels who
are now looking down on us from heaven or from outer space."
He raised his wine glass. "To the dead, who we mourn and
remember. Let us learn from their tragedies."

Putin raised his glass high and we all joined him, then drank
to the ghosts.

He sat down and looked at me. Leaning in close, he whispered, "It is always sad when our loved ones die." Then he
brushed off his mouth with a napkin.

I felt dizzy. He could only have been speaking of Natasha. I
was an orphan. Vulkov was already dead. Natasha was all I had
in this world. He was threatening her. I stood up to leave
immediately, to get back to her, but he grabbed my arm with
his forceful judo grip and pushed me into my seat.

"It would be rude to leave now, comrade. President Bush is about to speak."

George W. Bush stood up to offer another toast.

"My fellow Americans. My new Russian friends. Welcome to Texas. You know, we have a saying we like to say here. We say 'Everything is bigger in Texas.' And that's true, which is why we say it. But there's something bigger than Texas, and that is the space above it. We're here to honor the men and women who helped conquer space for all mankind. In the foot-steps of Christopher Columbus and Galileo ... Galilee? ... the Galileo guy. In their footsteps we've walked and then walked further. We took, as Neil said, small steps for man and giant leaps for mankind..."

As he drawled on and on, my heart raced faster and faster. Putin sat stone faced, occasionally picking up his steak knife and twirling it around in his hand. Something was wrong. I had to get home to Natasha as soon as possible, but I couldn't flee the dais without causing a minor international incident. I was trapped, forced to listen to the incoherent babbling of a man who had almost choked to death on a pretzel.

Luckily, that thought gave me an idea. I finished off the water in my glass, then, trying to seem calm and measured, I cut off a large bit of my steak and bit it off of my fork. It was more than I could chew. I made a few gagging noises quietly. I coughed loudly. Then I made another gagging noise, loud enough to disrupt Bush. He stopped his speech and turned to look at me.

"Excuse me," I muttered, pushing my chair back and scut-tling away as politely as I could.

"*Dasvidaniya*," Putin whispered into the air behind me.

I walked briskly to the door, where an event coordinator tried to pat my back and ply me with water.

"I'll be fine," I told her, lying.

Once outside the door of the ballroom, I ran for the stairs. All I could think of was Putin's cold stare and what he would do to hurt me. Perhaps he could arrange for the elevator to get stuck while I was on it, keeping me trapped in Texas while he sent his goons after Natasha. So I took the stairs at a full run, with an urgency I hadn't felt since Afghanistan and the night in the Russian forest. The emergency stairs were marked with glowing green tape and the stairwell reeked of cigarettes.

On my floor, I burst into the hallway, scaring a young man at a vending machine, who dropped his can of cola to the ground, where it began spraying soda all over the floor.

"Sorry, you startled me!" he said. I was in too much of a hurry to apologize.

I opened my room, happy to find that my electronic key still worked. I'd half expected Putin to have used an electromagnetic device to wipe my wallet clean. Grabbing my overnight bag, I ran back to the stairs, once more frightening the young man, who now dropped a second can of cola.

I took the stairs two at a time, wondering in my head what would happen to Natasha if I fell now, breaking an arm or leg in a Texas hotel stairwell. But I did not fall. I made it to the second floor, where I exited the stairwell, hoping to avoid any of Putin's men who might be looking for me in the lobby. All the way across the building, after seemingly endless corridors of soft plush carpet, decorative end tables and boring landscapes, I found a service entrance, which took me into a kitchen and then into the hotel's indoor pool. A few night swimmers stared at me with my suitcase and military uniform. I ignored them, forced open a window and pulled myself onto the gravel of the roof. Just beyond an air conditioning duct, I found the hotel's carport. Scurrying across it, I dropped my bag to the parking lot below. Then I grabbed the edge of the roof and dropped down to the decorative grass. An airport shuttle driver looked at me with curiosity.

"I was here for the astronaut dinner, but it was boring," I said. "Are you going to the airport?"

"I leave in two minutes," he said, looking at his watch.

I handed him $200.

"Can you leave now?"

He pulled the small silver knob on the end of his watch, advanced the minute hand twice around the face and pushed the knob back in.

"Time to go!" he said.

I dug into my bag and found my cell phone, but it could not connect with any of the American providers, and so it was useless to me.

The Texas night was big, as the President had said. Not nearly as big as the sky over Afghanistan, or the deserts of the Middle East. What was largest as we drove past was the people. Great fat wads of flesh tucked into blue jeans and cowboy boots. Then giant cloverleafs of highway swung us around and off the streets of pedestrians into great expanses of concrete without sidewalk, where giant towers of sodium light glowed downward to the steel carriages below.

It smelled like gasoline and barbecue. The radio blared with the drone of a Southern preacher.

Just this night, I say ... just this night ... we are called. All of us are called! By God! The highest power! God calls us with his love. I said, God calls us with his love. He calls us back home, to His house, the most awesome house on earth, the church. If you haven't visited the house in a while, maybe it's time for you to return. Return home. Somebody misses you there. That somebody is the One who makes it all possible ...

Thankfully I was saved from salvation by the dying radio signal, and the driver switched over to a country station. Patsy Cline told us that she was crazy. I knew how she felt. Love had made her that way.

As we approached the international terminal, I unbuckled my seatbelt and grabbed my bag. When he pulled to a stop, I hopped out of the unfolding door and ran inside. Luckily my credit limit was high, and my titanium American Express card still worked. I bought a ticket to New York, and then another to Moscow. It would still be a day and a half until I could get home.

In the abandoned corridor of the nighttime airport, I found a pay phone. It took some amount of negotiations with a couple operators to finally place a call to Russia. After all that work, however, nobody answered at our apartment. I tried to figure out what time it was in my home country. Maybe Natasha was on her way to work. Next I called her gallery, but ended up leaving a message on the answering machine there.

"Natasha, please call me back. My telephone is not working here, but leave me a message. I will be back home soon."

Just before my flight took off, I purchased a book from the airport book shop that had been recommended by Oprah. Probably due to my nervous state, I could not make any progress on the book, although perhaps it was because her books are aimed at people searching for meaning in life. But there is none. If Oprah really wanted viewers to enjoy reading, she should have picked one of my space adventure novels.

In any case, I had nothing to distract me on my flights. Instead there was just the throbbing in my brain, the worry which buzzed louder than the jet engines and the night sky. I couldn't hear a thing.

New York was a blur, a race across airport terminals and

then the waiting, the horrible waiting. I was like a father in the hospital while his wife is in labor, helpless but terrified. I suppose these days they let the husbands into the delivery room with their wives, but that is not what I mean. Some metaphors exist in a certain time and we must allow them their anachronisms.

It seemed like the flight to Moscow would never depart. Pacing back and forth in front of rows of blue plastic chairs, I tried to eat a muffin but couldn't keep any food down. I lurched into the men's room and vomited in the toilet. The motion sensor did not recognize my head (it was used to looking at asses) and flushed while I was still on the floor with my face pointed into the porcelain bowl. It was like I didn't exist. Luckily the airport travel store had bottles of mouthwash and I was able to cover up the smell of puke with mint.

Then more waiting.

Finally the PA system choked to life and a steward announced boarding by rows. My throat was in such pain I could barely answer questions like, "Did you have a nice time?" as I made my way onto the plane. In the small corridor that reached from the airport to the side of the plane, I tried to run ahead of the other passengers as if this would get me to Russia sooner, but a small family blocked my way and I was forced to wait.

"Magazine?" offered a woman at the door of the airplane.

"No, no," I managed to say.

They say the back of the airplane is statistically safer, as if the fraction of the percentage of chance should encourage you to request a seat in the rear of a jet. But what that really means is if the plane crashes, you'll die slower and more painfully. My seat was in the front, since the only unsold ticket available was in the expensive business class section. They plied me with magazines and chocolate, offered me drinks, plumped my pillows and handed me hot towels.

In my frantic state, I gripped the armrest like a drowning man.

"First time flying?" asked the well dressed man next to me.

"Not at all..." my answer was interrupted by a sudden need to vomit into the air sickness bag. We had not even left the ground yet. This man turned back to his magazine and did not get to hear about my numerous flights and my journey to outer space. *I was a cosmonaut, I was not scared to be flying!*

Except that I was. For a brief moment, I saw the plane crashing, breaking up somewhere over the Atlantic ocean. I pictured the horrific trip down, screaming, helpless, watching the sea approach through the parting clouds, the waves racing up to meet my flailing corpse. And what terrified me was not the death. It was that I would not be able to find Natasha and rescue her from Putin's thugs. I had a horrible vision of her, in our home, crying on the couch at the news that I was dead, when suddenly two shadowy men burst in and took her away.

The plane must not crash. I must make it home to find her.

Although I turned down every drink offered to me, I did accept an eye mask the stewardess presented. I pulled the window shade shut, and blocked out my eyes with the mask. I could not sleep, but I could concentrate on what needed to be done.

First: call her as soon as I landed. If she was at work, I would take a cab to the gallery. If she was at home, I'd direct the car there. Then, I'd pull her into the backseat with me and tell our secret code words, letting her know it was time for us to leave immediately. The cabdriver would be confused as I asked him to circle back to the airport he'd picked me up at 20 or 30 minutes before. Then we'd buy a ticket to the country of her choosing. I guessed she would pick Paris, where she could pursue her art and we would be relatively safe from Putin's reach. Granted, America would be even further and even safer, but I would be happy wherever she wanted to go. In France I could keep her safe. She spoke enough of the language to help us settle in. I imagined us in a small apartment on the fourth floor of a building on the Rue d'Something, like characters in *Breathless*. I'd have a small desk where I write my novels on a typewriter (for some reason in this fantasy I'd replaced my laptop with a typewriter) and a stooped-back woman would bring us baguettes and jam each morning before Natasha headed out to her studio. Perhaps we have a son who gets into mischief, cutting class to visit the cinema, kissing teenage girls in the park, and all three of us taking sandwiches and bottles of wine on weekend getaways to a small country home we also keep, beside a lake, near bales of hay and seagulls.

20 / TERMINAL

The flight was long and unbearably comfortable. I wanted the rest of the world, the other passengers, to share in my discomfort, but the immaculate carpets and clean white interior were soothing, and the service staff kept them well plied. After a few hours of my French reverie, I tried to read a magazine. I scanned pictures and indecipherable cartoons in *The Economist*. I looked at gadgets in the catalogue before me. Finally I settled for watching a movie on the small television screen in the back of the seat in front of me. How I would have liked such a small television on my space craft instead of that copy of *Moby Dick*.

The movie was dark and twisted, and I had trouble following it. Apparently, it was the sequel to an earlier film about a serial killer whom the filmmakers wished for me to support in his efforts to live in beautiful Italian obscurity. But another evil man was trying to find him and feed him to pigs. Also, for some reason, a woman in America was also looking for him. He must have been quite a charming man in the first film, this *murderer.* Then at the end of the film, there is a small banquet at a waterfront home where the characters eat the brains of another character. The film's gallery of murderers and misfits reminded me too much of Putin's Russia, and I lost interest, except to notice that the house where they ate reminded me of Jack Ryan's house in *Patriot Games.* That Jack Ryan was a great hero, almost like a fictional American version of myself.

After an eternity, we prepared for landing, and the stewardesses distributed customs papers. I filled them out dutifully, though I had nothing to declare but disdain for our country's leader.

The longest part of any flight is the waiting after you land, but before you can leave the plane. Some passengers spend the time removing their bags from the overhead bin and buttoning their jackets. Others read calmly as if they wouldn't mind another hour or two on the airplane. This time, I stood, my one bag in hand, at the front of the plane staring bitterly at the door and the attendant who would open it once she received approval from the pilot. She smiled blankly at me and I tried to smile at her through my sweat and urgency.

Then the pilot's voice came on the intercom and told her she could open the door. She turned the wheel and pushed it out into the night, and I ran past her, up the corridor into the airport. Ignoring all the welcoming faces, the cardboard signs with surnames, the gangster's apprentices with gel in their hair, it was straight through the terminal to the roadside, the chaotic mess of cabs and drivers, a sign of the missing communist dictators. We did not have freedom where it mattered, but we had it in the worst places. Municipal offices and traffic patrols. Fire houses and food banks. These were all free to be as shitty and disastrous as they pleased – while they had been bloated but effective in the height of the Cold War.

Choosing a car under such circumstances is no easy task. Don't take the shiniest newest model, it probably belongs to a novice. Likewise, an old steel beast will probably be driven by a knowledgeable old soul, but the machinery can't be trusted. Instead, pick an economical car, a few years old, but in good repair. Most often it will belong to a trusty driver, a man who takes care of his vehicle, is ambitious enough not to be driving Soviet era scrap, but not so wildly misguided as to have wasted a small fortune on a luxury car that will soon wear out with repeated trips to and from the airport.

This time a 1996 Ford Taurus caught my eye. A little older than I was looking for, but in great shape, which is no easy task in a country that has so few cars of that kind.

The driver was smoking and reading a newspaper on the steering wheel of his car when I rapped on the glass of the passenger side window. "Where to?" he asked.

"Moscow and back. You seem reliable."

"Hey, aren't you..." his question trailed off.

"I am. And I'm in a bit of a hurry to pick up my wife for a trip. I'd be obliged if you could help me."

He threw the paper into the back and unlocked the door.

I got in, my bag on my lap, and we were off. He drove to the left, up onto the curb, around the tangled mess of other cars, and then onto the wet gray pavement ahead.

"I was just reading about that stupid war," he said.

I dug my phone out of my pocket and turned it on, but the battery died.

"This may sound strange, but is there any chance I can use your phone? My battery died while I was in America. I'll pay you for the minutes."

"I'd be happy for a hero such as yourself to use my telephone."

He unplugged a car phone from the car's cigarette lighter and handed it to me.

First I dialed home. Nobody answered.

Then I dialed her office. Again nobody answered.

I left no message this time.

Perhaps they were busy and screening their calls? I realized that Natasha would not recognize the strange number I was calling from. Now I had no way of knowing where she was.

I gave the driver the address of her art gallery. Chances were that she was at work.

"How was America?" he asked me.

"It's a loud place. Every street sounds like money."

"That is not a bad sound. I wish I heard it more often," he said.

"Of course. Money is not bad. And the crowds there ... you never feel alone in America. At least, you are never so alone as you are in Russia. We are the loneliest people on earth."

"That is true," he said. "But at least we are all alone together."

The roads merged, traffic converged, lights passed in the rear view and soon we were approaching the city. Into the arteries of Moscow he steered us, ever closer to the nice part of town where her gallery resided. Just as I began to feel good about things, we got stuck in traffic. He was skilled enough to weave us in and out and inches closer despite the slowly freezing river of cars around us. It looked like an accident ahead, with sirens wailing. But also something in the air tasted acrid. He turned on a small radio, and scanned across the channels until he found what he was looking for – some sort of police band. Long gaps of silence were ripped apart by short bursts of information: robbery in progress ... pause ... possible suicide ... pause ... two alarm fire downtown.

"That's it," he said. "There's a fire up there. I don't think I can get you much closer."

I looked hard ahead and knew, through the black smoke I could now make out, that it was the gallery ablaze. That's why we couldn't move any further. Our destination was burning. I looked around madly. We were still fairly packed into the road with cars on all sides of us.

The driver looked at me sympathetically.

"Listen," I told him. "I need to get to my wife. I know she's not in that fire. I just know. I hope she's at home. Can you get out of this mess?"

"Eventually, but not very fast."

I told him our address.

"I'm going there on foot to make sure she's alright." I handed him 200 American dollars. "Can you get over there as soon as you can?"

"Go find her. I'll make it there somehow."

I dug through my bag, pulling out my passport. I could run faster without the rest of my clothes. I realized I was still wearing my uniform. Here I was, a soldier about to run madly through the streets, just as I had been so many years ago when I first joined the army.

"Wait."

I turned back to the car.

The driver handed me his personal phone from inside his coat pocket.

"Just in case you need it. My car number's in there under 'Car.'" Then he handed me a pack of cigarettes and a book of matches. "Just in case."

"Thanks." I didn't have time to explain that I didn't smoke.

"Good luck," he said, already cranking into reverse and beating down upon the horn.

I ran.

Through wet streets and alleys, in front of piles of trash, around homeless old men and women, I ran first through the bad part of town, then into the gentrified Moscow, where bums gave way to business men, garbage bags to recycling bins, empty lots to private parking garages. My feet burned with blister; I was still wearing my dress loafers. It was the longest run of my life, not in distance but in emotional miles. Again, the finish line was marked by the flashing glare of sirens. Just as the fire engines had gathered at the art gallery, now there was a municipal police car in front of our apartment, and the unforgiving black shape of a K.G.B. vehicle.[1]

Still running, I pushed past the patrolman, screaming that I lived here.

Up the stairs in a hurry, I would deck the cops, free her from their grasp and we'd run together.

But no one put up a fight.

The patrolman at the top of the stairs didn't swing at me. He grabbed at me, but not as an enemy.

He tried to hug me.

And then I knew.

"I'm sorry," he said.

A plainclothes detective appeared.

"You don't want to go in there, Ilya," he told me. "I was the first one on the scene. It's terrible." He looked familiar, his skin parched and cracked like a dry riverbed.

But he could not stop me. Nothing could.

I dragged the patrolman with me into the bathroom, where I could see a crime scene technician was taking photographs.

"Don't touch anything!" he yelled, not knowing what was happening.

"It's the husband," I heard the patrolman say. "He's the husband."

She was there in the tub.

"She must have fallen and hit her head." The detective was
in the doorway. "A tragic accident. But we'll run an autopsy to
be sure."

Everything went white. It was like being kicked in the head
by a mule. I threw up in the toilet. The technician groaned. The
patrolman backed out of the room. I looked at Natasha's body,
her skull fractured, her arms pointed in unnatural directions,
blood in the bath water, the floor soaking wet. If I had been
more awake at that moment, I might have asked, "How do you
fall when you're sitting in a bathtub?" or "Why is there such a
mess all over the room if she fell alone in the tub?" or "Who
called the police if she slipped and hit her head and died?" But I
did not ask any of these questions. Instead I looked at her and
her broken body, her limbs splayed sickeningly. And on the tile
floor beneath her lifeless hands I saw two things: a bottle of
shampoo and her pink plastic razor. She must have grabbed
them as she was being murdered and held onto them until the
moment of her death. A last message to me. It was time to go.
Don't mourn me, her message said. *Run*.

The white heat in my head vanished.

"Can I use your telephone?" I asked the detective. "I need to
call her family."

"I'm sure they'll be informed," he said, puffing up his chest.

"I should be the one to tell them," I said.

"Ahh, yes. I suppose the old chemistry teacher should hear
from you himself." I recognized him suddenly. *Peter Sukharin*.
To the patrolman, he said "Ilya and I were schoolmates in St.
Martyrsburg." He winked at me and blew me an air kiss, then
handed me his phone.

He was so intent on reminding me of the past that he didn't realize how little sense my request made. There was a working telephone in the other room, where the patrolman was sitting in my Eames chair.

"Are you alright?" he asked.

"Yes," I murmured. "I just need to..." I pretended I was too distraught to finish the sentence. I made my way towards the stairwell as if to get better reception and privacy. As soon as I was out of sight, I took the battery out of his phone and tossed it into the base of a decorative plant in the lobby.

On the street, I found a half empty vodka bottle in the gutter. The alcoholics of mother Russia are there for you in your time of need. I doused some booze around the gas cap of the patrol car, then crammed a lit cigarette into the hinge of the refueling door as a fuse. I did the same to the black KGB menace. Then I stepped across the road to the opposite sidewalk, where I pretended to make a phone call. After a few minutes, the Sukharin's face appeared in my window. I waved grimly at him, as if I was talking to Natasha's parents. When he turned away from the street, I pulled out the cab driver's telephone and called his car.

"I'm almost there," he said as soon as he answered.

I gave him the address of a building two blocks away and told him to meet me there instead. Across the street, both cars caught fire.

And then I slipped away.

21 / VOYAGER

"Dark was the night, cold was the ground"
—Blind Willie Johnson[1]

That night I cried for Natasha, cried a sea of tears in the trunk of a car, in near infinite black, but not suspended like a child unborn, instead beaten and battered like a child born unto a violent world, tossed about by the stones and bumps in the road. And so my tears splashed about as the cab driver took me north towards Finland in his private vehicle.

In older times I'd have been denounced in the newspapers and on television, branded a traitor by the state before it killed me in some unmarked icy field. Uncertainty and celebrity kept me from that fate. Putin's dog-fighting thugs could not risk accusing me of crimes in case I escaped to the West and broadcast my actual fate back through media connections. Instead, they ignored me. My records disappeared from stores. My novels vanished from shelves.[2] And they hunted me at every airport, every seaport, every border crossing.

But in the worst days of Stalin's terror, in the shadow of the Iron Curtain, a garden of protective angels had grown, men and women, sometimes children too, who spirited dissidents and refugees out of the danger of the U.S.S.R. and into the welcoming arms of the United States. Most of them were old, and happily retired from their noble professions now that the walls had ostensibly come down. Yet they remembered the old ways: the tunnels and the holes in fences, the border patrolmen who drank too much, the shallow waters where you could swim to safety on a good night, if the stars were on your side and the moon was there to guide you.

And so I climbed quietly from the steamy trunk of a Yugoslavian vehicle into a muddy brown field, then ran low across the ground to a freezing bay. A wrinkled old man smiled at me along the water and handed me a sealed plastic bag full of bread and chocolate, a musty neoprene body suit, a snorkel, and flippers.

"Get away from his horrible place," he said. "And find your freedom."

"Thank you."

"Josef took my boy." He pulled out a gray snapshot of an optimistic teenager, worn away by his worrying thumb over the years. Then he put the photograph back in his pocket. "Josef?" He spit on the ground.

I shook his hand and changed into the suit. I left my military uniform in the dirt.

"There's a rock, just barely out of the channel." He pointed out into the night towards it. "Stop there and eat. You'll need the energy."

He looked around us into the sharp summer night.

"I don't think they watch the bay too closely anymore, but you can never be too careful." He slipped into the shadow of a tree, out of the reach of the moonlight. "I'll watch your journey and make sure you are safe."

I shook his hand again, then crept towards the water. At the edge of the land, I pulled on the flippers and slipped out into the water. I checked the night sky, the unchanging lights of space, once my tormenter and now my guide as I fled the only homeland I'd ever known, towards the uncertain horizon in the gently lapping waves and current. My country disappeared behind me once again.

In the water I cried, my tears lost in the sea like so many Russian tears throughout history.

On the other side of the bay, crawling up onto the shore, I shed my skin and walked towards some lights. It was a small fishing village, mostly closed for the night, although a few late night workers cleaned and gutted their catch along the wharf. They glanced at me, then returned to their work, as if they had seen far more unusual things in their time than a man in his underwear lurching towards the saloon at the water's edge.

Inside the brown musty bar, a woman with a ruddy face welcomed me and poured a beer. Clearly I could not pay, as I had no wallet. She called into the back reaches of the kitchen, and a few minutes later, her husband appeared with an olive green wool blanket, which he wrapped around my shivering body. When I finished my beer, the woman handed me a bowl of seafood stew which I ate hungrily.

One other patron was sitting at the bar, watching all this with some amusement. He ordered me a shot of rum. "It is the spirit which warms the best," he said, in broken Russian.

The sugary sweetness masked the razor-like burn of my throat, although I felt it a few moments later.

The woman spoke to the man at the bar, and he translated for her.

"You can make sleep in the guest bedroom," he said. "They have a son who is away at the school."

"Thank them for me. I have lost everything tonight."

He spoke another few sentences to the barkeeper.

"Many people lose everything on the way to here," he said after a while. "It has been a while since somebody came across the channel, but many came before, during the Darkness."

After another beer, I followed the woman up into a guest room which was still made up for a small boy, although I could tell by the effects gathered on the small dresser that a young man had recently occupied the space. Underneath posters of dinosaurs and Michael Jordan were concert tickets and photos of attractive teenage girls. Some action figures on top of a toy chest had been arranged in sexually explicit poses that would amuse a 20-year-old.

I fell onto the bed and passed out.

In the morning, the bar matron cooked up a dish of eggs and fish for me, along with some coffee. We walked into town – she had dressed me in her husband's old clothes – and I was recognized by some Russian tourists. They asked for my autograph. I told them to give my regards to Russia, as I would never return. At hearing this, they giggled with confusion and continued on their way. Eventually we found our way to a small travel agency run by a beak-nosed, white-haired American. The bar owners waited outside as he took me into a back room.

"I haven't been in the business in quite some time," he said to me in English. I raised my eyebrows.

"What business?"

"The defectors' game," he said in Russian. "I worked for the C.I.A. and helped welcome and debrief Soviet refugees in the 1970s and '80s. Silvija brought you here because she didn't know where else to take you. During the Cold War, she helped shuttle defectors across the bay with her husband, in his fishing boat. That's why the bar stays open so late at night. Of course, they haven't needed to stay open late in recent years, but they'd picked up the habit. When you turned up in the night, it was rather nostalgic for them, but they knew what to do."

"You're not in the C.I.A. anymore?"

"Not officially, although I still have ties and they send me a bit of money every year to keep this place open, just in case. I'm an actual travel agent, you know, although business alone wouldn't pay my rent here, without Uncle Sam helping out."

He reached into a desk drawer and pulled out an old manilla folder.

"Most of these papers are out of date," he said, "but can I interest you in a holiday in the United States?"

He handed me the folder. Underneath brochures advertising the California coast, the splendors of the Grand Canyon, and the nearly crime-free streets of Manhattan, there was a blank passport, and a small fake mustache, mostly worn to shreds by time.

"You don't really need that, of course. But it's something interesting, isn't it?"

He took the folder back and returned it to the drawer.

"Are you interested in going to America, Ilya?"

"You know my name."

"And your story. Well, most of it." He was sorting through some papers with the digitized black printing of a fax machine. "Apparently you've made an enemy of our friend Vladimir Putin," he said, skimming the report. "We should probably get your wife out as soon as possible."

"She's dead."

He dropped the report.

"I'm so sorry. Was it ... ?"

"They killed her. That's why I left."

"I wish there was something I could say. I'm truly sorry."

We sat there in silence.

"I'd like to go to America," I said, finally.

"I can get you there."

Later that day, I boarded a small private plane and flew to Heathrow, where a young embassy attache greeted me at the airport. After a few months at a safe house there, he put me on a commercial jet to JFK.

I arrived in New York just as summer was giving way to autumn.

And then, despite the turbulence and violence, the crazy world around me and the way it seemed we were all falling to our deaths somehow, I made a home somewhere in America. I settled down in a place which I cannot reveal. Because Putin still runs Russia with his iron fist and empty heart, and no Russians are safe from his deadly reach. I have trouble sleeping. I lay awake in bed, alone, reliving my life and, I admit, often crying.

Some nights should last forever but never do, while others you wish to throw away.

In my apartment last night, I could hear the garbage men rumbling through the streets picking up the remains of yesterday. The sounds entered my dreams and I had a nightmare that I was home in St. Martyrsburg, riding my half-bicycle through the street when my shadow disappeared with the all-encompassing white light of an atomic blast somewhere behind me. I turned and saw a mushroom cloud, then began pedaling faster and faster as if to outrun the apocalypse. I woke up in a sweat, my legs pumping furiously despite the lack of pedals in my bed.

Not every nightmare is worth describing. Usually the fear and panic is intensely personal, non-conveyable to non-dreamers. In any case, I will try to tell you more about the night. After waking, I looked out my window and saw the great mechanical beasts and the ant-like men grabbing bags full of trash from piles upon piles upon the long fallen snow. A blizzard had prevented pick-up for a week, and so the process was slow and noisy. Between the chaos and the rapid heartbeat of my nuclear dream, I doubted I could get back to sleep.

Leaving the bedroom, I took refuge on the fold-out sofa in my living room. For Russian readers, it is probably shocking to discover a great hero of the Soviet living in such modest conditions. Yet, in my city, which I cannot name for fear, the price of living is astronomical, and most of my fortune is held prisoner in Russia. So I opened up the couch and prepared for a restless night in front of the television. I opened a six pack and drank myself into a stupor watching old black and white movies. If I couldn't find peace through natural means, I would beat myself into submission with drink. Eventually, whether through the alcohol or through sheer exhaustion, I did give in and slip under, despite the noise of the sanitation crews and the growing light of the morning sun.

In this second fitful sleep I had a dream more terrifying than the one about the bomb and end of the world: I found myself in a great Czar's palace, not one I had been in before, with great high ceilings and art masterpieces on the wall. There was a social event in progress, and I clung to the walls to avoid people. In the way we know our dreams, I knew that this was taking place during the height of my fame and yet I felt as shy and scared as I do now in my life of hiding. For all this, however, I did not know I was dreaming. Looking for an alcove to keep me away from socializing, I found a small shelter, but it was occupied. My Natasha was in there with another man who was on his knees, proposing to her. I did not know him, but she seemed to know him and to truly love him, so I could not argue. It seemed rude to interrupt, so I waited until their intimate moment was complete and then offered my congratulations. I was truly happy, for a moment, for Natasha, because she was happy. And then she and her fiancé wandered off and I was alone in my formal wear. I fell back against the wall of the alcove and my happiness abandoned me as I realized how alone I now was without her. I felt like a ghost haunting the palace, with as little life in me as a long dead nobleman with unfinished business that could now never be completed. My friends were there: Fedor, Lev, Evgeny, Vulkov, who was young and full bodied. They toasted to Natasha's happiness and made plans to attend her wedding. Certain missions would have to be rescheduled, leave granted, but all of them would be there. I could not speak. I sank further back into the wall, cold, shivering, my vision clouding with the white fog in front of me, this time it was the wall itself which I was becoming entombed inside, and though I felt hollow and cold, I felt what was left of my heart racing with shallow rhythm, more terrified now than I had been when I tried to outrun the mushroom cloud in the previous dream. Fire and doom fall down equally at the end of days, but loss of love is a personal evisceration, and loss of a lover to greater happiness cannot be righted or corrected. If the love of your life is truly happy, then you must be happy too, even if you are alone and miserable.

I woke up gasping for air. My head ached from the drinking. On the coffee table in front of me was a glass of water and a bottle of Advil. I do not know where it came from. I would like to think Natasha brought it for me in the night, to comfort me, but I know that she is dead and gone. Perhaps I had gotten it myself in a drunken haze and forgotten. Or maybe, I can allow myself to hope, that the ghost of her is in my apartment looking after me.

If that is true, then we are finally together again, and I can be happy.

It seems to me now that, like all stories of the past, this is has been a ghost story.

I believe in ghosts.

NOTES

EPIGRAPHS

1. From *18 and Life on Skid Row* by Sebastian Bach.
2. From an address to the Politburo, November 13, 1986 (cited in David E. Hoffman's *The Dead Hand*).
3. This slight inaccuracy may be blamed on the author's childhood in the U.S.S.R. without access to American pop culture. The sentence quoted here is actually from the poster for Ridley Scott's film *Alien*, not from George Lucas or his *Star Wars*. Also, it should read "no one can hear you scream," not *dream*.

CHAPTER 1: I Am Borne

1. It seems unlikely that Zamyatin was alive for the launch of Sputnik. If so, he would have been in his mid-20s when the Soviet-Afghan war started, not a teenager. It is possible that he lived in a region where the state media rebroadcast the launch of Sputnik at a later date to muster further enthusiasm for space travel. See Chapter 3, note 4.
2. Zamyatin seems to be confusing the narrator of David Bowie's song "Space Oddity" with Bowie's character Ziggy Stardust. Although Ziggy Stardust was a bisexual alien from outer space, he did not communicate with Ground Control like the character in "Space Oddity."

CHAPTER 2: Moscow, We Have A Problem

1. Mr. Pibb, a knockoff of Dr. Pepper, was not nearly as successful as the other items on the list.
2. Although I could find no record of a secret space program, it does seem possible. For instance, the Ventspils Radio Telescope remained a secret until 1993 when Latvia became independent, and the Soviet Perimeter System, also known as The Dead Hand, is described in Hoffman's 2009 book of the same name.
3. This seems to be a reference to the 1997 film *Face/Off*, where characters portrayed by Nicolas Cage and John Travolta swapped faces and identities. It is not clear whether Zamyatin thought the film was a documentary.
4. Here the author has clearly mistaken the fictional films *Papillon* and *The Great Escape* for documentaries. It makes sense, then, that he also believes *The Thomas Crown Affair* and *Bullitt* are documentaries about the same man.
5. Views toward domestic assault in 20th Century Russia were not terribly enlightened.

6. The author of *Moby-Dick* is Herman Melville, not "Herbert." This error is likely due to Zamyatin's possession of a samizdat copy with the incorrect author's name.
7. This is the plot of *Armageddon*, except with a whale. (*Armageddon* is the 1998 film adaptation of Eugene O'Neill's play *Anna Christie*.)
8. Ironically, American literature, as published in the twentieth century, was not nearly as diverse as the sampling Zamyatin happened upon, which included Allen Ginsberg's sprawling masterpiece "Howl" and Ernest Tidyman's 1970 novel *Shaft*.

CHAPTER 3: Nights in the Machinery
1. I have replaced a quote from Allen Ginsberg with this one from Walt Whitman due to copyright reasons. (The chapter originally began with a quote attributed to *Albert* Ginsberg. The incorrect name was most likely due to an error in his samizdat copy of *Howl and Other Poems*.)
2. Although he believes it to be fictional, Zamyatin is correct about the inscription on the base of the Statue of Liberty.
3. Zamyatin seems to have The Beatles and The Monkees confused.
4. Stalin died in 1953, which would mean Zamyatin was at least 27 years old when the U.S.S.R. invaded Afghanistan. It is more likely that his parents died later under another leader but the myth of Stalin still remained in the Soviet hinterland and the young Zamyatin was told Stalin was responsible even though he was no longer alive.

CHAPTER 4: The Neverending War
1. The author seems to have learned this quote incorrectly. Chief Joseph actually said "I will fight no more forever" when he surrendered to General Nelson Appleton Miles in 1877.
2. Probably due to mislabeled bootleg recordings from his youth, the author has confused the names of Neil Diamond and Paul Simon, who wrote "The Boxer" for an album he recorded with Art Garfunkel.
3. Drug use and killings among disaffected Soviet soldiers was a noted problem in this era. See Arthur Bonner, "Afghanistan's Other Front: A World of Drugs" in *The New York Times*, November 2, 1985.
4. "Single Ladies (Put a Ring On It)" by Beyoncé was a hit song in 2008 and 2009, which dates the manuscript to that era.
5. I could find no record of Confucius saying anything like this.

CHAPTER 5: When We Were Orphans Of The Floating World
1. The author must have confused *The Cowboy Way* (1994) with another movie, as it is not considered a classic by anyone really.

CHAPTER 6: The Mouth Of Hell

1. I could find no record of this interview or any article about Zamyatin in the entire history of *The New Yorker*.

CHAPTER 7: Wind of Change (Love Punches Me In The Junk)

1. Skid Row singer Sebastian Bach identifies as a man, but Zamyatin may never have seen a glam rock musician in person before, hence his confusion about Bach's gender.
2. David Remnick describes this practice being used to make a Fats Domino record "on the bones" on page 336 of *Lenin's Tomb*.

CHAPTER 8: Scarcity In Star City

1. Zamyatin seems to have confused the musical *Oliver!* with the book *Oliver Twist*. He has also confused Charles Dickens with Emily Dickinson.
2. Czar Nicholas II and his family were executed by Bolsheviks in Yekaterinburg in July 1918.
3. He seems to be referring to the TV quiz show "Jeopardy!"
4. This conversation seems to have happened almost concurrently with the composition of "Right Here, Right Now" by Jesus Jones, whose lyrics touch on a similar sentiment. That song, written about Perestroika in Russia following the band's trip to Romania, was released as a single on September 11, 1990.
5. He may have confused Michael Jackson's famous *moonwalk* dance with a space walk of some sort.
6. Zamyatin's decision to remain in the secret space program may seem strange to present day readers. For a similar tale, see scientist Sergei Popov's involvement with Vector, the secret Soviet chemical warfare laboratory, which is described in Chapter 4 of Hoffman's *The Dead Hand*.
7. Lyrics copyright 1991, SpaceTunes LTD.
8. No record of this event has been found.
9. *Top Gun* and *SpaceCamp* are both fictional films, not documentaries, although in the propaganda-fed mind of a Soviet general, they may have been mistaken for documentaries.

CHAPTER 9: Heart of Darkness

1. Zamyatin may be confusing explorer Christopher Columbus with the television detective portrayed by Peter Falk.
2. This manuscript was written after the first three *Star Wars* prequels, which were generally ill-received, but before *The Force Awakens* and the subsequent prequels like *Rogue One,* which was relatively successful.

CHAPTER 12: The Downward Spiral
1. This is not how the phrase *coyote ugly* is used in America.

CHAPTER 13: Notes From The Underground
1. This is not a typo. According to a brochure, Space Discovery Theme Park only accepted payment in American dollars.
2. Warren Zevon's middle name was William. Zamyatin has perhaps confused his name with that of American politician Warren G. Harding or hip-hop artist Warren G. Furthermore, the concept of "splendid isolation" dates back to British policy in the late 19th Century, although Zevon released a song with that title in 1989.

CHAPTER 14: Write It Like Disaster
1. The author is again confusing The Beatles with The Monkees. Paul McCartney was in The Beatles. Mike Nesmith, a member of The Monkees, is the son of Bette Nesmith Graham, who invented Liquid Paper, not paper clips.
2. The roadie must have seen French philosopher Jean Baudrillard, although it is not clear what television program he was watching.
3. The driver of the car has confused Bob Woodward with Robert Redford, the actor who portrayed him in *All The President's Men*.
4. I could find no record of this interview being published in the online archive of *Novaya Gazeta*. Perhaps it only appeared in the print edition?
5. Vladimir Putin is a noted judo enthusiast.
6. The more common translation of this first sentence of *Anna Karenina* is "All happy families..." not "All abnormal families..."

CHAPTER 15: Lodestar
1. From *Look! We Have Come Through!* (1918) by D.H. Lawrence.
2. This seems to reference a famous conversation between Nick and Jay in F. Scott Fitzgerald's *The Great Gatsby:* "'Can't repeat the past'? he cried incredulously. 'Why of course you can!'"

CHAPTER 16: A New Day
1. During the time Zamyatin is describing, McDonald's did not yet serve all-day breakfast.
2. See "Car Bomb Injures 7 at Moscow McDonald's," *Los Angeles Times*, October 20, 2002. There have been several bomb explosions at McDonald's locations in Russia, due to both mobs and terrorism.

CHAPTER 17: Gorky Park
1. Ewww. This part is gross, right?

CHAPTER 18: In The Year 2000
1. There is no record of Plato having said this.
2. Passage from *The Space Wife* copyright 2000, Snyot Publishing, Moscow. Used without permission. But what are they going to do about it?

CHAPTER 19: Pravda Means Truth
1. Zamyatin seems to have grown up reading a Russian version of the comic strip "Garfield" by Jim Davis.
2. *Over The Top* was not related to the *Rocky* franchise, though it may have been marketed that way in some parts of Russia.
3. While defeating John Glenn, Zamyatin quotes Nikita Krushchev's famous declaration to capitalist ambassadors from 1956, although the original Russian declaration was probably better translated to English as "We will outlast you" or "We'll be at your funeral."

CHAPTER 20: Terminal
1. He probably means FSB rather than KGB, since the KGB dissolved in 1991. But he may have recognized the car shape from the KGB era and still considered it one of theirs.

CHAPTER 21: Voyager
1. "Dark Was the Night, Cold Was the Ground" is the title of a 1927 blues song by Blind Willie Johnson. In 1977, it was, along with other songs and information, encoded on a golden record sent into space by the *Voyager 1* probe.
2. This would explain why few in the West have heard of Zamyatin, despite his claims to immense fame in Russia.